Amelia Garland Mears

Idylls, Legends and Lyrics

Amelia Garland Mears

Idylls, Legends and Lyrics

ISBN/EAN: 9783744787567

Printed in Europe, USA, Canada, Australia, Japan

Cover: Foto ©Andreas Hilbeck / pixelio.de

More available books at **www.hansebooks.com**

IDYLLS, LEGENDS

AND

LYRICS

IDYLLS, LEGENDS

AND

LYRICS

BY

A. GARLAND MEARS

LONDON
KEGAN PAUL, TRENCH, TRÜBNER, & CO. Ltd.
1890

PREFACE

THE chief thought that possesses an author when launching forth his work on the sea of the world's favour, is, whether it will float gallantly along the current, bearing its burden of the golden grain of instruction ; the pleasant fruit of romance ; or the music of poesy to the homes of the people around, or will his barque be shattered against the rocks of dispraise, or be permitted to sink into the quicksands of neglect.

It is with this feeling I launch my little shallop on the ocean, laden, not with science or philosophy, or the studied phrases of the polished poet, but with the simple music of the love-song, or old love-story.

The object of music is to yield pleasure to the mind ; the design of poetry is the same ; it should appeal either to the imagination or to the emotions. Its true object is not attained when it becomes chiefly the vehicle for philosophical or metaphysical instruction, reaching only the reasoning faculties.

I do not attempt those deeps of erudition : nevertheless, in the perusal of the legends something may be learned of old-time manners, and the thought of our ancestors ; and in the idylls the pictures portrayed of human life and of human love I trust will prove pleasurable contemplation to the reader.

No one likes listening to a long symphony heralding a song ; or wearying speech before a lecture, or a lengthy preface to a book ; therefore I will not tire the reader with further argument for the *raison d'être* of this work.

THE AUTHOR.

CONTENTS

ILAMEA

A DRAMATIC IDYLL

B

ILAMEA

A Dramatic Idyll

ILAMEA

See, how the sun now dips his glorious rays
In yonder crystal lake, and changes its
Pellucid face to sheet of molten gold!
How grand and beautiful his state, to sit
Enthroned on high, far into distant space,
And know that life in all its varied forms
Throughout the universe subsists upon
His smiles!

COUNT

Now, rather watch the fleecy clouds, which weave
And interweave with one another, like
Fair soul with soul commingling close, that
Seek no new condition for continuance

Of bliss, but sweet propinquity.

Fair lady, even so would life near thee

Be one long dream of joy.   Thou fill'st the space

Encircling thee with influence divine,

That gives my soul a strange new element

On which to live.

Ilamea, I love thee ; chide me not,

My sweet, for Love is peremptory—prompt,

And will bide no hiding.   Why should I try

To put on some disguise ? Thou knowest full well

In sweetest thraldom I am daily held,

And bright the moments speed when thou art near.

How quickly time hath fled since errand of

My own brought me to Rome ! When just returned

From roaming distant lands, Fate sent me here.

While on my proper business, oft I heard

Of the beautiful Ilamea ; she

As talented as beautiful, as chaste

As either.   Then good Fortune smiled ; I met

This queen of women, her I made my friend ;

Friendship hath ripened into love, yes, love

All strong, abiding, fervent, pure, to last

A long eternity.   [*Count kneels.*

Mine is no passion born of mere desire,
Because thou art so fair.   Ripe Womanhood
Becomes thee, who so full of knowledge art,
And versed in works of lettered heroes great,
Thyself no less.   And I have studied well
The deep imaginings of thine own pen,
And there reflected shines the beauty of
Thy soul.   Nay, blush not thus, I know not how
I should express a thousandth part of all
My thoughts concerning thee.   Can little babe
To its fond mother tell the reason why
It clings so closely, frets that it may lie
Upon her bosom soft ?
Ah, no ! it is mere instinct at the first ;
It hath no power of thought or speech ; its cries
Are Nature's eloquence.   Even so, unused
To framing language suited to my thought,—
In such a case as this,—I needs must plead
An infant's helplessness, and throw myself
Upon thy mercy.   Know, a cause so new
And strange as this unutterable joy,
This gradual change—completion of myself—
This absorption of another soul in mine,
Is inexpressible, and utterance fails ;

I did exist before, but now I LIVE,
For Love hath made Ilamea mine own !

ILAMEA

                         [She motions him to rise.

Oh, say not so, my lord, and cease to plead
Thy suit.   I must not—dare not listen it.
On me the sun of Love may never shine ;
Know then, nor love, nor wedded bliss, nor aught
Of happiness can ever be for me.
Henceforward I must tread my path alone ;
'Tis vain to say thou lovest me ; if 'twere
Now possible to give a thousand times
More love to me than what thou sayest,
I could not take it.

COUNT

This surely is a jest, Ilamea !
'Tis the cruel coquetry of thy sex
That's bubbling up within thee ! Yet I thought
Thee far beyond such trifling. Cultured, clear
Thy mind ; thy soul all perfect—beautiful,

And free from petty thought.   Most true thy
   heart,
And good, its motions governed by pure love.

Now tell me hath another gained thy love?
What is this mystery—what hidest thou?
Is it honourable to treat me thus?
Oh, surely thou hast seen how my poor soul
Hath been wrapt up in thee!   If thou but moved,
Mine eyes would follow as if magnetised.
All other women's beauty faded where
Thou wert.   Thy voice breathed music to my
   soul ;
When thou didst sing a sweet romance for me,
Where Love told some pathetic, tender tale,
Thy dear voice trembled ; thy white bosom heaved
If once thine eyes met mine.   Impossible !
Thou canst love none but me.

ILAMEA

It is impossible to love thee not ;
'Tis even as thou sayest.
My lord, I'm in a great dilemma now,

For all the weary years of my young life
Must be gone through in lonely solitude,
And all my natural affections quenched ;
For Honour says I needs must pluck thee from
My heart, and cast thee out.
Oh, Holy Mother, how can I do this ?
How can I make this cruel, cruel wrench ?
'Twixt Love and Duty—rather should be said
'Twixt Love and Law—there comes a struggle
    great.
My lord, I am not free ; I wear the yoke
Of marriage—bonds that only Death relieves.

Ten years ago I was a happy girl,
Although an orphan ; placed all safe 'twas thought
In quiet convent school, therein to stay
In strict seclusion till I was of age.
My liberty attained, I would be free
To choose the veil or enter marriage state
With full consent of my two guardians.
'Twas known throughout the convent I was rich ;
The same was talked of in the village too ;
But of the will and testament, exact
Provisions no one knew, save these old men—

A priest and layman.   Now, our convent stood
Hard by the village—quiet, grey, and old,
Secluded and embowered within tall trees,
And high stone walls encircling these.
Ah, those were happy days !   To me the nuns
Appeared like angels pure ; they thought of naught
But God and Jesu's Virgin Mother.   Thus,
Their love of Heaven to prove, they gave them-
      selves
To teach and train us children.   Oft I stood,
And gazing upwards to the vault of heaven
I wondered if the angels there our nuns
Resembled aught.   The painted pictures of
Sweet saints had wings, and harps of gold, but
      these
Were 'tired in darkest garb, as if our world
Were type of death, and sin, and hell, or all.

Anear the village dwelt one Carlos, gay
And profligate, yet handsome, tall, well-made.
His means all dissipated, he was urged
By strong necessity to find a mode of livelihood.
He sought my hand that he might get my gold ;
A low confederate of his did wait

Upon us girls.   She whispered in mine ears
How grand a thing to gain a gallant's love.
Tempted by her and him, and teased, and pressed,
At length I did give way and fled ; a priest
As vile as he then made us man and wife.
But fifteen summers had sped o'er my head
When that villain base decoyed me thus.
Oh, what a wretched life he led me then !
Completely baffled, foiled, when he had learned
His marriage brought no wealth (without consent
The whole was lost ; the convent gained my lands),
Then how he raved, and swore like madman wild,
And made my life a sea of misery.

I had no friends.   Shut out from all the world
From early childhood, I knew no pitying soul
To whom I could appeal.   He hated me.
A woman base as he held all his heart,
And daily urged him on to leave me.   I
Had hoped our little babe would, when the time
Was come, his hard heart melt.
One day—'tis graven on my brain with fire—
He came no more.   We lived alone, we two :
Our simple meal was spread, of which I would

Not taste till his return.   I filled the place
Of wife, and thrall—even I, the heiress of.
Fair Italy's fairest lands.   No handmaid now
To wait upon my will.   He knew full well
Mine hour I looked for, day by day, but yet
He did desert me.
In my solitude, still watching for him,
The pains of travail overtook me straight.
That long night I lay wrestling with my pain,
With none to help.   (The memory of it makes
My whole frame shudder.)
Then, in my dreadful agony, I prayed
That I might die.   The anguish of my soul
Exceeded many times the travail-pains.
'Twas like a spell of hell that awful night,
My mind and frame with torture torn, and soon
My strength was spent.
Then I remembered that another life
Might claim my care—that I must live for one
Who struggled now for life ; and so I braved
For its dear sake the terrors of that night.
Oh, how I longed for day ; that some stray soul
Might haply touch the latch and bring me aid !
When morning came a little child, to whom

I oft gave alms and cheerful words, peeped in.
What joy!   She ran all fleetly to a house—
The nearest one—and thus my life was saved.
But, ah, that spark of life was quenched which I
Had looked to light the utter darkness of
My home, unblessed by one small ray of love!
That gift of God to cheer my desert-path
Was lost : the babe, so strong erstwhile within my
     womb,
In its unaided struggles for its life
Was slain, and with it gone my dream of love.
How my hot soul in strong rebellion rose,
And in my heart I thought that God took heed
Of naught : that cruel wrong its rampant course
Would run for ever here !
Then utter weakness held me down ; I lay
For weeks 'twixt life and death, all cold and white.

When I revived, and hue of health came back
To my wan cheeks, I vowed a solemn vow
In deepest bitterness of soul that I
Had done with him for ever.   Rumour said
His paramour with him had fled away.
I cast aside his ring : I would not own

His name.   I left the place.   I told my tale
To my lay-guardian, who in pity gave
Me portion of my fortune.   I came here
To Rome, and gave myself to work, and hard
I studied daily.   In the course of time
My writings brought me much renown.

When I attained full womanhood, and came
Of age, I pleaded for my fortune then ;
The king the hand of justice forced to make
The priests disgorge my wealth.   This attained,
I had no end of suitors.   Vain their wish !
I closed my doors 'gainst all intruders ; few
Intimates I made, and secluded dwelt.

I heard that in another hemisphere
My husband wandered lawless—wild,
Entirely lost to me.   I know not where he is,
Nor whether he be dead, or living, now.
'Tis strange that Providence should watch so well
O'er wretches such as he : they seldom meet
Untimely end, but live to make us feel
That laws which govern the moral world
Are past interpreting.

I have no more to tell. In Friendship's guise
Thou cam'st to me, and cheered my solitude ;
'Twas thus that thou didst force the citadel
Of my proud heart, and made thyself
Its conqueror.
The circumstances of our life, how strange
They twist and turn ! One moment ask we
For a thing, the next we do refuse it.
An hour ago I longed to see thy face,
And, now, thine absence I must needs entreat.
These wretched contradictions now place
Me under hard conditions.
I willingly would give my life for thee,
But cannot yield mine honour.

COUNT

Oh, dearest, think what thy resolve doth mean
To me—thyself ?
It means the wreckage of two lives which thou
May'st save. No longer dost thou duty owe
To monster vile, whom legal contract calls
Thy husband. Get thee writing of divorce ;
'Tis soon accomplished ; and rid thyself

Of such base creature.
A covetous heart like his would burn to live
With thee again if wind of rumour brought
Him tidings of thy good condition.

ILAMEA

If once he came to Italy again,
'Twere not so easy to discover me.
The name I bear hath been assumed for this
Sole purpose, having no remedy.   All
The tribe of learned lawyers say I have
No case, as I hold proof of naught:
'Tis but too true.   That he hath left me for
A space, but shows desertion.

Our Holy Church forbids to be annulled
A marriage where the fault is venial, light.
'Tis naught to mar a woman's life, it seems,
If she be only wife ; the marriage vow
Doth cover all iniquity.

How bitter doth the heart become when thought
Reverts to bygone wrong !   Bygone ! alas,

It hath grown now an ever-living wrong !
An ever-present misery !
The Church's theory is good, and wise,
And very beautiful ; for marriage should
Be sacred, indissoluble.   The fault
Must lie where this is desecrated.

COUNT

Yea, truly, for a world of perfect beings,
This doctrine would be excellent.

ILAMEA

Now go, and let the widest earth divide
Us twain : yet know, each time thy life-pulse beats,
My heart gives answering motion.

COUNT

Like a beautiful star hast thou shone bright
Before mine eyes, and then retreated far
Above the heavens, never to come again.
Or, as some goddess sweet, too pure for sphere
Like this, thou'rt here and then away again

To thine ethereal home.   Ilamea,
Thou taughtest me to love in manner that
My deepest dreams could give no picture.   Why
Has Fate thus drawn me hither, making me
Her sport ?   I ask, why taught thou me to love ?

ILAMEA

And dost thou say 'twas I who taught thee Love ?
Methinks the lesson first was given by *thee*.
But what is this philosophy of love ?
Now, let us reason.   Was either taught at all ?

Who taught the lark to soar up to the clouds,
And in their bosom pour his happy song ?
Who taught the ocean in softly swelling waves
To kiss the glitt'ring shore, while making low
And melancholy music with sad voice ?

Who taught the gentle zephyrs to caress
The new-born roses shyly bursting forth,
While warm soft rays of sunshine pure
Expand their lovely petals to the kiss ?

Who taught the dew to kiss the lily's cheek,
And delicately leave a tear-drop there,
To show the soft, sweet tenderness of love?

Why all this strange attraction? 'Tis Nature's law
Which irresistibly impels, and leads
With forces so unutterably strong,
And yet so hid,—so wrapped in joy, concealed—
That whence it comes we nothing know, nor why,
We only know it is that power called Love.

Oh, mighty monitor! oh, mystic power,
That rulest, teachest ev'ry human heart,
Whatever be its outer case, or form,
'Tis insignificant!   The coarsest churl
Beneath thy happy influence and mild
Forgets his rudeness : instant greatest change
Takes place, and he is gentle, thoughtful, kind.
The cold philosopher, who naught believes
Save what to him is measurably sure,
And who, with proud disdain, and lofty smile,
Doth scorn existence of a spirit-world :
He sees no soul in man ; no God above ;
No Heaven.   To him eternity but means

The space of time the sun will glowing pour
His glorious rays upon the earth, and all
Is darkness after : man is surely doomed
To blank annihilation.

                              Yet only mark
How changed his words when strongly moved by
        love ?
Materialistic forms of speech to him
Are cold, unmeaning, empty—void.
For now a hidden force bursts forth in strength,
And lights upon him as a cloven tongue,
For God himself descends, and leaves on him
His spirit, baptizing him with FIRE !

And lovely woman, shy, retiring, proud,
Doth melt to softest tenderness when Love
Holds sway within her bosom ; while ev'ry nerve
In new and thrilling ecstasy is moved,
And quiv'ring, trembles at thy mystic touch.

Her very soul—no longer hers—goes out
To meet that other with such strong desire
That their two souls, like pair of liquid streams,

Might join as one ; united, onward flow
Beneath the varying shadows of long years,
And thus through all eternity glide on.

Or, longs their two existences might grow,
And blend together, like sev'ral coloured rays
All merged in one, do straightway form a light
Of glittering white, whose beauty fills the earth.

Ah, yes, Love comes to ev'ry one alike,
Unerring finds his way to ev'ry heart,
And on each various character outpours
Such strange and subtle influence ; such change
Effects upon the mind and course of men,
We can but look, and wonder.

                              Say'st thou yet·
I taught thee love, when thou dost know full well
I fain would break the bonds that bind me strong
To thee ?   I fain from me would cast afar
The chains invisible surrounding me,
And making me their prisoner.   The more
I struggle with my bonds, the more I'm bound ;
And yet it is captivity so sweet,

A thraldom so delicious, that at times
I long for liberty no more, and ask,
And only ask, to live for Love and *Thee.*

COUNT

And must be wrenched apart such ties as these ?
Is it the will of Him,—who liberal gave
To highest, noblest part of His own work
Such beautiful conception of that which
Makes His earth like unto Heaven—to close
Love's purest channels, and repress the soul's
Most tender impulses ?
If Love, my sweet, forbidden be, at least
Let us be friends ; and we'll begin anew
The gentle intercourse, and kindly thought
Which opened our acquaintance at the first.

ILAMEA

No, no, it cannot be, for who can rule
His heart ? 'Tis very true that Friendship may
Oft ripen into Love, but never Love
Will turn again to Friendship. Cold its light,

And pale when set against the fire of Love.
Compare the rushlight's glimmer to the warm,
Effulgent rays of Heaven's bounteous sun,
And mark the difference!
                    Even such is Love to Friendship.

Yet, stay awhile, and let me hear thee tell
A little of thy history.   What came
To thee, when thou didst wander in those wilds,
And pathless lands where men do strive for gold ?

COUNT

As thou dost bid me, dear, I must obey.
I would not touch a topic such as this
Of mine own will.   Thy tender heart would melt
At pictures of such misery as those
I witnessed daily.   I have seen poor men
Drop down in sheer exhaustion on the road
From hunger and fatigue, with none to help,
And left to die in solitude.
Just picture, now, some lonely man who strove
To find his way to gold-fields, distant more
Than length of Italy thrice o'er ; all spent

The poor remains of his small substance, first,
In buying tools which soon were cast away
To ease the strain of such exertion.

His only food the leaves from off the trees, or
  shrubs,
Which bore no nourishment ; and long before
His journey was accomplished, Nature sank
Exhausted.

The piteous sight would make me stop, and
  fetch
Some water from the spring to cool his thirst,
And then, unwilling I pursued my way
Lest long delay might bring me sim'lar fate.

ILAMEA

How couldst thou bring thyself to turn thy back
Upon those wretched creatures ; thou wert rich,
And could command all help ! Oh, why didst thou
Not try to render better aid ?
Ah, me, most foolish questions, now, I ask !

COUNT

What use is wealth in such a case as this ?
These lonely places have no mart for food,
So far from habitation or abode
Of men.

I came across a set of ruffians once,
Who quarrelling among themselves did wound
Their own companion.
'Twas one against a number—most unfair.
I rushed upon them, striking right and left,
And succoured the poor fellow ; then to place
Of nearest refuge I conveyed him quick,
And through the long night watches tended him.
A burning fever coursed throughout his frame,
Effect of wounds most desp'rate—deep.
When morning broke he knew not where he lay,
Or who it was that stood beside his couch.
He took me for a woman : ' Beatrice !
Beatrice !' he called, then muttered something
        else ;
Anon, in his delirium wild, he changed
The name to Martha !   'Twas most strange to hear

First Beatrice, then Martha! Martha!
How hard to lie upon a tortured couch,
The hot blood parching ev'ry pore ; the mind
Its balance gone, all racked with phrenzied
    thought,
And feel no gentle hand of love is nigh—
No woman's tenderness forestalling all
Our wants!
I pictured in my mind some gentle wife
In Italy's fair land awaiting his
Return, he desolate, dying far away.
I stayed with him three days, in hopes he would
Survive his troubles.   Business urged me strong
To make no more delay.   Good fortune sent
Antonio, a fellow-countryman,
To whom I gave the wounded man in charge ;
I left him gold and bade him not to spare
Good pains to bring the man to life and health.

ILAMEA

Didst thou inquire of thy poor patient, when
Recovered somewhat, whom this Beatrice was ?
And Martha—hateful name—of whom he spake ?

COUNT

It was not meet to trouble him with speech
At such a time.   I know that doctors urge
Necessity of silence to keep the patient calm ;
Yet this I learnt that Beatrice was his wife.

ILAMEA

His wife !   Describe to me the wounded man :
Was he quite tall and straight, with piercing eyes,
And Roman nose, and lips all large and full,
Of sensual mould, and hair of darkest hue ?

COUNT

Now truly thou hast drawn his portrait well.
He had beneath his curls a little scar
Just o'er his temple, seeming remnant of
Old wound.

ILAMEA

My God !   It is my husband !   Then thou hast
Even saved his life—thou, his would-be rival !

Ah, surely Providence hath some strange modes
Of working out its methods.   Thus 'twas given
To thee to succour him, who was of all
God's creatures most in thy way.

COUNT

Thy husband !   Oh, it surely cannot be !
And have I thus bestowed upon a wretch as he
My pity, love, and care ?   A heartless cur,
Who innocence deceived, and vows despised !
Without one shred of honour ?   This is misery
All heaped on misery ; a cup brimful !

ILAMEA

Cease to reproach thyself for thy good act,
Nor think that it was meet to take on thee
The punishment of one whom God himself
Was scourging.   Wisdom infinite decreed
That thou shouldst save him for some purpose
    wise,
Beneficent.   'Tis all inscrutable.
Yet know we that however strange appears

God's ways to us, He surely in the end
Will justify Himself, and show His laws
To be most excellent.
Humanity is an attribute divine,
Which lifts man from the baser part
Of all creation, proving his sonship,
And title to the Fatherhood of God.
And when a sudden impulse made thee fly
To help the stranger in his dire distress,
Thou only didst obey the dictates of
That innate sense of right, transmitted thee
From out the Heart of God.

COUNT

    [He sees a man approaching them.

By all the saints in heaven this surely is
A season of surprises!   Antonio!
My good Antonio, whence comest thou?
I left thee in the Austral wilds to tend
That lawless vagabond.   Come near and give
Account of what thou'st done. Now, doth he live?
Oh, say if thou didst nurse him back to life,
And health.   Be quick—I urge thee to be quick!

Recount to this fair lady and myself
All that thou knowest.

ANTONIO

My lord, I did your bidding; long I watched
And tended him both day and night.   Oh, blame
Me not; 'twas ne'er through lack of care that he
Made no recovery—'twas his bad luck.
For days he raved in strong delirium,
And when this passed away he knew that death
Pressed hard upon him.   Oft I watched the tears
All silent trickle down his face when of
A fair young wife he thought—one Beatrice.
There was no priest to grant him solace in
His deep extremity.   He said his sins
Could never be absolved by God; that he
Was past redemption.   Solemnly he bade
Me seek his wife, and in the village of
Arbosso find his Beatrice, whom years
Agone he basely had deserted.   From
A quiet convent school he stole her, in
Good hopes her wealth would then become his prey.
He loved one Martha, with her fled away;

Then she deserted him in turn.   At length
He wandered with a lawless band who lived
By plunder.   In the end they turned against
Him, grudging him fair share of booty.   On
That night you succoured him, they thought to slay
Him outright.
He made me swear, before the breath of life
Had left his quivering lips, that I
Would carry to his wife his deep, heart-felt
Repentance ; the gage of which was this
Fair missal, bound in gold, with jewelled clasp,
Belonging to his wife.   In deepest straits
'Twas ever kept as token of her worth.
See here, in fair handwriting is the name
Now writ upon it !
He died beseeching God to grant *her* good,
Although He did deny him mercy.

COUNT

And so he lived to learn that deeds of wrong
Do breed a fearful progeny !
Even so the mighty God doth make the law
Of retribution just, to follow out its course.

ILAMEA

Say, rather he was guided unaware
By God of mercy, who thus made him shed
The penitential tear.   And now we know
There is no soul upon this earth which is
All vile ; none unredeemable.   The breath
God breathed on man in Eden carries still
A remnant of the fragrance all divine,
Which with his first faint inspiration came,
Bearing still the germ of His sweet purity.
The story of my husband's fading hours
From out my heart hath taken all the sting—
The bitterness which time hath ne'er effaced.

                        [*She weeps.*

Now turn aside, I pray, and let me have
Communion with my soul.   I feel as if
A lifetime I have lived in one short hour.

COUNT

Upon my bosom, dearest, lay thy troubled head,
And heart to heart we'll live anew our life :

For now I claim the right to comfort thee.
When sorrow's cloud doth rise, my sympathy
Will lighten it.   Even as the sun doth break
Through thickest mist, and sheds his rays around,
So shall my love now chase away thy tears.

As flowers fragrant odours breathe to air,
My love shall rise to thee as incense sweet.
Or, as the petals of a rose enclose
The vital part, even so will I surround,
And guard thee from the faintest breath
That seeks thy harm.   Thus in the casket of
My heart I'll keep thee safe, my precious gem.

Now, is every barrier broken down,
And Love is Lord of all!   From thy dear lips
Of ruby let me take my first fond kiss,
Wherein methinks doth lie the essence sweet,
The summit and realisation of
Deliciousness of love.

HONORIA'S LOVE

AND OTHER SONNETS

D

HONORIA'S LOVE

INTRODUCTION

OF all the various methods adopted by poets in giving a love-story, no one, as far as I am aware, has attempted such a task in sonnets which are the outcome of the lady's feelings.

Innumerable sonnets have been addressed by the lover to his mistress ; but few have undertaken in this form of verse the expression of the lady's sentiments under similar conditions.

In ' Honoria's Love ' are depicted the several emotions of the mind when under the influence of love ; each sonnet expressing a separate phase of that passion which is admitted to be the strongest of all human passions.

The baser feelings of jealousy and vexation— the usual accompaniments of an ill-fated love—are not treated here, for Honoria is above her sex in generosity and gentleness. Inspired by the deepest passion, her heart knows no reproach. Even at the moment of her desertion she shows no scorn towards her vacillating lover, whose easy, voluptuous nature refuses to combat with the obstructions which circumstances have placed in the way of their union.

Owing to the form of the verse, the eighteen sonnets are less a love-story than an exposition of the emotions.

I

LOVE'S ENTRANCE

OH, Kingly Love, when first thou didst enthral
My soul in thy sweet bonds, I hardly knew
Thy presence : filled with joy, what could I do
But gaze upon thy face, and at thy call
Give willing ear ; then straight before thee fall,
In meekness yielding loving homage, true.
What sum of bliss wrapped up in moments few !
Life's sweetest mystery is made my all.

Beneath thy flowing robes, where none could see,
Were chains invisible ; then didst thou take
And lace elysian unseen spells o'er me.
What boots it that impetuously I make
These struggles? Vain to strive 'gainst thy
　　decree ;
For Love is life. Life 's sweet for Love's dear sake.

II

LOVE AWAKENS THE HEART TO THE BEAUTIES OF NATURE

OH, how the glorious sunshine fills all breasts
With gentle thoughts !   The soft and balmy air
Now breathes delicious sweetness everywhere :
The fragrance of the new-mown hay contests
With scent of flowers ; and Nature now invests
The earth with beauty, life, and joy : all share
In mutual gladness, for Summer fair
Her longed-for, promised treasures manifests.

The rise and fall of waving corn awakes
Sweet rhythm, as swelling waves of ocean seem
To give the music of the sea, which breaks
In cadence soft.   The gentle wind now shakes
The murmuring leaves.   Thus willingly we dream,
And listen to the poetry Earth makes.

III

ATTRACTION

WHAT makes me love thee, dear?   I cannot tell :
I know 'tis not thy beauty ; nights and days
I, like some first-work painter, fondly gaze
Upon thy face, and scan each feature well ;
Then wond'ring seek to know whence comes the
    spell
That silent sends me to thy side always ;
At times unwilling, I would make delays,
And fain this strange and sweet enchantment
    quell.

The painted picture of a Christ I've seen,
How round his head a halo bright is shown,
As if the beauty of his soul had been
In fair effulgent light outside him thrown :
Thou art not circled by such luminous sheen,
But yet thou hast a radiance all thine own.

IV

LOVE'S MYSTIC POWER

Now would I closely analyse my mind
Like some philosopher ; fain would I try
To fathom mysteries ; discover why
Thou dost possess such psychic force, and find
If Reason leads me on, or impulse blind,
Or cunning culture of thy mind, that nigh
To thee I'm drawn in loving sympathy,
Like floating sound-waves in the wind.

There seems to me a magnetism strong
Surrounding thee ; as if an aureole
Of subtle influence doth crown thine head,
And overspread thee wholly.   Thus, I long
For thy sweet kisses ; while my very soul,
And conscience, heart, and mind by thee are led.

V

LOVE, THE UNIVERSAL LAW

As atom unto atom firmly lies,
Obeying blindly that great law which makes
Subservient even lifeless matter ; wakes
An energy, a force whose hidden ties
Bind animate or inanimate in wise,
True order.   See, the silver cloudlet breaks,
With others interweaves ; thus changed, forsakes
An individual existence, dies.

Wave follows wave in rhythmic lines, and one
By one they lose themselves in close embrace ;
Thus are we twain commingled ; our lives run
In closest sympathy ; we interlace
Our mind's emotions : now there hath begun
Creation new, to which past life gives place.

VI

DEVOTION

IF mine were wealth of worlds, or vast estate,
Or kingly crown of monarchs great, then know,
I, dearest, would on thee all these bestow.
My Prince of Love, I would not hesitate,
Were I a queen, to daily ministrate
So humbly to thy wants, if need be show
How much my love would willingly forego,
Myself extinguishing to make thee great.

Ah, yes, if I the goddess Fortune were,
My gifts on thee I gladly would outpour :
If I possessed the zone of Venus fair
I'd give to thee a form and face e'en more
Enchanting than Apollo's.   I would share,
Nay, yield to thee wealth, honour, beauty, power.

VII

DOUBTINGS

ALL brimming over, dearest, with my love to-day,
I knelt upon the grass ; I whispered low,
While closely bending to the flowers that show
The constancy of love, 'Oh, blue eyes, say
If he who gives me love, will love alway ? '
I listened, but the leaves that to and fro
Were swinging overhead, then seemed to throw
A melancholy shadow as I lay.

'Oh, hapless one,' then sighing said the wind,
' Thy heart for ever on its love must bide ;
He loves thee not, and thou—well, thou art blind.
Just then, the love-songs to each new-made bride
Were trilled from tree to tree. ' These have divined
The mystery of love ! ' my heart out-sighed.

VIII

LOVE, AN INSPIRATION

WOULD I dethrone thee, idol mine, my king,
If mine eyes ceased to win from thee thy love ;
Or if my voice's music failed to move
Thy soul in sweet accord ; and all I sing,
And all the minstrelsies my heart could bring,
Indifferent still found thee ?   'Twould but prove
An incitation deep and strong : above
Love's joys is that of Love's sweet sorrowing.

Ah, if mine eyes had never looked in thine,
Or I had never listened to that tone
Which flowed in soulful words, like rich, red wine
That quickens warm life-currents ; then, not one
Stray thought of passion's poesy were mine ;
For, thou their inspiration, thou alone.

IX

SEPARATION

MUST we two part?   Bound as we are?   Oh, no !
'Tis sundrance of myself! I would abide
At any cost for ever at thy side.
Oh, must for evermore life's river flow
In sep'rate channels, dried and shrunken go
To limitless eternity's dark tide ?
Henceforward must our life-path far divide,
And leave me in unutterable woe ?

How chilled the life-stream is that warmly ran
Erstwhile throughout the subtle, unseen ways
Of this my frame !   All seems so cold and wan ;
Life's warm and roseate hues that met my gaze
Are turned to ice : for in that blow began
The death-in-life to last my length of days.

X

RENUNCIATION

Now go; I may not strive with this decree
Which doth divide us two.   I will not say
I suffer : sound of speech shall not betray
My soul's incessant, tearless agony.
How often lowly on my bended knee,
Or in the occupation of each day,
I sue for my deliverance ; and pray—
'How long, oh, weary heart, is this to be!'

Yet know, the farthest limits of earth's space
But poor division makes 'twixt thee and me :
The motions of our mind are so allied
That when thou hast a thought it must give place
To mine.   'Tis held by the intensity
Of that soul-chain which space may not divide.

XI

DESPAIR

My darkness mock not, oh, thou orb of day,
Nor make the world so beautiful and bright,
While heavy clouds of deepest, densest night
Press down my inmost soul.   No single ray
Of hope doth pierce the gloom that fills my way.
Departed is my joy, my life's sunlight.
Like one struck blind the memory of sight
Alone remains ; so light is lost for aye.

Oh, how those light-winged mites of pleasure make
Mine utter joylessness more vivid, plain !
While trilling happy songs they straight awake
All nature to rejoice : the sweet refrain
In times past thrilled each nerve, as bright leaves
　　　shake
In summer wind, or quiver in the rain.

XII

REGRET

WITH what delight the traveller longs to see
The shores of other lands, and eager goes
Upon his way despising ocean foes.
But, weary at last, he longs to be
At rest, and pants for home regretfully.
Thus storm-tossed, heart-sick, longing for repose,
I seek some peaceful shelter which bestows
A share of calm on chastened misery.

The flowery shores of Love I smiling sought
In new-born joy, nor ever stayed to think
'Twas but a lovely mirage that was fraught
With rainbow beauties.   Just upon the brink
Of full possession all dissolved to naught,
And in the clouds I watched the vision sink.

XIII

LOVE'S INDESTRUCTIBILITY

THE days have multiplied themselves to years
Since visible reflection of thine eyes
Met mine ; though God propinquity denies,
Still art thou very nigh me.   All my tears
Have failed to blot thine image, which appears
Upon the mental retina, defies
Laws physical; and when I rest or rise
One solitary speech the silence hears.

And this my cry—' Beloved, I love thee still !'
Howe'er I strive iconoclast to be
Mine idol will not shatter.   If my will
Could change thy substance, and had power to see
Thee turned to limpid water, then my fill
Of life were given to cast myself in thee.

XIV

LOVE VERSUS REASON

As prisoner pining in his darkened cell,
And sighs to see the golden, glad'ning light ;
So longs mine hunger'd heart for one short sight
Of thee, mine absent one.   Could I compel
Thy presence here, by force of that strong spell
Which essence is and outcome of the might
Of love enchained, and still all infinite,
Would I refrain ?   My lonely heart, me tell !

Hath Reason power to move the quickened soul
To do its dictates ?   Or doth the lord of all,
Imperious, issue his command, control
All man's emotions ?   Make him humble thrall,
And servant to his will ?   Love 's not the whole
Of life ; though ofttimes Reason's reign may fall.

XV

THE UNDOING

Now, how must I unlove thee?   I do attest
The task of this unloving can't compare
For easy methods to the loving.   Where
The first is full of toil and strange unrest,
Of all things human, 'tis most manifest
The second 's like a slippery downhill snare,
O'er which all blindly stumble unaware ;
Nor wise, nor simple can the fall arrest.

In searching for the way through all book-lore,
I read that 'tis pre-eminently wise
To scan the loved one's faults, and closely dwell
Upon his blemishes, whom we of yore
Thought perfect.   But, how vain to thus devise !
Away they melt !   Unloving, love we more.

XVI

PEACE

I HAVE at last the victory achieved—
That victory over Love, beneath whose sway
My hot, rebellious soul could see no way
Of freedom good, nor means to be relieved ;
And all this weary time I had believed
The bondage must endure ; for day by day
My ever-changeful, helpless heart would say—
' Love 's gone at last ! ' Then find itself deceived.

On me a nun-like peace hath now ensued,
Serenely I can think of thy dear name,
And sink each foolish, fond solicitude
In deep oblivion.　The past's a dream,
For Love is dead, and buried now for good,
A thousand times I tell myself the same.

XVII

SUBDUED, BUT NOT DEAD

WITHIN my breast a meek submission reigns ;
Unruffled as the stars I see thy face,
Of which I keep the semblance, not a trace
Of those old byegone love-throbs now remains :
Nor is it moved by burning, jealous pains,
That oft in quick succession took their place.
I see thy fair handwriting, in this case
The written page mine eyes no more enchains.

Yet, this I know, if Fate should send thee here,
We must not meet ; there's not a doubt but all
My walls of strong defence would disappear ;
I could not trust my wayward heart this much,
If on mine ears thy deep, soft tones should fall,
Nor neutralise the magnet of thy touch.

XVIII

LOVE NEVER LOST

ALL crushed and broken are those tender flowers
That wilful Hope persisting strewed my way ;
And there before mine eyes Love's rosebuds lay
Blushing, and waiting soft refreshing showers
To ope their petals sweet, in summer hours,
And bask in light and beauty while they may :
But just at brightest bloom they passed away,
And dying perfume breathed amidst their bowers.

The flowers are gone ; their fragrance still remains
All hid within my breast as incense rare ;
Though Love's departed, yet its influence reigns,
And gives more gentle thoughts the soul to share ;
Beneath its gen'rous power the heart attains
A sweetness fair, that else were never there.

TO AMY

ON HER TWENTY-FIRST BIRTHDAY

THIS day hath dawned for thee, my darling sweet,
Which often thou hast longed for in the past ;
Thy childhood's o'er, and thou hast gained at last
Fair womanhood's estate ; for thee replete
With health, and joy, and love ; gifts truly meet
For God's dear children.   Now o'er thee is cast
The glory of life's sunshine ; now thou hast
The fragrance of life's flowers at thy feet.

Thy smiling lips breathe sweet content ; thine eyes
Of clearest blue bespeak thy happy thought ;
For in their depth a tender beauty lies,
That e'en we think a glimpse of Heaven is caught,
Drawn as it were from out the far-off skies,
Which makes thy life with love for ever fraught.

TO J. W. S.

On his Birthday, March 31

WHEN Winter's frosts had safely passed away,
And all his course of storm and tempest run,
Then birds and flowers peeped forth to meet the
　　sun ;
For Spring-time came with bounding steps to say
Her pleasant mission was to make earth gay ;
And raising fairy wand, she thereupon
Commanded Life to spring, and one by one
The earth disclosed sweet charms each new-born
　　day.

'Twas thus midst budding trees, and sunshine brave,
The wooing of the birds, the building of each nest,
New-wakened Life to thee a greeting gave,
In mystic music all her love expressed,
Forecast of joys that I would wish thee have,
Thy length of days ; the purest, sweetest, best.

FAITH

YE countless, far-off suns that form a scheme
Unfathomable ; hung above the blue
Of high-vaulted heaven, and sending through
The skies your inextinguishable beam ;
Now say if Heaven and Hell be all a dream,
And but a myth the vast hereafter, too,
Yet ye remain all steady, constant, true,
For ever kept alight by power supreme ?

Is there no God ?   If so, then let your light
Now totter ; your empyrean fires go cold ;
No longer glist with scintillation bright,
Ye mysterious spheres of molten gold !
Now let your glory fade, and turn to night,
In darkness all the universe enfold.

THE EVANGELIST

'GOD IS LOVE'

OH, sweet-voiced messenger, now thou dost go
To spread the olive-branch of peace each day ;
At once rejoicing, pitying ; on thy way
Thou breathest gentle thoughts that surely flow
From out the Fount of God's own love, and glow
With light divine.   A mingled two-fold ray
Illumes thy face ; for in thy heart doth stay
A depth of human love most good to know.

Thou dear enthusiast !   Inspired by love
Speed on thy way, and strike the desert stone
Of hardened heart of man ; now gently break
That flinty rock, and by thy sweetness move
To penitential tears.   Thy work alone
Will bring thee love—'tis all for ' Love's ' dear
    sake.

EDAIN

AN ANCIENT LEGEND OF IRELAND

LIST OF IMAGINARY ILLUSTRATIONS

I. Early morning. A beautiful woman (Edain) bathing in a lake, which is surrounded by trees—chiefly willows. In the clear lake is reflected the rosy clouds. Behind the trees stands a man (the king) in an attitude of astonishment, mingled with delight, as he gazes on the maiden.

'He wandered on until his steps unwittingly drew near
The willow-sheltered lake, where bathed Edain all void of
    fear.
With eyes transfixed he stood amazed, and mute
With joy ; for quivered ev'ry nerve with love all absolute.'

II. Edain is crowned the Queen of Erin, and, seated on a golden throne at the king's right hand, she receives the homage of the nobles.

'And all the nobles in his court paid homage to her there,
In twofold honour, Erin's queen, and queen of beauty rare.'

III. The fairy king, disguised as a minstrel, and the King of Tara are seated at a table on which is placed the chess-board. The checkers are made of gold and silver alternately, the angles of which are richly illuminated with precious stones. The Queen Edain is entering the room. The minstrel looks at her, spell-bound with surprise at her extraordinary beauty.

    'The glory of her loveliness
      Enraptured all his soul ;
    His senses, steeped in joy, no more
      Were under his control.'

IV. The royal hall. The banquet over, the guests are standing about in groups, or seated on low benches covered with cloth of gold. The princes of Erin, in flowing hair, are crowned with golden circlets. The queen is seated in her royal chair at the king's right hand, while the minstrel (who is invisible to all others) is singing his love-song in the ears of the queen, and playing softly on his golden harp. The Chief Poet, arrayed in his robes of white, is seated on a dais at the opposite side of the room, surrounded by his train of fifty minstrels, or minor poets.

> ' Most beauteous lady, come with me
> To my palace made of gold ;
> Thy bed shall be drooped with diamonds rare
> And glitter with wealth untold.'

V. Beautifully shaped horses, with golden bridles, and shod in silver, are leaping over the high wall the king caused to be erected in order to starve them to death, so as to revenge himself on Midar. The chiefs of Erin running after them, in hopes of catching them for their own use.

> ' The horses were of noble blood,
> And leaped their barriers high ;
> Nor bolts, nor bars, nor prison walls
> Could spoil their liberty.'

VI. The king's warriors and workmen are all vigorously engaged in digging down into the hill, situated in the ' Sacred Midde' (centre) of Erin.

> ' And now the king's brave warriors
> And workmen, one and all,
> With spade and pickaxe bore the earth,
> To reach the palace wall.'

VII. Summer's night. Moonlight. An immense number of fays and fairies are diligently engaged in filling up the pit.

Some are striving to carry stones nearly as big as themselves, while others are filling wheelbarrows ; those nearest the pit are shovelling in the soil. They present a very grotesque appearance.

> ' But daily, as their task went on,
>   Their labour proved in vain :
> As fast as e'er the pit was made,
>   Each morn 'twas filled again.'

VIII. Fairyland. King Midar's gardens. Fays and fairies reclining on moss beds, which glitter like emeralds. Fairies wandering in the maze of beautiful avenues. Fountains playing at every turn, showing rainbow hues. Minstrels, dressed in glistening gossamer, with harps, are seated on the branches of noble trees. The whole illuminated by myriads of tiny lights suspended from the branches of the trees. The lamps give out every imaginable colour, the effect on the scene being most gorgeous.

> ' The spirit-music floating from
>   These sylvan seats above,
> Was tuned to poetry divine,
>   Whose themes were all of love.'

IX. Midar mixes them. Fifty fairies are seen filing out of the castle gate, all exactly alike, and all perfectly resembling the queen.

> ' In dress, and face, and form, all like
>   The beautiful young queen ;
> So nearly they resembled her,
>   No difference was seen.'

X. The king gazes bewildered at the file of lovely women. At the sound of his voice, Midar's spell on Edain is broken. She looks at her husband with a countenance lit up with joy.

> ' Her prisoned soul burst through its chains,
>   And lit with love her eyes,
> As gazed she on her husband's face
>   In warm and glad surprise.

> ' He knew her by her look of love
>   And drew her from the crowd,
> And kissed her, raised her on his steed,
>   Then back to Tara rode.'

XI. Fifty warriors have each a maiden mounted on horseback behind him. To prevent their escape they are strapped to the soldiers' waist-bands.

> ' Securely fastened to his waist
>   (A curious cavalcade)
> Behind him, mounted on his horse,
>   Each warrior has his maid.'

XII. Tara's Gate. The warriors, glancing behind at their prisoners, are utterly amazed to find that they are *non est.* In the distance the fifty fairies are seen melting into mere shadows, which become fainter and fainter.

> ' And when they turned them to alight
>   At Tara's palace fair,
> Lo, every maid had vanished quite,
>   And melted into air ! '

EDAIN

An Ancient Legend of Ireland

Introduction

THE romantic and poetic nature of the Irish may be seen in their beautiful fairy tales, or ancient legends of Erin, where historical events, and fanciful fairy lore are most romantically mingled. It seems as if the very beauty of the country helped to inspire a poetic feeling in its people, and stimulate their imagination ; for every glen and mountain has its own history, each of which is made dear by its association with some national hero who was held in honour in the days of old, when Ireland possessed her own kings and native chiefs.

The annalists of Ireland claim for their country a civilisation extending over a period of three

thousand years. Long before Romulus founded
Rome Ireland had her college at Tara, 'where
the Druids taught the wisdom of Egypt; the
mysteries of Samothrace; and the religion of Tyre.'

The Irish believed, as did most civilised peoples,
in a race of beings, partly human, partly supernatural; beings midway between man and the
angel. The Persians called these peris, the Greeks
demons, and the Irish the Sidhee, or fairies. These
latter are said to be very fond of beautiful mortal
women, and use their supernatural powers to wile
them away to fairyland. This belief has given
rise to many a beautiful fairy-tale. The fairies
are said to have their palaces beneath the hills
and lakes, where they hide all the treasures of the
earth. They enjoy perpetual youth, and are un-
acquainted with death or disease, living a life of
pleasure, and revelling in dance, and music and
song; nevertheless, they are not perfectly happy,
for they know they are doomed at the Day of
Judgment to complete annihilation.

In the following verses I have adhered faithfully
to the incidents given in the old legend; nevertheless these form but the framework of the story;

for the filling in of the details are partly the work
of my own imagination and partly information
culled from the best historic sources. In this way
I have endeavoured to give a more vivid picture
of those ancient times for ever passed away.

EDAIN

'Twas dawn of day, in his majestic beauty rose
  the sun
Behind the ancient hills of Erin.   Dewdrops one
  by one
Now slowly disappeared ; caught up, absorbed by
  every ray
That glinted through the shady glens, filled with
  the misty grey
Of Night's dark curtain.   Like some beauteous
  mirage in the lake,
The purple-tinted clouds appeared to move about,
  and break
In myriad forms and shapes.   Before the heat of
  summer sun
Had spread, and in the early cool, the maid Edain
  with none

To see, herself unrobed, and springing in the
  glitt'ring sheet
Of limpid water, bathed all free in this secure retreat.

Save the soft clouds none saw the rounded limbs
  alternate gleam
With shell-like tint upon the wave, or vanish like
  a dream :
Her breasts like two fair doves in gentle palpita-
  tion rose
With each lithe motion ; for her silken hair confined all close
Naught of her charms concealed. Th' exquisite
  beauty of her race
Was gloriously expressed in ev'ry curve of her
  sweet face.
No peri half so fair ; 'twas glimpse of heaven to
  see her eyes
Glow with the light of midnight stars set in the
  archèd skies.

From Tara's halls the king had wandered forth in
  quiet mood,
To list to love-songs of the birds in this sweet
  solitude :

To drink the morning air ; to watch the rising sun
soft glow

O'er every dell, or mountain top, or valley far
below ;

He wandered on until his steps unwittingly drew
near

The willow-sheltered lake where bathed Edain all
void of fear.

Then suddenly he stopped and gazed upon that
vision fair,

His heart beat fast and full, and he could scarcely
breathe, nor dare

He move a limb. With eyes transfixed he stood
amazed, and mute

With joy ; for quivered ev'ry nerve with love all
absolute.

He turned him round and fled ; this new-born
feeling quickly brought

Sensations of strange bashfulness. Then back he
came and sought

With swift impatient steps to see this naiad of the
lake

Who held such empire, that he could yield his
    kingdom for her sake :
But, lo ! the maid was gone ; in vain explored he
    everywhere ;
The sylvan glens, the shady woods he searched
    with anxious care ;
He homeward turned ; perturbed his mind ; with
    strong emotion rent ;
' Who was the maid ? How came she there ? ' he
    asked with wonderment.

Though parted from her presence there remained
    before his sight
The image of Edain, that seemed like some fair
    dream of light :
All things to him were changed ; the soothing
    sounds of minstrelsy ;
The pleasures of the chase ; of banquetings and
    revelry ;
Now lost their charm ; a melancholy man in all
    his thought
The king became, without Edain all pleasures
    were as naught.

At length the king's decree went forth through all
    his wide demesne
That sweet Edain be brought to him, and made
    fair Tara's queen ;
Now sate she on a golden throne upon the king's
    right hand,
And fame of all her loveliness was spread through-
    out the land ;
And all the nobles in his court paid homage to
    her there,
In two-fold honour, Erin's queen, and queen of
    beauty rare.

    King Midar the powerful chief
    Of Tuatha-Danann race,[1]
    Loved far beyond all of his kind
    A beauteous woman's face.

[1] It may be somewhat confusing to the reader to find
that the Tuatha-de-Dananns (a race of the earliest historic
settlers in Ireland) are treated in the legend in the two-fold
character of fairy and human being. The following will
explain this apparent anomaly. The first historic settlers in
Ireland were a pastoral people, called Firbolgs. The next

He longed to look on sweet Edain,
    Behold her features rare ;
And see how far a mortal may
    Transcendent beauty bear.

'Twas told him she was wondrous fair,
    More lovely to the sight
Than any fairy who e'er danced
    Upon a beam of light.

Then he disguised him cunningly,
    As wandering minstrel dight,
And came to Tara's halls, and sued
    For shelter on one night.[1]

were the Tuatha-de-Dananns, a large, fair-complexioned
and very remarkable race. 'They were warlike, energetic,
progressive ; skilled in metal-work ; musical, poetical, acquainted with the healing art, skilled in Druidism, and
believed to be adepts in necromancy and magic.' Owing to
their superior knowledge the Dananns were credited to
possess supernatural powers which in course of time converted them by the imagination of the Irish into fairies.
'From these two races sprang the fairy mythology of
Ireland.'

[1] In ancient times it was the custom in Ireland to render
hospitality to every bard who demanded it ; for it was held
to be a sacred duty for both king and commoner to entertain

No song sang he, no epic gave,
　　But to the king straightway—
'A game of chess, my sire,' said he,
　　'I beg of you to play.'

'And who art thou that I should play
　　A game of chess with thee?'
The king demanded of the bard
　　A little haughtily.

'Try me, I am a worthy foe,'
　　The minstrel quick replied;
'I have no check-board,' quoth the king,
　　Unable to decide.

''Tis in the chamber of the queen,'
　　Explained he to his guest;
'It is not meet to enter now,
　　And spoil my lady's rest.'

him. 'A train of fifty minor poets always attended the
chief poet, and they were all entertained free of cost where
ever they visited throughout Ireland. The Chief Bard was
borne on men's shoulders to the palace of the king, and
there presented with a rich robe, a chain, and a girdle of
gold. Of one bard it is recorded the king gave him in
addition, his horse and armour, fifty rings to his hand, one
thousand ounces of pure gold, and his chess-board.'

That challenge was given the king,
 The Queen Edain soon heard ;
Forthwith she sent the checker-board
 To please the stranger-bard.

The checkers were of rich red gold,
 And silver, white and fair ;
And every angle was bedecked
 With jewels rich and rare.[1]

The chessmen were most weird and strange,
 For they were deftly wrought
From out the bones of enemies
 Who centuries had fought,

[1] A manuscript of the twelfth century contains this description of a royal chess-board :—' It was a board of silver and pure gold, and every angle was illuminated with precious stones ; and there was a man-bag of woven brass wire.' The ancestors of the king to whom this board belonged used chessmen made from the bones of hereditary enemies. A recent writer says—' The game of chess was frequently referred to in the old bardic Tales ; and chess seems to have been a favourite pastime with the Irish from the most remote antiquity. The royal chess-board was very costly, and richly decorated.'

With Tara's kings [1] in bitter hate ;
  And thus from out the dead
A monument of victory
  Their conquerors had made.

Then from her chamber Queen Edain
  Came forth her guest to see,
But while she gave him welcome meet,
  He trembled visibly.

He gazed with ravished, dazzled eyes
  Upon that vision fair ;
The pow'r of utterance had fled,
  And speechless he stood there.

[1] Montalembert says—'Almost without interruption, up to 1168, kings, springing from its different branches, exercised in Ireland the supreme monarchy—that is to say, a sort of primacy over the provincial kings, which has been compared to that of metropolitan over-bishops, but which rather recalls the feudal sovereignty of the Salic emperors. Nothing could be more unsettled or stormy than the exercise of this sovereignty. It was incessantly disputed by some vassal king, who generally succeeded by force of arms in robbing the supreme monarch of his crown and life, and replacing him upon the throne of Tara with a tolerable certainty of himself being similarly treated by the son of the dethroned king.'

The glory of her loveliness
   Enraptured all his soul ;
His senses steeped in joy, no more
   Were under his control.

A strange emotion suddenly
   Came o'er the lady too,
She paled, and quivered like a leaf,
   Then silently withdrew.

'What are the stakes ? ' the king inquired,
   The minstrel answered free ;—
'Let him who conquers name the prize,
   Whatever it may be.'

'Agreed, agreed !' exclaimed the king,
   And then the game began ;
To make successful the campaign
   He wisely laid his plan ;

All skilfully he played his game ;
   With care the pieces moved ;
But played the bard more cunningly,
   Who victor final proved.

‘ Now, name the prize ! ’ the good king cried,
  ‘ The game is surely thine ! ’
‘ The Queen Edain,’ the bard replied,
  ‘ I fairly claim as mine ;

‘ Twelve months this day, I'll take away
  The prize thou didst award.’
Then suddenly was seen no more
  The strange mysterious bard.

The king, aghast at this demand
  Beyond all parallel,
Felt sorely straitened ; deep perplexed,
  And down his countenance fell.

Then instantly a grey-beard spake,
  ‘ Thy royal oath was given ;
Thine honour pledged to thy young queen,
  Which never may be riven.’

‘ Yield up Edain ? ’ exclaimed the king ;
  ‘ I ask the All-Good's curse,
If such I do while drop of blood
  My frame doth still traverse.’

The monarch kept a strict account,
    Whene'er the day should be,
And gathered round him all his court
    To bear him company.

And then he royal banquet made
    Upon this fatal day,
And summons sent to vassal kings [1]
    That none should stay away.

The prince of fair Mommonia, and
    Cannocia in the west,
Lagenia and Ultonia, were
    Each one an honoured guest.

---

[1] In ancient times Ireland was governed by a supreme monarch and four vassal kings. The country was divided into provinces, or kingdoms ; to the north Ulster, or Ultonia, to the south Munster, or Mommonia, to the east Leinster, or Lagenia, to the west Connaught, or Cannocia. Over each of these provinces reigned a vassal king who was subject to the supreme monarch. At one time Leinster alone paid a triennial tribute to the King of Tara of cattle to the value of 130,000*l*., 5,000 ounces of silver, 5,000 cloaks, 5,000 brazen vessels. The supreme king dwelt in and owned a distinct district—the antique 'Sacred Middle' of Ireland, represented by the counties of Meath and West-meath, which surrounded the royal residence of Tara, celebrated in Moore's 'Melodies' : some ruins of the castle still remain.

Beside all these the monarch bade
　　The minstrel-chief, and suite
Of fifty bards—well-favoured men—
　　To make the feast complete.

Above the nobles sat the bards
　　In honourable place,
All gifted men of noble mien
　　Endowed with every grace.

The minstrel-chief was centre of
　　This goodly, fair array
Of talent, genius, yet was he
　　More noble e'en than they.

He sat in state, resplendent in
　　His robes of purest white,
All clasped with jewelled brooches fair,
　　That glistened in the light.

To ask him to give song—declaim—
　　Such privilege none possessed ;
Not e'en the king ; nor nobles high,
　　Nor prince ; nor honoured guest.

The queen alone, 'twas e'er ordained,
   Should choose the epic, glee,
Or song of chivalry and love
   At royal revelry.

At times the venerable bard,
   When inspiration came,
Would sweep his golden lyre, or pour
   His soul in lofty theme.

And while the poet thus declaimed
   No sound the silence stirred ;
But all in reverence sate still,
   Nor ever uttered word.

And bravely all the chieftains looked
   With golden circlets set,
To crown their long and flowing locks
   Of brown, or glossy jet.

Antique they were, of classic form,
   And wrought all cunningly
In divers ways of workmanship,
   Most wonderful to see.

G.

And every chief his jewels prized,
For in the days of yore
Their ancestors these diadems
At war, or banquet wore.[1]

The fair Edain was richly tired
In robes of beauteous sheen ;[2]
A costly diadem of gold
Crowned Tara's lovely queen.

[1] 'Relics of a civilisation three thousand years old may be seen in the Royal Irish Academy. The golden circlets ; the fibulas (brooches) ; torques, bracelets, rings, &c., worn by the ancient are not only costly in value, but often so singularly beautiful in the working out of minute artistic details, that modern art is not merely unable to equal them, but unable to even comprehend how the ancient workers in metals could accomplish works of such delicate, almost microscopic minuteness of finish.'—Sir William Wilde.

[2] At this remote period ' the ladies wore the silken robes and flowing veils of Persia. The native dress was costly and picturesque, and the habits and mode of living of the chiefs and kings splendid and Oriental. The high-born and the wealthy wore tunics of fine linen of immense width, girdled with gold, and with flowing sleeves after the Eastern fashion. The fringed cloak with a hood after the Arab mode was clasped on the shoulders with a golden brooch. Golden circlets of beautiful and classic form confined their long flowing hair, and, crowned with their diadems, the chiefs sat at the banquet, or went forth to war. Sandals on their feet, and bracelets and signet rings, of rich and curious workmanship, completed the costume.'—Sir William Wilde.

At every portal, every gate,
   A guard full trusty, sure,
Was placed to keep all strangers out,
   And make the queen secure.

Around the palace walls were ranged
   Three lines of warriors, brave ;
A triple cord of chosen men,
   Who swore the queen to save.

Yet, when the hour of midnight came ;
   The pleasure at its height ;
And gallant nobles homage paid
   To win their ladies bright.

Within the midst of this gay throng
   Appeared the bard again,
And no one heard him, save the king
   Sing softly to Edain.

No bard so beautiful as he,[1]
   All glorious his attire ;
While deftly swept he harp of gold,
   And glowed his eyes with fire—

[1] Every bard was handsome. 'They were gifted, learned, and beautiful; even genius was not considered

THE MINSTREL'S SONG

' MOST beauteous lady come with me
　　To my palace made of gold ;
Thy bed shall be drooped with diamonds rare,
　　And glitter with wealth untold.

' Delicious nectar from dewy flowers
　　Shall be given thee all thy days ;
And crimson red are the lover's lips
　　That would kiss thee, sweet, always.

' And thou shalt sleep on the gentle down
　　That comes from the butterfly's wing ;
Thy wine-cup shall be the lily fair ;
　　Thy lover the Danann King.

enough without beauty to warrant a young man being
enrolled in the ranks of the poets. A noble, stately presence
was indispensable ; and the poet was required not only to
be gifted but handsome. Then, he was promoted through
all the grades until he reached the last and highest, called
" The Wisdom of the Gods."'

‘ And nightly thou shalt be lulled to sleep
   With a soothing, dreamy strain,
And the music floating through the air
   Shall come to thy dreams again.

‘ And delicate scent of balmy flowers
   Shall o’er thee shed incense sweet,
Culled from the gardens of all the earth,
   To render thy joy complete.

‘ And thou shalt be my fairy queen
   Endowed with eternal youth,
For ever and aye thy love I’ll be,
   If thou wilt be mine in truth.

‘ Then come with me, come, sweet lady mine,
   To my palace made of gold,
With ivory floors of creamy white,
   All beautiful to behold.’

Thus with his golden harp sang Midar to Edain ;
In low seductive voice he uttered this soft strain ;

Then drew her tenderly from out her royal chair
And pressed her to his heart with none to interfere :
He led her down the hall amidst the courtly throng
His presence none perceived ; none heard his sweet
　　　love-song :
None save the king, who sat immovable—fast
　　　bound—
Struck dumb by Midar's spells : as soon as he had
　　　found
His freedom, then he upraised him, in anger fierce
He bade his horsemen follow ; uttering a curse
Upon the sorcerer, he scoured the country wide ;
' Come back, Edain, Edain ! ' impetuously he cried ;
The echoes of the hills took up the mournful strain
In seeming mockery replied—' Edain—Edain ! '

The monarch message sent to all the kings around,
And bade them kill and slay, and utterly confound
All of the hated Tuatha-de-Danann race,
And leave of all their forts e'en not a single trace ;
And royal Danann steeds should perish in their
　　　stalls ;
For 'twas the king's command to build up all the
　　　walls.

The horses were of noble blood
   And leaped their barriers high,
Nor bolts, nor bars, nor prison-walls
   Could spoil their liberty :[1]

Of noble form these fiery steeds,
   With golden bridles dight,
Their hoofs with silver gaily shod,
   Shone in the bright sunlight.

The chiefs of Erin now forgot
   T' obey their king's command,
To find where Midar kept Edain,
   And spoil the Danann band ;

To capture for himself a steed
   Each chieftain vainly tried ;
To mortal man these would not yield,
   But ran the country wide.

[1] It is said that the Tuatha-de-Danann horses were a breed of noble animals found only in ancient Ireland, where they flourished for several centuries : they were distinguished for their beautiful shape, and high mettle. 'The last of this race at the death of its owner refused to submit to a base-born churl ; threw the groom, killing him on the spot, and galloped away. Finally he plunged into the lake and was seen no more.'

The king in hottest anger raged ;
    His heart with anguish stirred ;
To see his warriors and chiefs
    So disregard his word.

He straightway issued a decree
    That the Druid chief who dealt
In spirit lore, should cast a spell,
    And find where Midar dwelt.

The Druid over Erin searched ;
    His charms cast all around,
For, lo ! the penalty was death
    If Midar were not found.

At length it was revealed to him
    That Midar's palace bright,
Was hidden deep down in the hill,
    In Erin's centre, quite.

At once the king's brave warriors,
    And workmen, one and all,
With spade and pickaxe bored the earth
    To reach the palace wall.

But daily as their task went on,
   Their labour proved in vain,
As fast as e'er the pit was made,
   Each morn 'twas filled again.

And now the monarch sorely felt
   All baffled in his quest
And sat heart-broken on the hill
   Refusing food, or rest.

At midnight on one starry eve
   While lonely he stayed there,
He heard a soft mysterious voice
   Come floating through the air:

And then 'twas told him how to break
   Th' enchanter's wily spell,
And how the pit could sure be made,
   And all the work go well.

Oh bravely, bravely sped they on
   Until the palace bright
Was seen to glitter through the earth
   All in the broad daylight.

And soon they reached the palace gate,
  When lo ! they saw a train
Of lovely women filing out,
  All like the Queen Edain.

Then, what a gorgeous scene burst forth
  Upon their ravished sight,
Enchanting gardens teeming o'er
  With every delight !

The turf was velvet to the touch,
  And glowed with beauteous sheen,
Like sparkling emeralds glittering fair
  In many hues of green.

Delightful flowers of brilliant dye
  Filled every gay parterre ;
While balmy odours from sweet shrubs
  Were wafted through the air.

Far up the height of noble trees,
  And glittering among
Their foliage, were a myriad lights,
  Like stars in heaven hung.

Each lamp gleamed with a wondrous fire ;
   (No two alike were there) ;
A multiple of colours shed
   Their lustre ev'rywhere.

No eye before such radiance saw,
   And no one could divine,
What mystery made these tiny lamps
   So constantly to shine.

At every turn a fountain played,
   In thousand colours dight,
Like many rainbows merged in one
   Sweet cloud of beauteous light.

And resting 'neath the spreading trees,
   Or wandering through the maze
Of lovely avenues, were seen
   The fairies, and the fays.

Upon the stately linden trees
   Were scattered here and there,
The fairy minstrels, robed in white
   Of glistening gossamer.

The spirit-music floating from
  These sylvan seats above,
Was tuned to poetry divine,
  Whose themes were all of love.

The perfumed air was parted with
  Delicious melody,
That swept the ear, and filled the soul
  With thrilling ecstasy.

The halls within were soft illumed
  By radiance that was spread
Of myriad diamonds clustering thick
  In branches overhead.

Indignant that these soldiers bold
  Should view his fairy hall,
King Midar caused a thick dark cloud
  To cover over all :

Yet when he saw his conquerors close,
  Their victory to protract,
He fifty beauteous fairies sent
  The warriors to distract.

In dress, and face, and form all like
    The beautiful young queen,
So nearly they resembled her,
    No difference was seen.

For Midar this enchantment made
    In hopes he might retain
The winsome woman whom he loved,
    And struggled hard to gain.

The king was sorely puzzled now
    When gazed he on the scene,
He could not recognise his wife,
    Nor say which was the queen.

Then with the concentrated force
    Of love, and wild despair,
In mighty tones his voice cut through
    The dense and darkened air.

' Edain, my love, my life, come forth,
    Throw off thine awful yoke ;
Reveal thyself, my joy, my light ! '
    Thus pleadingly he spoke.

Now, when she heard her husband's voice,
 Her heart gave sudden thrill ;
It broke the spell that bound her down,
 And held in bonds her will.

Her prisoned soul burst through its chains
 And lit with love her eyes,
As gazed she on her husband's face
 In warm and glad surprise.

He knew her by her look of love,
 And drew her from the crowd,
And kissed her, raised her on his steed,
 Then back to Tara rode.

And now the gallant warriors were
 Unable to refrain
From much contention 'mongst themselves
 Which should a maiden gain.

The sight of so much loveliness
 Their souls set all on fire ;
Their hearts were witched by fairy charms,
 And burned with strong desire :

But Might asserted now its Right ;
   The strongest soon agreed
Each warrior should a maiden take,
   And place her on his steed.

Securely fastened to his waist,
   (A curious cavalcade)
Behind him, mounted on his horse,
   Each gallant had his maid.

But when they turned them to alight
   At Tara's palace, fair,
Lo, every maid had vanished quite,
   And melted into air !

Though Midar loved fair women well
   He ventured ne'er again
To trouble Tara's Halls, or try
   To steal the fair Edain.

THE BURSTING OF 'CONE-MAUGH LAKE,'

JOHNSTOWN, U.S., MAY 31, 1889,

IN WHICH 14,000 PERSONS PERISHED. THE DISASTER TOOK PLACE AT HALF-PAST TWO O'CLOCK, IN EARLY DAWN.

THE busy town was hushed, and silence reigned
Around, upon that eve of leafy June ;
And sweetly Nature nestled everywhere.
The bird-song hushed, the hum and chirp
Of each wee wingèd thing that flits on earth, through
    air
Had ceased ; and weary men who toiled all day,
The labour-sleep full deep and dreamless slept.

In light repose a babe lay on the breast
Of many a tired house-mother. Young Love
    came

H 2

All decked in pearly robe of rainbow hues
To whisper pæans sweet to maidens fair,
And steep their senses in a new delight.

The restless little children slumb'ring lay
Within their cots, while pleasing dreams
Brought dimpling smiles to play all lightly 'mong
Their roses.   Nature, empress first and last
Of all the universe, did then enforce
Her gentle law, and saw that ev'ryone
Of all her various subjects rested.

But, hark !   What is that cannon boom that rends
The air with awful roar, more fiercely than
The concentrated sound of myriads of huge
Field-pieces, belching forth their fire and death ?
Is this artillery of Heaven that bursts
Upon the ear in new and forceful form ?

Now comes the rush of mighty waters—see,
They leap along their course like chargers spurred
To agony, expending all their strength
To compass full destruction of some foe,
Or hungry tigers springing on their prey

They light upon each unresisting cot,
And ev'ry homestead thought so safe erstwhile
Is now submerged within the angry flood.

Then terror strikes at every heart ; it is
As if the mighty ocean broke its bounds,
And now no longer moon-kept thrusts away
Its chains, engulfing all it reaches.

See, riding down the vale in fullest speed,
The horseman brave to give the sleeping town
An instant's warning ; valorous he sped,
The huge flood following, and fronting him
The town.   He hears the waters rush, he turns
Him round ; he sees himself pursued
E'en by a mighty moving mountain chain,
Whose huge dimensions gave momentum great.

With pallid face he spurs his steed—' On—on !'
He urges him, ' or else a town is lost !'
But while the words were on his lips, both horse
And rider were to quick destruction whirled.

Now bravely stands one woman at her post,
And sends electric summons to each place,

Within the radius of the waters' course,
To warn them of their danger.   'Save thyself!'
The answering message said ; but still she plied
The needles, while the waters onward came
With giant strength.   ' This message is my last !'
She trembling wired ; one moment later rushed
In fullest force the torrent wild, and swept
Away in one vast wave that noble soul.

But her brave deed will live : no hero great
Hath better won his laurels bright, than she
Who willingly laid down her life to save
The many from destruction.   Henceforward men
Will say,—' Ah, seldom woman's courage fails
When those she loves are found in danger :' here
No selfish love inspired her soul, 'twas done
All bravely for the public good ; and in
Long years to come the children shall be told
With quiv'ring lips this woman's gentle deed,
This tale of noble self-devotion.

Now high upon the roof a mother stands
Surrounded by her children ; wond'ring if
Avenging God another deluge sent.

The building swayed and rocked, moved by the
    force
Of that mad water-mountain. Suddenly
It tottered over. In the flood herself
And one brave boy now struggled. 'Swim for
    life!'
She cried as she upheld him clinging close
To floating thing, which swirled and danced
    around.
With blanching cheek and beating heart the boy
Obeyed ; then turning his white face to hers—
'Mother,' said he, 'you always told me God
Would keep me safe ; will He protect me *now* ?'

Alas, poor mother, that long ling'ring look
The loving child gave thee is all thou hast
To dream upon ! Now, widowed, childless, 'reft
Of all the seven, weep thine eyes away ;
The light of life from thee for ever fled,
All blighted and extinguished thy heart's joy
In one short moment.

Impelled with awful force the floating wrecks
Of all the hamlets round come riding on

The wave, alive with shivering souls who cling
With death-tight clasp to their unstable aid.
On—on the waters rush with mighty swell,
And soon the town is even with the ground,
And ev'ry habitation as completely wrecked
As if an army vast with vengeful force
Had swept it with great cannon.   Onward goes
The flood, which carries now the wreckage of
A town, together with the remnant left of all
A goodly town's inhabitants.

Now mingling with the waters' rush and roar
Are heard the shrieks of terror-stricken souls,
Who cling in wild despair to aught that floats
The frightful current.   Snow-white locks of men
Bent with the weight of years, are mingled with
The full rich brown of youth.   And childhood's
    gold
Is gleaming in the morning sun, that lights
Those cruel waters that last day of May.

All innocent of danger ; void of fear,
A child plays on the floating timber ; laughs
Full merry as he dances down the wave

In all the joy of childhood, happy—free—
In full belief this ride on chance-made craft
Was pleasant sport for dawn of summer's day.

Still rushes on the flood, until the bridge
Is reached ; the wreckage is too vast to pass
Beneath its arches.   Suddenly is made
A barrier of piled-up heap of homes
Demolished—shattered—all that goes to make
A goodly town, and clinging to this mass
Are thousands souls who swell the block the bridge
Hath made, and forms one firm stupendous dam.
And thus the coming current losing vent
Falls back upon the town, which now becomes
As deep submerged as ocean bed ; as void
Of human habitation, or the sign
Of human hand as what the sea traverses.

But see !   A flame is flickering through the pile
Against the bridge : it gathers strength—it spreads
All o'er the mass ; and volumes of dense smoke
And tongues of fire are leaping from that heap
In which are wedged a multitude of souls.
Oh, God ! Now hear the shrieks that fill the air ;

The moans of dying in their agony ;
As if a thousand martyrs to the stake
Made fast, were slowly, horribly consumed.

Or has the Earth disclosed at last a Hell,
And in the midst of all the torrent's rush
Belched forth its fierce and fiery fumes
Upon the hapless beings gathered there ?
To flee the torture of this hell, those free
To move their limbs leaped from the writhing mass
To end their torments in the deep dark flood.

.   .   .

Abated now the fury of the flood ;
But who shall dare approach that awful pile
Still burning, smould'ring dense?   And now no
        sound
Doth issue from its depths ; no groans—no cries—
No signs of life ; an awful stillness reigns.
Though hope is lost yet every man hath now
Become a hero.   Day by day they struggle on
To free the loved remains from hellish place,
Though naught but ashes, or charred limbs will
        meet
Their dazed, dimmed eyes, and sickened hearts.

And this is all
That's left of manhood's strong and stately prime ;
Of womanhood's sweet beauty !   Hoary age,
And tender infancy are mingled in
One mass, and none can say—' She's mine !' for all
That goes to make a woman love one man,
Or man to love one woman far above
All other, are now extinguished, and full
Obliterated all life's beauty.

Oh, saddened men, why seek ye your beloved
Among the charred remains that strangely fill
This floating charnel-house ?   Shut fast your eyes,
Nor let the hideous vision haunt your sight
Throughout the weary, solitary years
That ye may call your own.   Let Memory
Alone, before the mental retina
Bring faces sweet and fair ; whose eyes looked
     love
To yours ; whose smiles were as a household sun
Which spreads its warm, refulgent rays around.
Whose souls were as a book all fairly writ
With tender thoughts, and deeds, and all
Those sweet solicitudes that Love begets

In woman's heart, and leaves to blossom there.
Thus contemplate ; and in the earnest strife
That falls to men who live their lives through-
    out
Now bury this Dead Past in deep oblivion.

TO J. F. T.

Birthday Ode

Once more the earth with swift unerring flight
Hath sped her course around her glorious lord,
Who sits enthroned above the Heavens, and sheds
On many worlds his warm effulgent beams :
To each their proper season duly gives,
Bestowing riches, beauty, life on all.

Again the earth is clothed in russet dress,
And Autumn brings its many-shaded hues
Of golden brown ; more beautiful than spring
In all its youthful freshness ; now the heart
Is stirred with aspirations pure and good
By all this wealth of loveliness around.

'Twas thus, dear friend, at such a beauteous time
Thou first didst ope thine eyes, and saw Heaven's
    light ;

When Earth breathed poems sweet, and softly
    sang
Her mystic songs in every rustling leaf.

Yes, then thou cam'st, all innocent of what
Life means.   Thou hadst to learn that even joy
Brings pain.   That hid beneath the cup of bliss
There lies some bitter element we hate ;
And fain would we untasted leave those dregs ;
But still no choice is left :—the full, deep draught,
Or none.

      Wrapped in sweet unconsciousness of all
Existence means ; its duties, crosses, joys,
Its vast responsibilities, thou breathed
The breath of life in gentle sleep.
How much unwearied love and care
Have fondly been bestowed on thee since then !
So much its magnitude were all in vain
To realise, until thy time doth come
To lavish pure paternal love on bright
Young hearts.   It is a compensating law
Our Mother Nature doth enforce that what
We cost we pay again in full : in turn

We render too that self-forgetting love ;
That patient, true devotion we received.

To what can I compare thy glad, young life
Emerging just on manhood's sober years ?
'Tis like a tree that's now attained fair growth
And covered o'er with scented blossoms sweet
Gives promise sure of richest freight of fruit.

And yet one other simile is here ;
As year by year the tree doth form around
Itself a circle, showing the vital force
Within is ever working out with strong,
Unceasing energy, that first great law
Of Nature : that power inherent, to build—
Construct, and give unto itself such grand
Proportions—such wealth of noble beauty,
So let thine energies be put to high
Pursuits, to elevating deeds : to that
Which cannot fail to give the toiler true
A glad and sweet content.
And may each sep'rate phase of thy career
Bear honourable marks of thy life's work
Which seeing, all can say 'THIS MAN HATH
     LIVED !'

APOSTROPHE TO THE OCEAN

OH, surging ocean, wide, and wild, and grand!
An angry despot thou, and harboureth deep
Strong enmity to Earth.   Fain wouldst thou rob
Her every treasure.   Now, wouldst thou engulf
The glistening beach, anon, the smiling fields:
How many forest wilds hast thou entombed
Since first thou wert begotten?
In far-off age, while yet the Earth was young,
Thou mad'st a bed for thy tumultuous head,
'Midst spongy reeds as great as forest trees,
And tangled brakes which drew their breath
From rank and humid atmosphere.

Now white with foaming rage in furious storm
Thou fill'st man's heart with apprehension deep;
Awe-struck, with fascinated gaze he sees
White-crested waves, like thousand monsters huge,

Rush on in quick succession ; gaping wide
With cavernous mouth, to swallow up their prey.

Then terror-struck the white-sailed ship doth flee,
As if she were some closely-hunted hind,
That running blindly on, doth trembling seek
The quiet shelter of some friendly cave.
But long before 'tis reached her eye-balls strained
With longing gaze, are glazed in grim, cold death.
The quiv'ring limbs her great embarrassment
No longer testifies.   The fearful strife
Of death-agony is past ; she breathes no more.

Even so the laden ship so fair, and strong
Erstwhile, is now resistless torn by grasp
Of Ocean's arms ; she gasping sinks therein.
No more will gentle zephyrs play within
Her fair white wings.
No more to shores whose odorous breath
Delicious scents the balmy breeze, she'll sail
With graceful mien.   The Sea, with envious eye
Hath cruelly despoiled her.   Down she sinks
With all her living, breathing treasure closed
Within her.

I

And thou, oh, Sea, assumeth placid calm,
As if no crime were thine ; like innocence
Thou weareth smooth and happy brow, and trust
Again is given to thy deceitful face.

Now slowly comes the rolling mist all dark
And moist.   It is thy heavy breath which fills
The broad expanse.   In volumes huge and dank
It spreads itself, o'er earth, through air, and like
A dark unsightly veil it hideth all
Things fair.

The numerous suns who myriad miles above
The sky, desire to send their far-off light
To earth, are now shut out.   Their scintillation
    bright
Is hid by black and murky mask.
And Cynthia herself can show no more
Her beaming, placid face, and her strong spouse
Through atmosphere has ceased to dart his rays ;
For all is steamy, cold, and vaporous.

The Heavens unhappy at such fate weep tears
Of sadness.   Winds moan and sigh, and all

Without is misery.   Birds hide their heads ;
Their song is hushed ; their pleasant warblings
    ceased,
For in this darksome time all Nature mourns.

SOUVENIR OF OXFORD

LIKE echoes oft repeated through a chain
Of mighty hills, reverberating far,
Whose voice so strangely multiplied doth leap
From peak to peak ; or as a train of dear
Sweet visions, each one brighter than the last,
So thy remembrances, fair city come
Before mine eyes, and ever in my thoughts
Are imaged forms so life-like, real,—true—
They take a tangibility so clear,
That fain I would persuade myself once more
I live, I move among them.

      Now I glide
Most softly o'er the rippling waters bright
Of lovely Isis ; where the willows bend
With graceful mien from rich and verdant banks,
And seem to watch their own reflection fair

In drooping modesty.   And blue forget-me-nots
Shy peeping from their em'rald beds, now set
My heart aglow.

Imagination fondly takes me next
Beneath the cool deep shade of noble trees,
Which clothed in beauteous dress of green stand
    forth
All radiant in their freshness, new and bright ;
Suggesting thoughts for utterance too high,
Too deep for words to give expression true.

And now the soul in tend'rest rapture turns
To dear associations of the past ;
For mem'ry quick recalls how genius trod
That very path long time ago, in grave
And serious contemplation.

Again the scene is changed.   I see uprise,
As vivid antique pictures, forms distinct
Of venerable piles, whose ancient walls
All ivy-covered ; fair, and shapely domes,
And arches curiously carved, inspire
Me straight with rev'rence deep ; I bow me down

In meek humility ; my soul is stirred
With loving wonder at the mighty Past.
And looking back through centuries, I see
What warm enthusiasm, zeal, and love
Have done, how much they have attained !
How each succeeding generation made
Sweet Learning its own mistress, framing thus
A scheme of evolution broad, and true,
And perfecting.

Thou city of religion, then, farewell !
Of realism, beauty, learning deep ;
Of pleasure, labour ; prejudices old,
Ideals new : but ever shall these last
Strive hard and struggle ; surely in the end
Their victory over ancient notions gain ;
Which like old men all ready for the grave,
Shall gently pass away from ev'ry mind,
And only by the new and vig'rous be
Remembered long for their antiquity.

THE LOVE OF UTHER

OR, LEAVES FROM ANCIENT ANNALS

THE LOVE OF UTHER

OR, LEAVES FROM ANCIENT ANNALS

PART I

DEATH OF AURELIUS

UPON his royal couch Aurelius [1] lay
All sick, and they who loved him, day by day
Soft whispered to each other—'Would that some
Deep learnèd man of healing art could come
And ease our king ; for sorely straitened we
To see him peak and pine all helplessly
At such a troublous time.   Those Saxons vile,
Led by Pascentius, invade our land, defile
The peaceful homes of Britain.   Yet the bold,
Strong Uther, brother to the king, doth hold
The conduct of the war, and all valiantly
Will lead the army on to victory.'

[1] Aurelius Ambrosius, King of Britain, A.D. 484.

So hoped the Britons; but the Saxons grew
More bold, and flattered they themselves anew;
That Fate had favoured them with fortune fair
To lay Aurelius low in time of war.

Then Eopa to the invaders came,
And spake,—'What the reward, and what the
    name;
What will ye give if there be one who'll slay
The smitten king, and thus no more delay
The laurels that be yours?'   Pascentius said—
'Oh, that I could find a man inbred
With such brave resolution!   I would give
A thousand pounds of silver; and while I live
Make him my friend; and if the crown I gain,
He shall centurion be, while I the king shall reign.'

To this the Saxon Eopa replied,—
'I am well skilled in Physic; but beside
All this I know the manners—speech
Of Britons, and in their own tongue can reach
The court and king.   If thou wilt swear an oath
To well perform thy word, I give my troth
That I this part all faithful undertake.'

Pascentius readily complied—' I make
This covenant most solemnly with thee.'
He swore the oath ; 'twas sealed ; and silently
The Saxon left the presence of the son
Of Vortigern.   Before the day was done
The wily Eopa had shaved his head,
And in the habit of a monk had sped
To Winchester, armed with a mighty load
Of drugs, he hied him to the king's abode.

Then, with an air of holy sanctity,
And look of wisdom suiting his degree,
He simulated sorrow ; great access
Of sympathy for King Aurelius :
And offering his services to heal
The stricken monarch, promised with great zeal
To quickly bring him into health, and make
The fount of life with vigour to awake.

All willingly they listened him, and gave
Unhesitating the liberty he crave.
Then led him to the king : with anxious air
He soft approached the couch ; with tender care
The baleful draught he bade the monarch drink.

' Drink !' said he, 'and sleep ; to-morrow thou wilt
      think
Thou never hadst a pain ; thy sickness seem
To be some vague, and half-forgotten dream :
Now lie thee still, and fear not ; court sweet sleep,
Let silent slumber soon thine eyelids steep.'

The poor drugged king now slept, and ever slept,
Until the life-stream in its courses kept
No action : then, they knew the king was dead,
And Eopa, the false physician, fled.

Then in the heavens a mighty star appeared,
Most brilliant its light, and strangely weird
In shape : for, darting forth a fiery ray
This ended in a dragon, whose jaws lay
Gaping ; sending forth two other rays of light,
Of which one reached to Gaul ; one beaming bright
Upon the Irish Sea, was finished by
Seven other rays of less intensity.

And all the people wondered ; and great fear
At sight of this strange star spread everywhere.
Even the gallant Uther now betrayed

Disturbance of his mind, as all dismayed
He gazed upon the fiery orb while on
His march to Cambria.   'No comparison
Bears this to aught I've seen ; now quickly go,
Bring Merlin, the magician, for I would know
The full interpretation of these signs,
If evil doth portend our harassed lines.'

Thus Uther spake, and Merlin,—who following
The fortunes of the war that he might bring
Good counsel unto Uther,—then lifted high
His voice, and with a wail, and woeful cry,
While tears adown his cheeks their channels made,
Uttered the words of prophecy, and said—

'Alas, alas, the king is dead !   Now woe,
Now death, now doom is on us all, for lo,
The king is dead !   Yet, Uther, that bright star
Doth signify thyself : take heart ; this war
Shall end in thy renown, and thou shalt reign
All over Britain, and the crown remain
Most steadfast on thine head ; for, from thee
Shall spring a son most potent, that shall be
A monarch great, whose rule shall reach as far,

And wide as doth the rays of yon bright star.
Thou art the dragon ; and the other ray
That emanates from thee is picture of the sway
Of thy fair daughter, who in turn shall bear
Her husband royal sons, whose every care
Shall be to win their subjects greatest good ;
And rule all Britain with solicitude.'

And Uther, scarce believing all was true
Marched on to battle ; valiantly drew
His forces nigh Menevia,[1] where lay
The Saxons.   Fierce the battle raged all day,
And each side suffered keenly : 'twas most long,
And bloody ; in the end the bold and strong
Pascentius, with Gillomanius were slain,
And all their forces routed from the plain.

And Uther followed even to the sea,
Where th' invaders sought their ships, to flee
The swift pursuer.   Messengers soon came
To camp, who brought account of that vile scheme
Which slew the stricken king. Then, Uther went
His way to Winchester, where reverent

---

[1] St. David's, Wales.

Bishops, abbots, and persons of degree
Assembled were in great solemnity
To render to the dead the sacred rite,
With all the pomp, and honour requisite,
For royal obsequies.   And in the tomb
Reared by Aurelius, whose stones had come
From Mount Killarius, the manes were placed ;
A monument [1] that time hath not effaced.

Succeeding this in great magnificence
The crowning came, and conference,
Where with one accord they Uther chose for king :
And Merlin's prophecy remembering

[1] The monument of antiquity now called Stonehenge. According to the legend these stones possessed medicinal properties, and were brought over from Africa to Ireland by giants, who used them for healing-baths ; whence Aurelius, by the magical aid of Merlin, had them conveyed to Britain, and constructed into a mausoleum for himself. Francis Palgrave says—'The temples in which the Britons worshipped their deities were composed of large rough stones disposed in circles, for they had not sufficient skill to execute finished edifices. Some of these circles are yet existing ; such is Stonehenge, near Salisbury ; the huge masses of rock may still be seen there, grey with age ; Stonehenge possesses a stern and savage magnificence, the masses of which it is composed are so large that the structure seems to have been raised by more than human power.'

King Uther caused two dragons of pure gold,
In likeness of the star which had foretold
His power, to be constructed.   One he gave
To Holy Church ; the other he would have
As lucky talisman to take at ev'ry war
In memory of the strange prophetic star.
And both were finest wrought, all skilfully
In veriest workmanship that be :
Then was ' Pendragon ' added to his name,
Or ' Dragon's Head,' by popular acclaim.

PART II

THE BATTLE

MEANWHILE, the enemy now bore
On luckless Britain.   Octa, bound no more
By treaty made with King Aurelius,
The Saxon army joined most treacherous ;
Who pressing message unto Germany sent
For troops to swell their numbers, and augment
Their heavy forces ; which exceeded far
In numbers Uther's troops ; and everywhere

They ruin, desolation, spread around,
And ravished, razed fair cities to the ground.
With this vast army Octa then made waste
The northern provinces ; urging great haste
He sieged the places fortified, and sped
His way to York, so thither Uther led
His forces : gallantly he made onslaught
Upon the bold marauders, courageous wrought
Heroic wonders.   Now, from his chariot leapt
The British warrior, and fiercely swept
The Saxon lines with long, and glitt'ring sword ;
While the skilful charioteer in keen accord
His well-trained steeds would swiftly turn aside
To give good space for prowess ; there abide
The issue of the struggle, and give good aid
If worsted were his comrade.   Full well arrayed
With numerous piles of javelins, a line
Of charioteers in steady discipline
Came tearing through each Saxon rank,
And with deft aim the pointed weapons sank
Deep in the breast, or mayhap at the head
Of many a stout barbarian ; who red
With streaming gore, and weak with deepest wound
Would spend his ebbing strength on all around

K

With fierce, and deadly thrusts.   In contest close
The short sharp sword of these barbarian foes
Proved instruments death-dealing : swiftly down
They mowed the Britons, whose corses white were
     strown
Upon the reddened plain.   Yet all that day
They unremitting fought, until the grey
Of evening, on the tempestuous scene,
Closed for a brief night's space the conflict keen.

Thus, were Uther's legions by th' invading force
Outweighed in valour. However brave their course
Throughout the fight, the Saxon dogs devoured
The struggling Britons. The remnant overpowered
At length some safety sought, to flee the slaughter
     made
For Hill of Damen, where the friendly shade
Of Hazel trees fair sheltered the pursued,
And rocky caverns in centre of this solitude —
The wild beasts' lair—the soldiers did impress,
As harbours welcome in their dire distress.

No sleep that night pressed down the lids of king
Or commoner ; for what the morn would bring

Made tremble every heart.   Night nearly spent,
The king to all his consuls message sent
To hold a council ; when assembled gave
To Gorlois, the Duke of Cornwall, first leave
To make his motion.   Being of them all
The eldest, bearing ripe experience,
The king accorded him pre-eminence.

' This is no time for ceremonies fine,
Or speeches ; for unless we well combine
Our chance is lost ; our lives, or freedom gone
If we keep still till shines the morning sun.
But rather let us rise while darkened night
Our scanty numbers covers o'er from sight ;
And keeping well compact make rush and raid
Upon the enemy, who all dismayed,
And taken by surprise, will haply prove
Our victims, not our victors, by this move.'

Thus spake Gorlois, the duke : with one consent
The council well received his argument.
Collecting all their troops the rugged slope
The warriors descended, and high with hope
All silently and soft pursued their way

To where the heavy-sleeping Saxons lay,
And pounced upon their guards ; who instantly
Proclaimed approach of coming enemy
With loud-voiced bugles.   Swift they pushed their
    course
Towards the Saxons ; with vehement force
Rushed right, and left, and ruthlessly they hewed
The half-awakened men ; who nearly nude,
And all unarmed ran madly here and there
In 'wildered, wild confusion ; for where
A Saxon missed one sword, he straight would fall
Beneath another.   Thus were slaughtered all
King Uther's foes ; of all their hosts scarce one
Remained, to tell how Britons lost, and won.

　　　' Firmly hath the archer fixed his bow ;
　　　　　Like wind the cunning arrow
　　　Cleaves its wingèd way towards the foe
　　　　　To pierce him to the marrow.

　　　' Iron warriors hurled the javelin
　　　　　With force all full unswerving ;
　　　Cord-like swells the knotted muscles in
　　　　　Each limb, good purpose serving.

' Scythèd chariots swiftly hew their way
　　Through the lines unheeding :
Helmèd knights in all their war array
　　Their chargers boldly speeding.

' Scythe, nor spear, nor dart, nor glitt'ring sword,
　　The bold marauders vanquished ;
But the arm of God, the mighty Lord,
　　The heathen dogs [1] extinguished.

' Weep for your dead, oh, women, weep as rain,
　　Nor stay the wild emotion ;
For you ne'er shall see your pagan men
　　Come sailing o'er the ocean.

' Stark and stiff they stay upon the plain
　　With faces upturned lying ;
Curse nor caress shall never again
　　Come from the lips of the dying.

' Weep, weep, oh ye women, weep for aye,
　　Though the western wind is blowing
Over the sea this dawn of sweet day,
　　No white sail shall be showing.'

---

[1] The Britons applied to the Saxons constantly, the
epithets—' dog,' ' barbarian,' &c.

Thus sang the thankful Uther, giving God
The praise ; while the legionaries raised the
    sod,
And reverent laid beneath their own dear dead.
Then marched they on to London ; thither led
As prisoners Eosa and Octa, who stirred
The Saxons with great confidence ; whose word
Brought hosts of fresh invaders.   News of raid,
And ravage, and rapine was quickly laid
Before the king that Caledonians were
For ever lawless, plundering ; void of fear,
Undisciplined.   Then Uther with much care
Quelled the contumely ; punished the pillager,
And straightway made strict laws of equity
To govern his dominions steadily ;
And forcibly their prompt obedience brought
That all might live in harmony throughout.

And mild-eyed Peace proclaimed her gentle
    sway
All over Britain ; and mingled with the Bay
Meek olive-branches decked each warrior's
    head,
And o'er his brow an ambient glamour shed.

A sheen more honoured ; of nobler sort,
Than all the laurels that can grace a court :
For kings, proud Conquest is most glorious art ;
For subjects, Peace doth play the better part.

PART III

THE BANQUET

AND when the Ides of March drew near, the king
Would have a royal banquet ; issuing
Invites to his nobles ; and all the fair
Of Britain's daughters Uther summoned there,
And bade he graciously each high-born guest
To grace his court, do honour to his feast.
Being the festival of Easter-tide
King Uther thought to honour it ; beside
'Twas his desire to meet his subjects face
To face ; gain their esteem, give royal grace ;
And thus by mutual affections bind
The Ruled, and Ruler in harmonious mind.

The king arrayed in royal robes and crown,
Covered with glory ; justly-earned renown,

In great solemnity, and pomp, and state
The Church's festival did celebrate.
From every city fair the nobles came
To greet the conqueror with loud acclaim :
All gentle blood of Britain now essayed
To show him honour.   Many a beauteous maid
All bright with gems, in rich apparel tired,
To royal grace would gladly have aspired.

The royal banquet set 'neath silken tent,
Was costly, rich ; on scale magnificent :
On silver vessels of beauteous design
Were delicacies served, and dishes fine :
In glistening wine-cups of pure gold did shine
The red, or amber juice of choicest wine.
And silken couches from Damascus' loom
Were ranged in Roman style all through the
        room : —
For simplicity of the Briton's home
Was changed for luxuries of conquering Rome—
And costly tables of sweet-smelling wood,
Brought from Eastern groves, vied with the food
In yielding delicate odour.   While breath
Of fresh spring-flowers, woven with green heath,

Delicious fragrance shed throughout the air,
And made a multiple of perfumes there.
The whole was blended with harmonious sound ;
For melting music swept the space around :
Thus cultured art enhanced th' enraptured sight,
And every sense was steeped in sweet delight.

And all the stateliest in the land were there ;
Long trains of lovely women ; and every fair
Was led by noble knight of high renown,
And braves, and beauties in one phalanx shone.

Of all the glittering galaxy none saw,
The equal of the lady of Gorlois : [1]
Of queenly mien, of loveliest form, and eyes
Like gems set in translucent skies.
And all the beauty of the court was dimmed
By fair Igerna : to Uther's eyes she seemed
To stand a peerless pearl ; a diamond divine ;
Beyond all price, and fitted most to shine

[1] This name I take to be Gallic, and have consequently given it the modern French pronunciation as in *Dunois*. The pronunciation of old French is as entirely lost to the French of the present day, as Old English is to us, therefore only the modern style can be safely given.

In kingly coronet of the Great on earth ;
A prizeful jewel of unbounded worth.

Upon her beauty Uther gazed with eyes
That saw no other ; all women she outvies
In every gentle grace.   Her voice now thrilled
With soft delight his ravished ears, and filled
His listening soul with music's harmony
Sweet as the rippling water's melody.
And heedless Uther knew not this was Love,
Which took away his strength, and sweetly wove
Around him mystic chains, that gave
A mingled joy, and left him veriest slave.

Only to Igerna the king's discourse
Was e'er addressed ; his care at every course
Of tempting viands to send most delicate
Of the dainties to this fair lady's plate :
And when he quaffed the ' cyathus ' of wine,
His toast was fair Igerna.   To enshrine
Her in most honour, as oft he filled the same,
He drank to every letter in her name.[1]

[1] This was a Roman custom. To give extraordinary
honour to a person the Romans at a feast would drink a

His smiles to sweet Igern alone were given
All through that festive day, and when the even
Drew on, and revelry began, he sent
Her golden cups by his own confidante.

And while the king was bound in love, the song
Was sung, the harp was strung the whole night
  long.

THE HUNTER'S SONG

I

'THROUGH forest, over heather,
Regardless of all weather,
  I range a hunter bold,
The sylvan woods I'm keeping,
With pearly dew-drops dreeping
  To be my own stronghold.

cyathus of wine as often as the number of letters contained
in the name of the person toasted. The cyathus was a
certain measure that held the allowance of pure wine which
was always mixed with a fixed quantity of water.

II

' And when the skies are looming ;
Her cannon Nature's booming
  Through darkened firmament ;
I watch the lightning sunder,
'Midst crashing of the thunder,
  The trees magnificent.

III

' Though quick the woodcock's flying,
My bow and arrow plying
  I reach it in a trice :
The boar that's madly rushing,
And thick-set brushwood crushing,
  My needs help to suffice.

IV

' In truth, I'm monarch royal,
For subjects none so loyal
  As those the woods bestow :
No jealousy assails me,
My dog he never fails me,
  My sceptre is my bow.

V

' The pure and crystal fountain
That trickles down the mountain :
　My thirst doth soon allay :
Day vanishes so fleetly,
And evening comes so sweetly,
　I scarce feel them glide away.

VI

' Before the stars are gleaming,
While yet the sun is streaming,
　Its glories from the west :
While his crimson rays soft glimmer
Through the trees with elf-like shimmer,
　I seek my mountain nest.'

THE POET'S SONG TO HIS LADY

I

' COME to the woods while day is brightly beaming
　And songsters fill the air ;
The earth is filled with life and beauty, seeming
　A paradise so fair.

II

' The flowery mead in gayest colours smiling
  Reflects the sun's bright beams :
The brooklet sweet with murmurs soft be-
      guiling
  Sends forth the purest streams.

III

' At eve we'll watch, when day is calmly
      closing,
  The sunset 'neath the hill ;
And feathered choristers are soft reposing ;
  And all is hushed and still.

IV

' The blue skies gemmed with stars that
      beaming brightly
  O'er this fair world of ours,
Sends whispering winds to play so lightly
  Their music 'mongst the flowers.

V

' Fair beauty and sweetness now are pervading ;
  Filling the earth and sea ;
Ah, whether sunshine, or even's soft shading,
  All teems with good for thee.'

THE MINSTREL'S SONG

I

' AH, Music and Song, how I love ye twain well !
Now, come and cast over me your sunny spell !
Come hither, your charms unto me now reveal ;
Come ravish my senses, and make me to feel
The care that surrounds and oppresseth the mind,
Is fled by the flow of your measure combined.
Enhanced are the ripples of sound, that enfold
Mine ears, by the poet's sweet story that's told.

II

‘ Ah, how can the lover his heart disclose,

Which bursts with the fulness of love’s gentle
    throes,

To her he adores with his whole soul’s delight,

Without whom existence would be as dark night ?

’Tis sweet voice, and sweet verse that can tell his
    tale,

Express it with fervour that never can fail ;

Her heart it will melt at the soft witching strain,

While swells her white bosom with Love’s sweet
    pain.

III

‘ Two-fold is the beauty of Music, and Song ;

A foretaste of heaven while to earth we belong ;

They lift up the soul to ethereal bliss,

With ecstasy pure like a lover’s first kiss.

The heart-sick and weary most gently they soothe,

Life’s rough stony ways delightfully smooth :

Give courage anew to the warrior when faint ;

Softening the sinner ; inspiring the saint.’

PART IV

THE QUARREL

GORLOIS, the Duke, perceiving how the king
Paid court to his fair wife, with her took wing
At once to Cornwall ; nor did he crave
Permission thus to quit, but took his leave
Abruptly.   The king insulted in his court,
Vexed, and indignant sent a summons short
To quick return, and pay apology,
All due to host as well as royalty :
But th' angered, jealous duke was stiff and stern,
With scorn, most sullenly refused to turn
Him back again to court ; for well he knew
The prime, sole cause why this disturbance grew ;
He clearly saw 'twas not *his* grim old face
That thwarted Uther longed his court to grace.

Set at defiance thus King Uther swore
A hasty oath, and hotly vowed he'd lower
Gorlois' proud arrogance ; while furious heat
Filled all his blood, he bade his army meet.

L

Gorlois unswerving from his course, now placed
His vassals and his warriors in great haste
To stand a siege ; for no equivalent
Of men had he to the vast complement
Of royal troops commanded by his foe ;
He therefore made defence alone, to throw
Attack on Uther.   On the wild sea-shore
Was reared his castle of Tintagel ;[1] more
Strong, and inaccessible than any tower
Within the realms of Britain ; for its power
Was helped by rugged Nature.   Here frowned
The grey impenetrable rocks all round,
Like giants great emerging from the wave.
Sustaining solid walls of stone, that gave
No entrance there ; save by a passage small
And narrow, that three fighting-men were all
Defence the castle needed.   To keep secure
His wife, Gorlois within this fortress sure
Now placed her ; and in his wisdom thought
'Twere best to thus divide.   Said he,—' If aught
Of ill befall the town wherein I stay,
There is she safe, secure from all the fray ;

[1] The ruins of this castle still exist, and show that it
must have been a place of great strength.

Within Dimilioc the siege I can sustain
Till aid shall come from Erin o'er the main.'

The sun was sinking 'neath a glorious pile
Of crimson-tinted clouds, and for awhile
Bathed Uther's tents in richest tints of gold.
It played upon the rippling sea that rolled
In rhythmic motion on the smooth sea-shore,
And gleamed and glistened more, and more,
As wave succeeded wave in endless train,
Kissing th' expectant shore again, and yet again.

It lit the hedgerows with more vivid hue ;
It oped the blades of budding corn that grew
So tall, and waxed in verdant strength each day,
Till crushed by ruthless feet they dying lay,
Like children swept untimely from the breast,
By famine, sword, or pestilential waste.

And Uther in his anger fiercely warred
Against Gorlois, nor spared the fire, nor sword ;
Upon Dimilioc's fields he pitched his tent
With all the force of royal armament.

But pangs of conscience ever and anon
Depressed his mind, howe'er he strove to shun
Uneasy murmurs.   In his heart he felt
'Twas not the insult of the duke that dealt
A blow to kingly pride, but inward fire
Of passionate love that filled him with desire ;
Converting all the sweets, and good of life
To one long hellish stream of endless strife.

PART V

THE CONCEPTION OF KING ARTHUR

AND Uther sat within his camp that eve
In melancholy thought ; nor longer could deceive
Himself with reasons plausible to make
The siege continue.   Then, he to Ulfin spake—
Brave Ulfin his familiar friend, and said,—
' I'm weary of this war, and hate to shed
The blood of mine own subjects, though Gorlois
Hath given me scorn, I'll even now withdraw.
Oh, Ulfin, woe the day, and woe the hour
That e'er I saw Igerna ; for me no more

Hath life the shadow of a joy ; nor peace :
Lost to me the sweets of conquest, unless
I may possess Igerna.   In my heart
There burns a passion strong, whose counterpart
Hath no existence.   Now, am I consumed
With love all strong and powerful, and doomed
To bear a flame that hath no parallel
In all my past.   Oh, Ulfin, is it well
That I should die ?   Yes, death will prove
The inextinguishable force of love.'

While thus he spake his eyes grew dim, and dew'd
With tears, unlike his hardy habitude ;
His ruddy cheeks embrowned by sun, or rain,
Or biting wind, when camping in the plain,
Were paled and sunken by the lack of rest ;
Unerring witness of unquiet breast.
And while the fretted king the silence broke
His manly frame with strong emotion shook ;
And lowly bowed he down his mournful head.
Then Ulfin to his master sorrowing said—

' It grieveth me sorely to see my king
Sighing in sorrow all unavailing.

Oh, why dost thou dwell on the lady's charm
With unsatisfied love that can only harm ?
For safe is she lodged in Tintagel's town,
Girt by the sea-wave and thick walls of stone ;
And the bravest warriors of all thy train
Could ne'er make a breach, nor an access gain :
Now, let me call Merlin, the deep, and wise,
Who out of his wisdom might now devise
Some magical method to gain this prize.'

And Merlin was brought to the king that eve,—
For he kept with the camp that he might give
Good counsel to Uther, and lend his aid
With rare words of wisdom when came the need.
When Uther revealed the torments he bore
To Merlin, his friend and counsellor,
Then pained was the prophet to learn, that he
Was held in a hopeless supremacy.

But he comforted Uther whose soul waxed light
At the glorious plan he unfolded that night.
By my art,' said he, ' I will change thy face
To that of Gorlois, with his figure and dress :

And Ulfin will I metamorphosise
To Jordan, his comrade ; with this disguise
To Tintagel's gate I'll go with ye twain,
And order the guards to open amain.'

And Merlin, the Wise, by his magical law
Converted the king into Duke Gorlois ;
And he and his friends were disguised so well
When they came to the Castle of Tintagel,
That th' intelligent guards oped wide the door,
Supposing their lord had come to the bower
Of his beautiful wife that twilight hour.

Igerna, the fair, was so well deceived,
She ne'er hesitated, but straight believed
That she held in her arms her own Gorlois,
Who filled with delight, and rapturous joy,
Now kissed and caressed her the livelong night,
And tenderly told her when morning's light
Peeped over their heads, what risk might incur
In leaving his castle for love of her.
And love-songs sang he to softly beguile
His sweet lady fair, and win one more smile.

‘ Dearest, tell me which is first
    Of thy winning graces,
Rival beauties meet mine eyes
    In so many places ?

‘ Love circles round thy lips
    Like a cupid lying
In a rosy, coral bed,
    While his arrows flying

‘ Swift upon their dang’rous course
    To unsuspecting victim ;
Who is forced to yield himself
    To that fateful dictum.

‘ So in thine archèd brows
    Even there he’s hiding ;
Each mute unerring shaft
    In quick succession sliding.

‘ In every look of thine
    Love is surely peeping ;
Thine every motion proves
    That he’s never sleeping.

' Love lights those liquid eyes
   Till in very seeming,
The brightest star is shamed
   At their lustrous gleaming.

· Fringed lids shade their light
   With a tender veiling,
As cloudlets through the heavens
   'Neath the stars are sailing ;

' Hiding now their lustre bright ;
   Now their light revealing,
While through the firmament
   Rays are softly stealing.

' Yes, thou hast bound me quite
   To thyself securely,
By a thousand magic charms
   I am thine, most surely.

' Links fastened by such spells
   Never can be riven ;
Oh, what enchantment sweet
   Unto thee is given !'

Thus sang th' enraptured Uther, all untired,
By sweet deliciousness of love inspired ;
In bliss they spent a long dear night of love,
Like mated doves that coo in shady grove ;
Igern conceived in loyal love that night
The goodliest son that e'er saw the light,
Arthur, bravest prince that Britain ever knew ;
The kingliest of kings ; most gentle, true.

PART VI

DEATH OF GORLOIS, AND MARRIAGE OF UTHER

ERE morning broke the absence of the king
Was full discovered ; and what strange thing
Had now befallen him his legions made
A cause of wonder.   Gladly they essayed
To hurry on the siege, and make attack
Most desperate ; eagerly they longed to sack
Dimilioc's fair town ; themselves repay
For Uther's indecision and delay.

Gorlois, with scanty numbers now rushed out
Most rashly on the royal troops, and thought

To win his way victorious by a raid
All sudden on the foe ; fronting blockade
Of full-drawn swords he fell amidst the fight :
And every warrior, every wight
Each plundered as he willed, all unrestrained,
Nor deigned to share alike the booty gained.

Then messengers to Tintagel swift came
To give the duchess tidings of the same ;
Struck with surprise, she knew not how to act,
Nor reconcile the statement with the fact.
' My husband killed ! ' she unbelieving cried,
' And still my husband standing at my side ! '
' My sweet,' said Uther, ' sure thy husband's here ;
Come kiss me ere I go, and have no fear.'

All quickly Uther hied him to the tent ;
Ridding himself of all disguise, he went
To camp, to test the tale he thought so vain,
Of Dimilioc sacked, and Gorlois slain.

But when the king the staunch old warrior saw
Slain with a score of wounds, the Duke Gorlois :

Then lifting up his voice he wept full sore ;
' And art thou gone, Gorlois, the brave !   No more
Shall I behold thy stern and honest face ;
No more thine iron arm shall leave its trace
Upon thy foes.   Gorlois, thou diedst my foe ;
Deserved I well thy wrath.   Oh, now I know
The pangs of biting conscience, and my heart
Moved with remorse doth feel the stinging smart—
The bitterness of friendship wronged, know I ;
For thee I wronged, Gorlois, most bitterly.'

And when the king his fallen foe had mourned,
His thought to his heart's idol fondly turned,
And all his grief was changed to keen delight,
When he full realised how soon he might
Crown her his own fair queen ; nor did he wait
A length of moons for her to meditate
In darkened widowhood ; but strove to dry
With soft caress, and soothing minstrelsy,
The ever-welling woe that filled her breast
In strong tempestuous waves of deep unrest.

Like a pale lily beaten to the ground
By fiercest winds ; whose courses all unbound

Know naught of mercy ; so she bowed her head,
Nor heeded what her lover fondly said.

'Canst thou forgive, Igerna !   At thy feet
I humbly sue for pardon, and entreat
Thine ample mercy.   I would atone
My shameful fault, and sorrowfully own
I plucked the rose not mine ; which blushed in all
Inherent beauty : thus, did I forestall
The unexpected bliss that lit on me
With golden wings, and fixed my destiny.

'Now, like a rainbow merging from the cloud,
I see thy dove-like eyes shine through their shroud
Of mist, and greet me with a gentle gaze
Of God-like pity.   Or, is it thy dispraise
Of my unutterable boldness ?   Sweet,
Say by one dear smile, if all complete
Thou hast forgiven unseemly brimming-o'er
Abundance of my love, for evermore ?

'In kindness, cast not all the blame on me,
For man is not himself, when urgency

Of over-powering love doth master him.
Beloved, arise, merge from this sorrow dim,
And suffer thy sweet womanhood's dear sway
To meekly bend to Love, and me.   Away
With Grief ; let my fond kisses now beguile
Thy soul to burst through cloud to sunny smile.'

I

' Pale sits fair Igerna within her strong tower,
       And she weeps, and weeps for aye,
       For her husband she weeps alway ;
She mourns her dear lord with a sorrow all sore,
       Oh, she mourns him night and day !

II

' And the breath of her sighs fills the space around,
       And her sobs break through the air,
       As she wails and weeps up there :
Like a dark pall falls from her brow to the ground
       Her long waves of silken hair.

III

' All bedimmed is the rose upon her fair cheek,
And washed with the heavy rain,
Aye, washed and watered again ;
And fretted and changed to the pale lily meek,
With the tears, and sore heart-pain.

IV

' Oh, beautiful lady, now bind up thine hair,
Now bind it in shining braid
In coronet on thine head ;
Stay thy sad sighs, and cease thy sorrowful air,
And calm thee, for thy dear dead.

V

' For who is it loves thee, Igerna the bright,
Igerna my lily all pure,
With passionate love, and sure,
But thy sovereign lord, who sues for the right
To make his fair pearl secure ?

VI

' I will give thee one hour, my beloved, to weep,
    To weep one other sad hour,
    In the silence of thy bower ;
Then thy tears will I dry with kisses, and keep
    Thee ever, my own sweet flower.

VII

' Oh, sweet was the scent of the pure morning air
    That came o'er the bright sea-wave,
    And Tintagel's towers did lave !
But my love she is sweeter, more soft, more fair
    Than the breath the south winds gave.

VIII

' And hid in the casket of my deepest heart
    I'll treasure thee all my days ;
    My diamond worthy all praise ;
Thou gem of my crown set in golden art,
    And shedding divinest rays.'

IX

' Make thee ready, my love, for the marriage rite ;
    The solemn and sacred vow,
    Within an hour from now ;
Give joy to my soul, thou sweet star of my night ;
    Thyself on thy king bestow.

X

' And as the firm apple encloseth the seed
    All safely within its core,
    From frost and wintry show'r,
Until the ripe season of fair Earth's good need
    Shall succour it evermore.

XI

' Even so shall I shelter thee, love, from all harm,
    And nourish thee in my breast,
    Like dove in its own sweet nest :
No rough wind shall assail thee, or biting storm,
    Till the earth shall give us rest.

M

XII

' Then, cease thy lamenting, my jewel, my crown,
    Thou source of my soul's delight,
    Who changest my dark to light ;
Array thee in robes of the bridal, my Own ;
    And gladden my longing sight.'

One moment pale, then flushed with rosy red
Igerna's tear-stained face, while being led
All trembling towards the altar, by the king
In happy triumph.   And she fulfilling
Merlin's prophecy, gave to him her love
Unswerving, faithful : soon around him wove
In silent strength the sweet magnetic chain
Of wife, which throughout life bound close
    the twain.

CAEDMON

AN EARLY ENGLISH IDYLL

CAEDMON

AN EARLY ENGLISH IDYLL

INTRODUCTION

EVERY student of early English literature is familiar with the story of Caedmon, the peasant-poet. Historians give him a marked position in their writings as forming a distinct epoch in English literature ; for Caedmon, ignorant and unlettered, and belonging to a race rude and uncultured, rose out of the darkness that surrounded him, in a truly wonderful manner. A thousand years before Milton's time this Whitby peasant sang the epic of the Creation, the first 'Paradise Lost.' In vivid language is depicted the War in Heaven, the Fall of Satan, and his counsellings in Hell. 'Thus, Caedmon began the first in time, and among the first in genius the strain in English poetry.'

Caedmon was in fact our first English poet ;

our Early Milton. His verse is full of dramatic
power, and true poetical fervour. Here he sings
of Satan fallen :—

' Satan discoursed, he who henceforth ruled hell
Spake sorrowing.
God's angel erst, he had shone white in heaven,
Till his soul urged, and most of all his pride,
That of the Lord of Hosts he should no more
Bend to the word. About his heart his soul
Tumultuously heaved, hot pains of wrath
Without him.
" Then," said he, " Most unlike this narrow place
To that which once we knew, high in Heaven's realm
Which my Lord gave me, though, therein no more
For the Almighty we hold royalties.
Yet right hath He not done in striking us
Down to the fiery bottom of hot hell."'

The monks with whom Caedmon was associated
when he became an inmate of the monastery, were
acquainted with the Chaldee Scriptures, and gave
him the name of Caedmon, because his verse was
taken from that scripture—' In the beginning' the
Chaldee for which is ' b Cadmon,' thus, in every

sense it was a beginning, for it was the first dawn of Saxon genius in England.

Although Bede, and every historian downwards, give Caedmon due place in their histories, no poet has ever pictured the story of his hearth-life, or woven around him in imagination the probable incidents of his home, and immediate surroundings.

Bede informs us that 'Hilda received him into her monastery with all that he possessed.'

This implies either the possession of some little property, or family, or both. Being an elderly man at the time of his poetic inspiration, his family, if any, would be grown up. It was no uncommon thing at that time for married persons, in the enthusiasm of their new conversion, to give up husband or home for a monastic life, in order to promote the glory of God. Therefore, it is quite probable that Caedmon had a portion of his family living with him at the time he broke up his home to enter into the monastery.

The 'Idyll' presents a double picture to the reader; on the one hand it recounts those incidents given by the Historian, and on the other, it fills up those spaces left out by him.

CAEDMON

THE oxen and horses all slowly along
The summer-white roads, were now wending their
　　way,
Bearing their burdens, as they patiently toiled
Alongside of the hedgerows, which robed in their
Emerald dress—new gift of the fair young Spring—
All scented, and decked with the may-blossom
　　bright,
Were mingling their sweets with the newly-mown
　　hay,
And with ravishing perfumes filling the air.

The Beechen trees bursting their bud-leaves,
　　branched out,
Beflecking in shapes all bewildering,
The beautiful scene, with their shadows all
Shifting, as light clouds in the arch of the sky.

At a turn in the road stood a cottage, meek,
Where dwelt Caedmon, the churl, the dreamer, yet
    wise,
And all urgent to learn the new story of Christ,
And Creation.   His fathers, barbarian
Saxons by birth ; who worshipped Odin, as god,—
A dead hero ;—bowed them to sun, and to sea.
And Caedmon's dear gentle daughter, had now
    learnt
The new doctrine of love, from the God-serving nuns
Of Streaneshalch,[1] sea-town on our northern shore.

Overlooking the great rolling ocean, oft
Angrily lashed into motion, by north winds
And east winds, was the Abbey of Hilda, the saint ;
Hilda, the Princess, who rose as a Deborah—
Revealer of Truth, on the wilds of our northern
    shore.

Kings in humility for her counsel came,[2]

---

[1] Ancient name for Whitby.   'Streaneshalch' means,
Bede tells us, 'the Bay of the Lighthouse.'
[2] 'Her prudence was so great that not only indifferent
persons, but kings and princes came for her advice.'—BEDE.

Her wisdom-words drinking in reverence, deep,
And left her refreshed for their toil in the world.

From her teaching uprose
The Old Fathers, and heroes of gentle renown ;
Who quelled the wild passions of Northmen, brave,
Alone by the love that springs out of God's fount,
And laid for all time the foundation of faith
In the hearts and the book-lore of England.

Save his one daughter, Caedmon lived lone ; all else
Who belonged him were long since laid in their
    grave ;
And his thoughts were all God-ward, but bound
    his speech,
No utterance finding for the fire within.

When the gold of the sun turned to crimson, red,
And shadows fell long ; finished the toil of the
    day,
Then Edna, his golden-haired daughter spake out,
Saying—' Father, dost thou remember the feast,
Our good corl hath maken us ready to-night ?
We thither must hasten ; have share in the sport ;

For the harp and the song will merrily pass
The hours with good speed.   And the old-time
Love-stories, old Ulfin, our neighbour, will tell,
Who weareth his ninety long winters full well,
On his snowy-white head.

       'And cometh young
Ethwuld, the fisher, from Heorta,[1] to-day.
He longeth all greatly to join in the throng :
And sings he most sweetly the songs of the sea.
Now, look through the distance, and canst thou not
  find
The sight of his brown sail just dotting the wave?
Dear Ethwuld ! The daughters of Aegir[2] are now
Winging thee over the ocean, to help thee
To hie unto me.'

' My daughter, it doth not beseem thee to give
Such honour to sea-gods ; all idle this talk !
For only Almighty Lord reigns over all.

---

[1] ' Heorta ' or ' Heruteu ' ancient name for Hartlepool.
[2] In Scandinavian mythology Aegir was god of the sea,
his daughters, the waves. Our ancestors for long retained
their old superstitions, and kept them side by side with the
new faith.

So Ethwuld is coming to greet thee!   'Tis well ;
He is welcome to bed and to board this night,
For sake of his father, my friend of old-time.
But Edna, oh, set not thy heart upon him,
Nor think thee of marriage ; for fain I would see
Thee God-serving always, as the nuns who sing
    praise
To their King day and night, for love of His Name.

Then, swiftly uprose the deep blush on her cheek,
Which as quickly retreated, turning back on
Her heart, and leaving her pale as a white rose,
Whose petals untinted, and passionless, send
Only their sweets to the air.

                            ' Give up Ethwuld !
Desert him, who loves me as dear as his life !
I cannot.   'Tis now all too late to undo !
I love him, and holds he my true plighted troth.
Yet, father, I still would obey thee.   Take now
My promise.   If Ethwuld all willingly yields
His just claim, myself I will give unto God.'

Then trembled the tears within their casements
    bright,

As dew on the flowers, or cloud hiding the stars :

And stirred was her whole soul, and heart deeply
    moved

By contending emotions, filling her breast.

Full oft had she longed to live only to God,

And give Him heart-service. Advancement 'bove
    all

To dwell 'neath the roof of his holiest saint,

The sweet Lady Hilda ; exalted beyond,

And above all women.[1]   Who daily was blessed

By the poor ; revered by the wealthy and great.

That instant through the open door, Ethwuld's
    form

Across her vision came. In thoughtful tenderness,

Fearing lest to him the pleasure would be lost

[1] 'At Whitby Hilda was as mother to the child-princess,
the one-year-old daughter of King Oswald's brother and
successor, who grew up under her care, and became next
abbess after her. She was as mother in her little community,
and among the rude people round about, who long preserved
the belief that her form was at certain times to be seen in a
vision of sunshine among the ruins of the later abbey, built
upon the site of hers. She so much encouraged the close
study of Scripture that in her time many worthy servants of
the Church, and five bishops, are said to have come out of
her abbey.'—MORLEY.

Of that night's revel, she put away her grief,
Made good endeavour to greet him valiantly,
And meet him with a sunny smile.   He, man-like,
Knew not the difference 'twixt the brightness
  forced,
And the heart's true merriment.   Donning her
  hood,
She led the way athwart the fields to the abode,
Where now, the eager guests in full assemblage
  met.

When finished the repast, and the mead sent round,
And all had well quaffed : they straightway sate
  them down
In one great circle.   Thither was brought the harp,
And in the simple minstrelsy each took part.
One touched the strings with cunning fingers ; or
  one
Sang his heathen song, or told some Northland
  tale.

The stranger to honour most, the host now bade
Young Ethwuld sing the first.   Though embrowned
  his cheeks

By sun, and rough sea-wind, still, the flush rose full,
As straight he stood, and, with deep melodious
    voice,
He sang the song of his birthplace.

THE FISHERMAN'S SONG

I

' AROUSE thee, my mate, for ye western breeze
    Now blows fresh, and free, and clear;
Across ye white-foaming, and surging seas,
    And thou, our coble must steer;

II

' For long have we waited ye fickle wind
    To lend her light fairy wing;
But she with uncertain, and changeful mind,
    No help to us e'er would bring.

III

' And then we will hoist our one big, brown sail,
    To swell in ye morning's light;
And away with our nets, and a pleasant gale,
    We'll hie us with all our might.

IV

' We'll silently speed, as fishermen brave,
    Who toil on ye ocean wide ;
While bright waves our boat will merrily lave,
    As onwards we safely glide.

V

' But if ye false wind should change her soft tone,
    And furious send ye storm,
And wild beats ye tempest, whose angry moan
    Doth fill us with deep alarm ;

VI

' Our thoughts will then fly to ye dear old Bay,
    Where those who love us are nigh ;
While watching for us through ye livelong day,
    Their prayer will ascend on high.

VII

' Arouse thee, my mate, for ye western breeze,
    Now blows fresh, and free, and clear,
Across ye white-foaming and surging seas,
    And thou our coble must steer.'

Then full great applause was given Ethwuld's
    song ;
When, suddenly an old-time warrior uprose,
Regarding with scorn the theme of Ethwuld's lay :
' I will sing anent Great Odin's son, King Ring,
A lay learnt long ago in the old home-land.'

THE SCANDINAVIAN'S SONG

(The Choosing of a King)

' O'ER hill and vale the Bud-staff,[1] fleet,
    Calls to the Ting ;[2]
Prince Ring[3] is dead ; the people meet
    To choose a king.

[1] The bud-staff was made of wood, about a foot long, and
was carried from house to house for the publication of news,
or proclamations, which were inscribed thereon in runic
characters.

[2] ' Ting ' was an assembly first introduced by Frei at
Upsala, where the people met three times a year for sacrifice,
and also for the conduct of State affairs.

[3] King Ring ruled over Ringarike, a part of Norway.
These verses are translated from an original Scandinavian
Saga.

‘ The warrior takes adown his blade
     Of blue-bright steel,
Against his hand with care ’tis laid,
     The edge to feel.

‘ The maiden cleans the helm awhile
     With diligence ;
And blushes as she sees her smile
     Reflected thence.

‘ Then to the field the people hie
     Where bucklers ring ;
No tent was there, save cloudless sky
     O’er open Ting.

‘ Above all, Frithyof was descried
     With boy so fair,
’Twas royal child, close at his side
     With golden hair.

‘ A murmuring voice went through the
          throng ;—
     “ To lead the host
He knoweth not ; and is too young
     For Judge’s post.”

‘ The child is raised by Frithyof’s hands
    On shield of steel :
“ Here is your king ! on him depends
    The country’s weal.

‘ “ And ancient Odin’s image grand
    Before ye, see !
Descended from the royal line[1]
    Of Gods is he.

‘ “ My sword his country’s just renown
    Shall e’er protect ;
Hereafter with his father’s crown
    He shall be decked.

‘ “ Forseté, Baldur’s[2] son, I take,
    As witness, thee ;
If ever I this oath should break,
    Destroy thou me ! ”

[1] These kings invariably considered themselves descended
from Odin, and traced their ancestry back to him.

[2] ‘ Baldur ’ is god of light, and typical of all good.
‘ Forseté ’ is Baldur’s son by Nanna, the god of justice.
The sun is female in Scandinavian mythology ; the moon
male !

       ' And from the shield the child looks round
           With eyes all bright ;
       As eaglet looks from gloomy ground
           On Baldur's light.[1]

       ' But wearied now the youthful blood ;
           So with a bound,
       The boy in proudly royal mood,
           Attained the ground.

       'Then rang the voices from the Ting
           All full and free ;
       " We choose thee buckler's child[2] of Ring,
           Our King to be ! " '

And the merry circle grew merrier still
At thought of their ancient Fatherland, which
    had

[1] ' Baldur's light.' This expression refers to the eagle looking at the sun.

[2] ' Buckler's child,' is an expression alluding to the custom of ancient northern nations, who, when they had elected a king, raised him on a shield, and carried him round the host in a triumphal procession.

Given birth to Gods.[1]   And many a lay was sung
In great Odin's praise ; and Frigga, his fair wife ;
And strong Thor, their son—the Northern Trinity,
Which in Upsala's temple they had worshipped.
And Caedmon's poor heart was burning strong
    within,
As listened he long to these vain verses sung,
Which now he full disdained.   Still, he could not
    sing
The praises of *his* God.   Motionless and mute
Remained he there, all pained ; and dreading the
    turn
He plainly saw approaching.   Then, silently
He stole him from his seat ; and the merry band
Better served by tending to their tired beasts.

Then, Ulfin, white-haired man, all bowed by weight
Of many a weary winter, spake full clear ;
Recounting a story of a time within

[1] The religion of the Anglo-Saxons was a compound of
the worship of Celestial bodies and of Hero-worship, termed
Sabæism.   The worship of Odin was common to all the
Teutons.   He was their king from whom their science and
lore had been derived.   The song of the bard and incanta-
tion of the sorcerer had been taught by Odin.

His sire's remembrance.　A love-tale of a king,
Descendants, of whom these rough Northmen long since
All clean annihilated.

OLD ULFIN'S STORY

I

' As far northwards I wandered away,
I saw shining Heorta's fair Bay,
And I wended my way by the sand,
Till I came where the sea-robbers land.[1]

II

' I saw nothing but rocks all around,
And dark caves reaching far underground,
But no soul in that solitude bare,
Nor the sign of a being was there.

[1] This is the place now called ' Black Hall Rocks.' Believed to have been a great resort of pirates, on account of its facilities for concealment. It possesses a weird, wild beauty of its own ; being now a coastguard station, a few cottages relieve its solitude.

III

' 'Twas the heat of a bright summer's day,
Now, what think you I saw near the Bay?
But a beautiful maiden bathing all free,
Laughing and laving in the cool sea.

IV

' How she splashed and she dashed in the wave!
How the sound of her clear voice now gave
Sweetest echoes on echoes, whose shock
Silver-belled seemed to play on each rock!

V

' Glittered the sun on the scene so fair ;
Sending his rays through her golden hair;
Lighting the water with golden light ;
Topping the waves as they danced so bright.

VI

' Sparkled the blue eyes in their wild glee,
Brighter than sunbeams lighting the sea ;
Like a lily the limbs, fair and round,
Parted the waves at each merry bound.

VII

‘ Oh, what luck, lackaday, lackaday !
Now whom think you came passing that way,
But King Locrin, the brave, who traversed
Past the place where the maid was immersed.

VIII

‘ But the sight of the nymph in the sea,
Nude as the flowers that grow on the lea,
Never came to his eyes ; nor espied
Maiden’s garments hard by the rock-side.

IX

‘ Then, in soft dreamy mood sate he down,
Close to the robe of dark russet brown,
As if careful to keep in his sight
The lily-white linen, bright with sunlight.

X

‘ Horror-struck, and all under the sea
Dived the maiden as long as could be ;
But the day-dreaming king, from the spot
Never stirred even one little jot.

XI

' Sentinel unbidden still he stayed ;
Little dreaming what part would be played
By the rosy sea-nymph in her strait,
Growing crimson at thought of her fate.

XII

' " Oh, for the ribbons of dark sea-brown,
Thickly upon the broad beach now strewn !
Never a one will come to my hand
While full plenty lie there on the sand ! "

XIII

' Thus, Estrilda wailed out in her woe,
And the shame made her cheeks deeper glow,
And she prayed that the distant sea-weed,
Fate would float to her in her great need.

XIV

' Aegir listening the prayer of the maid,
Sent his daughters, the Waves, to her aid,
Who brought clusters of sea-ribbon, brown,
Over rocks, as they tumbled adown.

XV

' Aphrodite uprising from sea,

Than Estrilda no fairer could be,

As she timidly 'merged from the wave,

Robed in the raiment the sea-god gave.

XVI

' Now, from her waist of ivory fair

Hung the brown streamers, trembling in air ;

Hiding the limbs of shell-tinted hue,

While sea-zephyrs kissed, and parted them, too.

XVII

' Never in Britain beheld he before

Like of this Naiad, who 'thwart the sea-shore

Fleetly she fled far into a cave,

That opens its mouth anear the sea-wave.

XVIII

' " Gods !   Do I dream !   Or, see I aright !

Is this beautiful being of light,

Goddess come hither from Northland shore,

Daughter of Estrild,[1] whom all Northmen adore ? "

[1] Estrild was the god of love, in Northern Europe. The
heroine of this story was daughter of a Northern Prince, and

XIX

‘ Thus he cried, and he suddenly knew
That a fire swept its courses all through
Heart, and brain ; and he bowed to the ground,
Homage paying to her he had found.

XX

‘ And he loved with a passionate love
Northland princess, whose beauty above,
And excelling all women's, made glow
His soul with joy too sweet to forego.

XXI

‘ And around him she tenderly wove
Her heart’s truest, devotional love ;
And her bright eyes of violet deep,
Told the secret she fain would now keep.

XXII

‘ Then, Corineus raising on high
His great battle-axe, King Locrin drew nigh ;
Harshly in all the heat of his rage,
Cried—“ Die—traitor, die ! Or keep thy gage.

was evidently named after the god. The story treats of the
ancient days of Britain.

XXIII

' " Marry Estrilda, Barbarian vile !
My daughter desert, and shameful defile
Blood of fair Britain ; and basely break
Thine own pledge, for this strange woman's
  sake !

XXIV

' " Poor reward for the scars I now bear,
Remnant of wounds in many a war
Fought for thy sire !   Full well now I know
How much of gratitude kings bestow ! "

XXV

' To appease Corineus, Locrin sware
Guendolena to marry, and share
With her his crown ; so he kept the troth
Wrung by ambition, and forced by wrath.

XXVI

' But he loved with a passionate love ;
Love, that naught on this earth could remove ;
And daily and nightly his tears would start
For the golden-haired maid who held his heart.

XXVII

'Within a subterranean hall,
Faithfully tended by many a thrall,
This Northern princess was kept in state
For the love of the king could ne'er abate.

XXVIII

'His devotional duties as shield
Made he for his visits concealed
To his love ; by this cunning device,
Of rendering his gods sacrifice.

XXIX

'When Corineus died, he banished from sight
The lady he loved not ; and brought to light
His hidden Estrilda, all full of grace ;
Made her his queen in Guendolena's place.'

While spake the old man, all silent listened him ;
Not only for reverence of his great years,
But also for the strange love-tale he then told,
Which diversely charmed each willing listener.

Then missing Caedmon the company cried out
That he had basely treated them, and needs must
　　pay
Some forfeit, which only his own kin must answer
　　for.
To clear his debt, fair Edna, trembling, took
　　place
Among the singers, and lightly touching strings
Of glee-wood, she sweetly sang an old quaint
　　song.

THE SHEPHERD

Edna's Song

'By crystal fountains,
O'er grassy mountains,
　And pastures fair,
The shepherd speedeth,
His flock he feedeth,
And gently leadeth,
　The young with care.

II

'Few things he needeth,
Free life he leadeth
  In open air.
On God relieth :
The spring supplieth
  To him full share.

III

'His flock is biding
Where streams are gliding
  Beneath the shade.
The woods are seeming
With new life teeming :
The sun is beaming
  O'er hill and glade.

IV

'Evening 's advancing,
Shadows are dancing
  Over the hills.
The shepherd 's kneeling,
His heart is feeling
That God's kind dealing,
  All nature fills.'

Meanwhile the unhappy Caedmon full of shame
That he was dumb, and all powerless to sing,
Or, tell the tale in verse, as old Ulfin did,
Set himself to watch the cattle of the guests,
That while they made them merry, no harm
Should overtake the patient beasts which had
Conveyed the peasants from their more distant
      homes.

Weary of watching he laid him down to rest,
And gentle sleep soon peacefully pressed his lids :
But, the fire that filled his breast throughout the day
Still haunted the visions of the night ; and dream
Most wonderful disclosed itself before him.

He thought the great Almighty had come nigh,
As he lay there ; and in a majestic tone
Straight issued the command—' Caedmon sing !'
And unaffrighted answered he—' I cannot sing,
I left the feast because I could not.'   But, still,
The Being at his side said, ' Sing !'   Caedmon
      cried,
' Of what then must I sing ?'
' Of *Me* ; of all created things.'

And straightway the emotion of his mind
Found true utterance ; and all his soul was filled
With the poet's fuller conception, and all
A poet's beautiful imaginings.
The tongue, erstwhile all dumb for verse, burst
    forth,
And sang he sweetest songs ; yea, songs more
    sweet
Than mortal ever heard.
When morning broke he thought he had talked
    with God.

With this new inspiration filled, hastened he
To Lady Hilda, and audience humbly sought,
Which graciously she gave.   Then recounted he
His glorious vision ; rendering the noble verse
He sang with God beside his couch, which upon
His mind most vividly remained.   In deep surprise
The Lady Abbess listened, all strong impressed
With this most unexampled testimony
Of Power supreme.
Then she realised that this unlettered churl,
Who, in her presence shamed, and hesitating stood,
Was called to tell the wondering world His Work.

O

To Caedmon's mind, trained in humility,
'Twere presumption unsurpassed, but that he knew
A Higher, still, than Hilda bade him speak.

Willing to help the work which God commenced,
And further still to prove him, she council called
Of learned monks that they might witness how
This uncultured and unlettered man could sing
The epic of the great creation.

And one, by her command a scripture read
Which Hilda bade the poet turn to verse
To test his truth.   Next morn he sang again
The verses sweet, new-made from Holy text.
Then Hilda knew the peasant was inspired.
And now, she issued the command that he
Be taught and trained, giving him privilege
Of dwelling there, devoted unto God.

And Caedmon wept for joy that he so lowly, rude,
And of such mean condition should be thus raised
To high estate of holy monk, and dwell
Beneath one roof ; with wise, illustrious men.
And ever dedicated he both voice and verse

To themes all holy and sublime ; and none in all
His time sang verse so eloquent as he.

When Edna's soft voice had ceased ; her simple lay
Fell with a tender influence on the hearts
Of the heathen around ; of God knowing naught.
Beckoning young Ethwuld to follow eftsoon,
With quick step she wended her way through the
    wold
Illumed by the silvery light that outbeamed
From the night-lamp of heaven.
Looking upward, she gazed on the gentle orb,
That placidly shone from the blue arch above,
And ardently longed for the calm that dwelt there.

All through the revel she had hidden the pain,
And the tumult within her.   Now, the great strain
Of joy all assumed, and fictitious, was past,
She burst into passionate sorrow, and cried—
' Oh, Ethwuld, how hard 'tis to give up the world—
The world, oh, my love, that holds thee ! '

His footsteps approaching her swiftly, at once
Arrested her speech.

                    'My Edna in tears!
What ails thee, my darling, that after the feast
Cometh this sorrow?   Hath Edgar, or churl
Been rude unto thee?'
Then she told him her strait.   Her father's com-
      mand ;
Her gage to lead life of a virgin, to God
Devoted, if her lover would yield his claim.

Then Ethwuld turned white with the anger that
      rose
All rapid and fierce through his frame.   And the
      fire
That flamed in his eyes fell like shot ; or the
      point
Of an arrow that would pierce through heart or
      brain.
'Where is thy love, I would ask thee?   I well trow
How little thou carest for me.   Fool that I was
To believe thee!   Thy vows are as firm as sand
That shifts on the shore, or clouds that sail in sky!'

'Ethwuld, listen.   Lay not this blame on mine
    head !
The charge of the matter is *thine*.   With thee rests
The final decision.   Thou art the judge
Of my future.   Say, shall I live unto God,
Or, for thee ? '

' Ask thine own heart.   I prize little the love
All halting between two resolves.
Mayhap after marriage thou wilt rue, and then
Desert me for nuns in the end !   What a faith !
For they teach it is good to leave husband, or child,
For God and His work.'

Then Edna's eyes filled ; but after a space
She lifted her head, and indignantly said—
' Even so let it be !   No more of thy doubts,
I'll not rue *after* marriage, but *now* ! '

And homeward she hastened, and left him alone :
In bitter resentment, stern stood he there ;
Out on the common, his face fanned by the winds
That played in the soft summer air.
And wildly he wandered all night on the wold,

In utter distraction, driven this way, and that,
As he balanced the matter in his wild brain.
Consumed by the passion that held him, at once
He would beg her forgiveness ; next moment felt
'Twas too late. At dawn of the day, when streaked
With new gold was the sky, Ethwuld was seen
In the distance sailing away on the sea.

And all that long night Edna waited return
Of her father ; drowned in her own bitter tears ;
Wailing the loss of her love : full of remorse,
She chid herself vainly for taking the share
In so thankless a task.   Her father more fit
To tell his commands.   The whole blame of his
        wrath,
And strong indignation she placed on herself.
If chance had then brought him, she surely was his,
One soft word of love would have won back her
        heart,
And melted the dissidence raised by her faith.

But that word never came ; and the stream of her
        life

Took an opposite course.   Helpless, and heart-sick
She drifted along the flood of her fate.

When the sun had attained its meridian,
Caedmon returned to his home radiant with joy,
And delirium at thought of his newly-found gift.
For ever to him a rich source of delight ;
A continual blessing ; a cup at his hand,
Filled with wine inexhaustible, giving new life,
And bestowing the richest of joys.
A fount ever welling, that shrinks not, like friends,
When dewy streams of the world's riches are
    dried.
Unlike beauty which fades with the burden of
    years,
Time only enriches this storehouse, its fruit
All mellows, refines.

As a sun-ray meeting with glittering diamond,
Or, polygonous crystal, is many times
Multiplied, so Edna rejoiced full tenfold
In the glory her sire had attained, such joy
That shed multitudinous rays of sunshine
O'er the home and the heart of her sire.

And zealously Caedmon now pressed the nun's veil
On Edna, for health of her soul, and new faith
To advance, that the light of God's love might be
    seen
In the drear and the darkness around.
And her thought was of God, and daily her prayers
Went upward to Christ, and to Mary, for grace :
But her heart in deep yearning mourned mutely
    for love,
As to Ethwuld she sent her farewell.

EDNA'S FAREWELL

I

' THINK of me only as thy friend
    Whose memory is to thee,
As some sweet song that haunts thine ear
    With tuneful melody.

II

' My love shall be the poet's theme,
    Whose verses make the song ;
My heart-strings shall the music be,
    Vibrating now so long.

III

' The memory of mine eyes shall give
Thy strains their gentle flow,
And fill thee with emotion sweet,
That only poets know.

IV

' And my soul shall be filled with joy
The angels fair, might take,
Pure as the streets of gold, they tread ;
Clear as the silver lake.

V

' When over wave thy little bark
Glides on with fairy flight,
The picture on mine eyes is fixed,
And fills my inner sight.

VI

' If in the stillness of the night
I long for quiet rest,
The one recurring thought is thee,
An ever-welcome guest.

VII

' Where'er thou art, where'er I be,
  Ah, Ethwuld, 'tis the same,
The distance cannot shut thee out,
  I only hear thy name !

VIII

' Think of me only as thy friend,
  Who without doubt shall be,
The truest, tenderest of all,
  That God can give to thee.

IX

' And the thought of the love I bear
  Shall be as glad sunlight,
Or, as the kindly dew of heaven,
  That droppeth in the night.

X

' Or, like the fragrance of sweet flowers
  That comes from a garden fair,
Their odours, wafted incense-like
  Amidst the balmy air.

XI

‘ Or, the calm of a holy hymn
That falls on all around,
When through the lofty pillared aisle
Is borne the mystic sound ;

XII

‘ The waves of music softly steal
O'er tired hearts gathered there ;
Like echoes sweet from heaven, they come
All floating through the air.

XIII

‘ Oh, Love, the sweetest aim in life,
What joy is given with thee,
Thine essence every soul pervades,
Thou rul'st eternally !

XIV

‘ Let an altar for ever be raised
To the Power all must own,
'Tis meet that Love be deified,
The heart of man her throne.

XV

' As memories come in our dreams,
Shadow the pictures of old ;
So love, now all living and warm,
Will end like a tale that's told.'

All over the rugged steep, on which was reared
The Abbey of Hilda, the setting sun showered
His wonderful shades of deep gold ; which the sea,
Lying below, mirrored as fair as if 'twere
The face of a crystal lake.

        Looking down on the scene
Or gazing far into the distance at sails
That dotted the wave, Edna stood on the edge
Of the steep, lost in sad bewildering thought :
Only one night lay between her and the world ;
Next morn the seal would be set that fixed her fate,
And the inviolable vow would be given.

Now, deeply was stirred all her soul with the old
Agitating, retrospective regrets :

For in full force felt she the fault of her weak,
And wavering purpose ; which, justly brought grave
Self-accusations.
How different her method had she better gauged
The state of her heart, fully conscious of love,
Now, felt she the coil of her fate winding round,
All due to her own irresolute doing !
Pendulum-like, her will worked this way, and that.
In imagination full clearly the scene
Was enacted before her.   Yet, not the same.

In the unity perfect of knitted souls,
Whose purpose was firm, undivided, and sure,
The twain would have conquered her father's great
    zeal,
And melted him to set in its own true place
Th' irresistible altar of sweet human love.

In the midst of her musings, like a dream ap-
    peared
A white sail on the waterway which lightly bore
Towards the shore of Streaneshalch ; near and
    more near
It steadily came on its way ; till she discerned

The boat of her lover swift skimming the wave,
All lit by the gold in the sky.   Then her heart
Gave a bound, for she saw that young Ethwuld
    drew nigh :
And hastening all quickly he clambered the steep
Where Edna sat silently weeping in woe.
Like a lily her cheeks with heart-sorrow, and wan
With her anguish and grief.   But, now, the bright
    flush
All over her face was suffused, and her eyes,
New lit by the light that came into her soul,
Beamed their welcome to Ethwuld ; showing her
    heart,
At that exquisite moment, all bare to his gaze.

No tongue-knowledge seeking ; nor staying for
    word,
He kissed her in passionate fervour, and led
Her away to the sea.   And the soft summer wind
Full well knew it bore on its wings a new bride
To Heorta's wild shore.   And the sea-birds saw,
As they wheeled in the air in wonderful flight,
And told it the rocks rising out of the wave,
That the fisherman's bride was come to her home.

THE STORM

I

THE storm without is wild and strong,
    The rain in torrents beats
Upon the panes, and all along
    The dark deserted streets.

II

But for the dismal noise of winds,
    That shake the very floor ;—
Each gust some unseen crevice finds
    Beneath the bolted door,—

III

There would be stillness everywhere,
    For not a soul is seen ;
No children's voices fill the air ;
    All wears a woeful mien.

IV

The sparrows too, are mute and still,
No fluttering wings abound ;
Their cheerful chirps no longer fill
The house-tops all around.

V

And many a little nest this night
That's stood the summer's rain
Ere morning brings its cold, grey light,
Will ne'er be seen again.

VI

And many a mariner this day,
Who's been to many a shore,
Will never again be heard to say—
He's seen the like before.

VII

And many a ship that's sailed away
With swelling canvas bright,
And left behind the broad, smooth bay,
Will never see the light.

VIII

And many a careless, happy child
　All full of joyous glee
While gazing on the billows wild,
　Of the angry, boiling sea,

IX

Will know full soon, the one so brave,
　So loving, tender, true,
Whom mother prays her God to save,
　Is lost with all his crew.

X

And many a gentle wife, just now,
　Who's watching, hoping on,
Will something learn that shades her brow,
　And makes her cheek grow wan.

XI

And all along the yellow strand,
　And near ' the rocks,' I ween,
There's many a ship fast in the sand,
　And many a wreck is seen.

XII

For, oh, the Storm so cruel, cold,
 Ne'er cares what hearts it breaks ;
What lives it spoils remains untold ;
 What misery it makes.

MATERNAL DEVOTION

PART I

I

SWEET memories rise unchidden in my breast
Of thee, my darling : in Love's warmest nest
Securely art thou hid.   When thou art here
I cannot sing, nor tell what makes thee dear :
When thou art gone my bursting heart would move
In tend'rest measures of exalted love.

II

Communion close, and sympathy of thought
Brought us more near than Kindred could ; we
    sought
Ambitions high and true.   The noblest aims
Erstwhile didst fill thy soul, and all the names
Of men in bygone days, who won their state
Of honour, thy models were to imitate.

III

Thou art not only son, but brother—friend ;
The three all merged in one, and in these blend
Love, sympathy, and trust ; a triple cord
To firmly bind us twain.   Unframed the word ;
Unknown the thought to analyse this chain
Subtle—unseen.   Who can its depths obtain ?

IV

'Tis mighty, mystic Love that draws us nigh,
That sacred link ; that everlasting tie !
Ocean may rear between its broad deep wall :
The widest earth divide us far, yet all
Is naught to us.   The world may pass away,
And all things fail, but Love is bound to stay.

MATERNAL DEVOTION

PART II

I

MUSING and dreaming, here sit I alone,
Thinking of moments that long since have flown :
March winds are tumbling, and rumbling ; and
 rush
On their wild course, as if trying to crush
All that opposeth them ; conquerors free
In their mad flight they now strive hard to be.

II

Out of the Calendar, who would not own,
Insolent Ides, that he wishes thee gone?
None love thy boisterous, roughly-hewn face ;
Nothing that's tender therein can we trace ;
Season more balmy, delicious I'd sight
If I could rule the ethereal height.

III

Go now, rough March, and take with thee thy
　　train ;
Long I for sunshine, and summer's soft rain ;
Long I to dream and gaze into the sky
Wherein fairy cloudlets sailing on high,
Shimmer and shake in the odorous breeze,
Wafted so gently from the southern seas.

IV

Ah, far above these there's a well-loved face
Wealth of the world could never replace ;
When it is absent the hearth is a-cold ;
Sun's gladdening rays do not as of old
Flow round my heart with their life-giving beams ;
Nature is icicled even in dreams.

V

Song hath gone from me ; for there is no sound ;
Only my heart-sighs that echo around ;
Sits by my Solitude whisp'ring ' At last,
Sister, accept me, I'm all that thou hast.'
Unwilling to take her, bow I my head,
Wishing that dear one were here in her stead.

MATERNAL DEVOTION

PART III

I

SILENTLY sitting close imprisoned here,
And weary of all this solitude drear
The days of November hath brought.   I sigh—
Yet how vainly—for the beauteous sky,
For gossamer cloud ; for the sunshine fair
For the hum of the bee in the dreamy air ;

II

I look, and I long for the balmy breeze
That comes to our shores from the southern seas ;
The scent of the hay, the bright flowers so gay,
How I wish for one hour of summer day !
There's something I long for, far above these ;
E'en something more dear than the budding trees ;

III

For the cloud in the air, and the cloud in my breast
Now fill me with feeling of strange unrest ;
I long now to hear in these lonesome hours
The voice of my firstborn, more sweet than flowers,
More sweet than the songs which give me such joy
Are the tones of thy voice, my dearly-loved boy ;

IV

Fair harmony is the song of the birds,
A thousand-fold sweeter are thy heart-words :
Mine idol as babe ; in manhood the same,
Thou'rt part of my being, as the gold frame
Encircles a diamond, so art thou laid
Encased in the casket my strong love's made.

MATERNAL DEVOTION

PART IV

I

THOUGH cold and dark November
    Brings yearly the happy morn,
That ever I remember
    As the day that thou wert born ;
Yet bright it will be always,
    And beaming a sun shall be,
That sun is Love, whose warm rays
    Are surely lit up for thee.

II

Then faint not when aweary
    With many an uphill stride,
For oft the path proves dreary
    While yet it is being tried ;

But think of love so tender
That follows thee ev'rywhere ;
A love that seeks to render
Thy young life all free from care.

III

A love that is undying,
E'en when the quick pulse grows cold ;
The spirit endless sighing
Will outbreathe its yearnings old ;
And send in still small voices
The unforgotten refrain :
The soul even then rejoices
In watching, loving again.

THE CRY OF THE DESERTED ONE

I

OH, that I had some sweet magical charm,
  Some secret and powerful spell
To cast over him who enchants my soul—
  Over him whom I love so well.

II

If only a share of the deep, deep throbs
  That fill my tumultuous heart,
Were echoed in his to the smallest degree,
  To even a thousandth part.

III

Oh, then would it leap with supremest joy,
  Then hotly the wildfire would glow ;
Oh, then would the life-stream rush through my frame,
  Which slowly is languishing now !

IV

Ah, there was a time when the whisper of love
  Oft came from his lips all unsought ;
But now hath his heart grown cold as the sea,
  And my love for him is as naught.

V

Where then shall I find the magical wand,
  Or elixir worthy all cost,
To kindle again the fire of his love ;
  The love that is doomed to be lost.

VI

Ah, what is my beauty? my empire is gone—
  What care I for woman's soft grace,
When he who's my world, my life, and my joy
  No longer looks into my face?

VII

No longer dwells he on the sound of my voice
  Which he singled from out the world's throng ;
Its music is gone ; 'tis now like the lyre
  Whose strings are all broken—unstrung.

VIII

If only its chords were touched by *his* hand
How quick would the vibrating string
Give harmony sweet, for answering love
The lost music would surely bring.

IX

Oh, must I then cherish his image no more,
And banish him ever from sight,
And crush out the love that's sapping my life,
That's turning my day into night?

X

Can the sunflower forget the bright orb of day,
Her idol, her lover confessed?
And oh, can the rose forget the soft dew
That nightly doth fall on her breast?

XI

In the infinite future of love
His spirit will come to my side;
In the eternity endless I'll gain
That love which on earth he denied.

TO MY BROTHER

I

WHEN Autumn brings the russet leaf,
    And Earth is all a-glowing
With colours rich of yellow sheaf
    That in the fields are flowing
In waves of beauty, while the air
    In gentle zephyrs playing
Makes rhythm in the meadows fair,
    And lines of beauty laying.

II

Then Nature's poetry is sung,
    For Earth herself is trying
To make her music with sweet tongue
    In cadence softly sighing.

'Twas thus in sweetest time of year
  A little babe thou camest,
To fill thy niche, and unknown here
  On earth a place thou claimest.

III

And when the harvest moon shines clear ;
  With stronger lustre beameth,
Then memory brings thee very near
  And at my side thou seemeth
To list, and wonder as before,
  When thou to me appealing,
I told thee tales in days of yore,
  Of fancy, or of feeling.

IV

But soon I wake and find thee gone ;—
  'Twas but a spell of dreaming ;—
I here, thou there, and all alone,
  Above the great moon gleaming.
And yearly as the Autumn wanes
  My heart would fain be showing
Its love towards thee, and full contains
  A measure overflowing.

THE BATTLE OF LIFE

A FAIR young girl with a serious look
Sat pondering deeply over her book ;

And lifting her head in innocent grace
Intently gazed she in her mother's face.

' Oh, what is this " battle of life " ? ' she said,
' Where are the soldiers ?   By whom are they led ?

' Our Queen hath her warriors brave, I know,
But what is this army ?   Who is their foe ?

' With pennant and plume, and brave array
Are the soldiers dight on the battle-day ?

' With flashing sword and cannon, and lead,
Mow they down the living, heap up the dead ? '

' Ah, daughter, the men in the battle of life,
Do not meet on the blood-stained field of strife ;

' No sword is seen, nor pennant, nor plume,
Nor rolling thunder of the cannon's boom ;

' Nor charge of rifles, are heard on the plain,
Where combatants struggle for life or gain.

' Strange soldiers are some in this battle of life,
The young and the frail ; the widow, and wife ;

' Unequal the contest, yet on they go,
Their leader Necessity, Want their foe.

' And countless heroes now gone to their rest
Ne'er wore the Victoria Cross on their breast.

' More noble than they who have scaled the height
Of some dear ambition, kept well in sight.

' Yet the battles fought by these heroes great
Are seldom acknowledged by King or State.

' Oh, the garret all bare, and lowly cot
Give shelter to many brave hearts, I wot !

' The slim pale youth in his attic high,
Must face this terrible ordeal, or die.

· And many a woman shrinks not to yield
Her very heart's blood on this battle-field.

· The strain on her heart, and strain on her brain
Are more than human power can sustain.

· The weak and weary soon slip out of sight,
Crushed by the conflict they sink in the fight.

· Ah, yes, there are battles fought valiantly
'Neath poverty's shadow, with none to see.'

She finished ; a pause ; then the quiet air
Was parted by sound of a whispered prayer,

And the fair young girl on her bended knee,
Wept tears at these pictures of misery.

MY CHOICE

I

THE bard may sing of eyes so blue,
  And say that none compare,
With their sweet beauty, emblem true
  Of all that's good and fair.

II

And others sing of bright dark eyes
  That flash 'neath jetty brow,
While each glance with its fellow vies
  To make all hearts to bow.

III

But, oh, give me dear kindly eyes
  That beam with Love's soft light,
Which throughout ev'ry change ne'er dies,
  But gathers depth and might,

IV

With all the long, long, changeful years,
   Whose joy now comes, now goes,
And in each chequered phase endears
   The hearts wherein it flows.

V

Then give me eyes bright with pure love,
   Whose lovelight shines for me ;
And whose sincerity years prove
   The truest love to be.

NEW YEAR'S THOUGHTS

I

In ev'ry moment gliding o'er our heads
Insensibly are woven subtle threads
In life's own garment : year by year
Are tissues fashioned that we needs must wear.

II

And of these robes no two alike are made,
For each hath sep'rate tint of light, or shade,
Some glitter like a rainbow, beauteous, bright,
With pearly hues of everlasting light.

III

And daily we're invested by our deeds,
More real these than all beliefs and creeds,
For good or ill, they never fail to cling
More close to us than any other thing.

IV

And, lo!   Our life is numbered, not by days,
Nor counted by the years, but rather by the ways
And actions it hath wrought ; by these alone
The sum of our existence is best shown.

CHRISTMAS

I

OH, Christmas fair, oh, Christmas fair
  How sweet thou art to me !
Thy feath'ry flakes of falling snow
  That crown each hill and tree,
Like the Spirit of God descend
  In silent dove-like guise,
And light upon the hearts of men
  To make them pure and wise.

II

I love thee, beauteous, glist'ning snow,
  Emblem of Him who came
Clad in the innocence of heaven
  To give me His own name.
Love left his 'thereal home,
  Love lives with us to-day,
Love fills our hearts with God's own peace,
  Love ever lights our way.

WAITING FOR THE FIRST-FOOT

IN the North of England an old custom still prevails of having a first-foot for the New Year. It is supposed that good or bad luck is brought to the inmates of a house by the person who first crosses the threshold in the New Year.

If a female should happen to enter first it is considered an omen of misfortune; consequently, great care is taken that none but the favoured individual be permitted to go into the house at such a critical time.

The moment the New Year is ushered in, the expected first-foot enters, when he is received with hearty welcome.

In the following verses a poor girl, whose family have been undergoing the trial of trade depression, is awaiting the return of a reconciled lover. He is hastening homewards in order to make his appearance in the capacity of first-foot.

I

THOU'RT passing away from us, grey Old Year,
    Thy moments are few and fleeting;
All spent thy career, thy farewell is near,
    For now thy last pulse is beating.

II

Full many a grief thou didst bring, Old Year,
    My heart with much sadness steeping,
Yet Hope did appear, and dried the hot tear,
    And stayed the long spell of weeping.

III

The poverty-cloud that appeared, Old Year,
    Brought its train of miseries, making
So white the brown hair, with sorrow and care
    Of mother, whose heart was breaking.

IV

And weaker the little ones grew, Old Year,
    Though bravely hunger defying;
Ah, we had a share of trouble to bear
    When little Annie lay dying.

V

I never could hope, relentless Old Year,
   However foolish my dreaming
This night I would wear the smiles of good cheer
   With love-light mine eyes soft beaming.

VI

New gladness hath come to me now, Old Year,
   Instead of that time so weary ;
The longed-for New Year dispels every fear,
   And gone are thy days all dreary.

VII

There's someone returning to me, Old Year,
   Who left me in anger and sorrow ;
But the scalding tear shed over Love's bier
   Will shine as diamonds to-morrow.

VIII

A lucky first-foot is speeding, Old Year,
   As soon as the bells are ringing
To welcome the year, his step I will hear,
   To me a whole life's love bringing.

IX

Come in, oh, come in, with the glad New Year,
    My bosom with joy is glowing ;
Ah, yes, he is here, to me now more dear
    Than rivers of gold o'erflowing.

MEMORY

I

WHAT art thou Memory, the essence of the
    mind ;
Embodiment of all the faculties combined ;
The seat of all the intellect ; the moral throne ;
The lamp that keeps our love alight, when all is
    gone ?

II

Thou mausoleum of the heart, in which are
    urned
Our dead and buried hopes, those ill-spared joys
    that turned
The clouds of life to laughing sunshine, full and
    bright,
Whose every ray of bliss converged in one
    delight.

III

What subtle necromancy little children own,

'Tis felt in every footstep; 'tis heard in ev'ry
    tone!

Its influence still lives, though buried in the grave

Where memory hath laid the dear ones God once
    gave.

IV

Within the vault of memory are close entombed

Our dearest, best ambitions, blighted, long since
    doomed

To banishment perpetual ; yet here they stay

Fair relics of a goal for ever passed away.

V

Oh, memory is crowded with graves of ev'ry
    kind ;

The broken trust ; the stinging wrong that haunts
    the mind ;

Our wasted love ; the false deed done in friendship's
    guise ;

In this mysterious place each ghostly shadow lies!

VI

What art thou Memory, a vista fair of dreams,
Or, vision of the past in which our fancy teems
With fond illusions of sweet, sunny rose-strewn
    ways,
Crowned with the pearly beauties that belong
    youth's rosy days?

VII

Along the avenue of Time there rises now
A shining halo whose soft lustre doth endow
One darkened scene with sun, one glaring scene
    with shade
Thus looking down the distance, a pleasing
    glamour's laid.

VIII

And all throughout the way traversed long years
    ago,
Time strews enchantments fair, by which he may
    bestow
A multiple of joys to cover all the pains,
That in the grand sum-total only good remains.

LOVE'S MISERIES

I

OH, how I love thee, how I hate thee,
 Often wish thee far away,
 And endeavour day by day,
To teach, and charge my heart most straitly
 That my love is gone for aye.

II

My heart's emotions beat not even
 In their palpitating walls ;
 When thy deep voice gently calls
My name in love, 'tis taste of heaven
 That thy presence here forestalls.

III

But when I watch thine eyes all roving
 O'er the charms of ev'ry fair ;
 Like the bee who here and there
Is constant changing, always moving,
 Kissing flow'rets ev'rywhere.

IV

And I can see new passion gleaming
    In thy face, but not for me,
    Naught am I just then to thee ;
Then straightway thousand torments teeming,
    Gather round tumultuously.

V

High throbs my heart, but not with gladness,
    Moved with pain I know so well,
    Filled with hate I cannot quell,
And all the tumult, and the madness
    Make it feel a very hell.

VI

Then a weary feeling follows,
    And the joy my heart had known
    Into black despair is grown,
Full darker than the darkest hollows,
    Where the sun no ray hath thrown.

VII

Ah me, the agony of keeping
    Outward calm the livelong night,
    While its balm hath taken flight,
Oh, how my heavy eyes still weeping
    Gladly welcome morning light!

VIII

As limpid spring to parched wayfarer
    Panting in the wilderness,
    So the kisses thou dost press,
And love of which thou art the bearer
    Give new life in one caress.

IX

Impetuous as the torrent's motion
    Towards the vast unbounded sea,
    Dashing by each rock, and tree ;
Such is now my soul's devotion ;
    Wrapped in thee eternally.

THE IRISH MAIDEN'S ADIEU

ON LEAVING ENGLAND

I

WHEN other friends around thee smile
　　Whom thou hast known for long,
Give one stray thought to her, meanwhile
　　Who cheered thee with her song,

II

And warbled forth her simple strains
　　Of chivalry and mirth ;
Whose echo only now remains
　　To hover round thy hearth.

III

But even shadowy echoes bring
　　The sweetest recollection,
And Fancy oft will faintly sing
　　Songs of a rare collection.

IV

And I will conjure in my mind
 Sweet thoughts of Love, and Thee,
And music soft, in one combined ;
 Love's surest, truest key,

V

And carry back to Erin's shore
 A new and thrilling theme,
Wherewith to warble out once more
 The melody I dream.

VI

And as the lark 'twixt earth and heaven
 Doth trill its joyous song,
So from my inmost soul are given
 Its breathings all day long.

VII

Thus full of happy thought I'll go
 Bright as the gladsome day,
And as the streamlet loves to flow
 Make music all the way.

VIII

Soft murmuring sounds that sweetly fill
  The heart with new delight,
Like dancing, rippling, glitt'ring rill
  That flows down rocky height.

IX

Oh, Erin, land of sun and dew,
  Thou spreadst a spell o'er me,
And tender yearnings spring anew
  That draw my heart towards thee !

X

Thou land of trefoil emerald green !
  Thou land of daisied turf !
Thou land of waters bright, whose sheen
  Gleams 'midst white-crested surf !

XI

Ah, Ireland, country ever dear,
  Thy beauties now recall,
Thy sorrows even while still here
  And tears unbidden fall !

XII

As dreams of loved and long-lost dead
  Whose memories we keep,
So homes whose joys are ever fled,
  Their solitude I weep.

XIII

But, ah, why should mine eyes be dewed
  With tears which dull their light ?
Begone from me such mournful mood
  My smile shall e'er be bright.

XIV

My song shall henceforth be of mirth ;
  My lay of truest love ;
My ardent soul shall e'en give birth
  To strains that all hearts move.

XV

Tho' fairer face thy heart shall gain
  When I am gone from thee ;
Ah, then, let memory still retain
  One sweet, stray thought for me.

XVI

And as night spreads her softening shade
    O'er earth, and sky, and sea,
Remember her the Celtic maid
    Who loves, but must leave thee.

THE SAILOR'S SONG

I

OVER the breezy, rippling sea
  We sailors merrily go,
With all our canvas spread so free,
  While gaily we shout—' Yah, ho !'

II

None so merry as we, and light,
  The rolling sea our world,
All gilded by a sun so bright,
  That gleams on the sails unfurled.

III

We have perils, God knows, our fill,
  But why should we feel alarm ?
Duty and Love inspire our will,
  Give the courage to our arm.

IV

Over us the resistless storm
    Low, our gallant ship would lay ;
Our head is cool, as heart is warm,
    And safely plough we our way.

V

True, there are times when all unsought,
    Welling upwards to our mind,
There come great waves of yearning thought,
    For the dear ones left behind :

VI

Though the wide, wide ocean may part
    The mariner from his home,
Still, constant and true is his heart,
    Wherever his ship may roam.

VII

Over the breezy, rippling sea
    We sailors merrily go,
With all our canvas spread so free,
    While gaily we shout—' Yah, ho ! '

TO JAMES WATSON SEWELL

BORN MARCH 31

(*Acrostic*)

J UST as boisterous, blust'ring March is dumb,

A nd knoweth full well that his hour hath come ;

(M erry made he in his wild, wilful glee,

E ncircling the valley, and bending the tree ;

S miling and scowling by turns now did he

W in the good-will of the frost-bound Earth,

A s she opens her arms to welcome the birth,

T hat brings her soft showers, and sunshine, and
      flowers ;)

S o thou wisely waited not the few hours

O f dying-out March ; thy Fate safely rules

N ot to let thy *début* come on Day of All Fools.

S ecuring a star more lucky to shine

E ver upon thee with soft rays divine.

W hen Night spreads her veil all over the sky,

E ven then thy good star, tho' hidden from eye,

L ights its lustrous lamp ; for thee surely burns,

L oving and watching and warning by turns.

MISCELLANEOUS POEMS

TOO MODEST BY FAR

A Kiss-in-the-ring Incident

(*Ballade*)

THE ring was formed, a pretty sight
   To see the maidens dark, and fair
Stand blushing, and pretending flight,
   And make-believe the kisses were
   Too much for modesty to bear ;
And yet they slily wished for one ;
   And each girl longed her turn was there
To give a kiss when fairly won.

Among the merry group that night
   A bashful swain refused to share
The blisses that were his by right ;
   To take a kiss he could not dare,
   Before the world, and gaslight glare,
'Twere sacrilege in sight of sun !
   ' And, still,' he thought, ' why need I care
To give a kiss when fairly won ? '

So with good courage, manly might,
　He took his place with jaunty air,
And gazed around on maidens bright ;
　But mercy ! ere he was aware,
　Some sadly mischievous betrayer
The kerchief dropped at him in fun ;
　Oh, where his brave resolves, oh, where,
To give a kiss when fairly won ?

O'erwhelmed he sank on nearest chair ;
　The cannon's mouth he might not shun,
On woman's lips 'twere harder far,
　To give a kiss when fairly won.

FRIENDSHIP

(*Ballade*)

I THOUGHT thee friendship all divine,
   I worshipped thee as a being fair ;
My heart I made thy living shrine,
   I was thy slave, and I would dare
   All things to do without one care.
I saw thee with enchanted eyes,
   But now those eyes are opened—there—
Ah, me, is too much friendship wise ?

Why should I waste this heart of mine
   On tinkling brass or empty ware ?
No longer will I wish and pine
   For that which is by far too rare.
   Ingratitude is hard to bear,
And cold neglect from those you prize ;
   Experience says each passing year
' Ah, me, is too much friendship wise ? '

And is this Nature's best design
  That human love be poor and bare,
And must my heart itself resign
  To the ascetic's cold despair?
  True faith be found not anywhere—
No kindred soul to sympathise?
  I would myself this question spare—
' Ah, me, is too much friendship wise?'

ENVOIE

Oh, Friendship, fickle, light as air,
  I'm still thy slave to idolise;
The cynic's wisdom I'll not share,—
  Nor ask—' Is too much friendship wise?'

THE MONKEYS

(A LECTURE)

In Holy Writ it is enjoined
   That men should love their brothers ;
I trust this lesson on your part
   You learn with all the others.

For men and monkeys are the same
   The scientists now tell us ;
If this be true, we sure must treat
   The monkeys as our fellows.

The structure of their tender frame
   You cannot help from seeing,
Essentially is just the same
   As that of human being.

They grin, they squabble, steal, and learn
    Tricks that are very naughty ;
And if you gave cigar and cane,
    Like gents they'd grow quite haughty.

Whate'er the difference may be
    'Twixt man and little monkey,
I cannot see, no more than ' Tit '
    Saw in her darling donkey.

She loved him well, she led him forth
    To sylvan, leafy bowers ;
She beauty saw in his long ears,
    And wooed him with bright flowers.

'Tis true 'tis but a fairy scene
    Imaginative feeling
Doth spread before us, yet we know
    With real life 'tis dealing.

How many a woman good and fair,
    Intelligent and clever,
A donkey for her idol makes,
    And worships him for ever.

And if one raised the sorcerer's veil
   That Cupid's ever casting
Before her eyes ; though clear she sees,
   She loves to everlasting.

And thus the world goes round and round,
   And matches human beings ;
Strange incongruities are found,
   And all by Fate's decreeings.

THE MAIDEN'S CHOICE

OR, THE AMERICAN GIRL IN ENGLAND

OH, she was fair, as fair could be ;
Her step was light, and quick, and free ;
Her golden hair shone with bright hue,
And roses bloomed 'neath eyes so blue.

Oh, whom will this fair maiden wed,
This maiden with the buoyant tread ;
Oh, whom will she in wedlock take,
Whom now will she her husband make ?

How earnestly the young man wooed
And for her hand he warmly sued ;
His words of deep and faithful love
A maiden's heart must surely move.

Oh, she should be his star so bright,
Filling his home with 'thereal light ;
His heart's own idol ; his desire,
Of whom his soul could never tire.

' His goddess fair,' he said, ' his life,'—
All merged in one sweet title—' wife.'
His aim her happiness on earth,
If she would share his home and hearth.

The maiden listened for a while,
Then turned away with coldest smile,
She told him she preferred to be
Just as she was, with fancy free.

He went his way, only to dream
That she was good as she did seem,
But, oh, his heart was very full,
And all the world seemed cold and dull,

For want of her whose beauteous face
He thought endowed with ev'ry grace ;
He hoped 'twas but a passing whim
This anguish deep had laid on him.

And then another suitor came,
Whose wealth was his untarnished name,
Unblemished was through life his path,
But riches none, alas, he hath!

In this case too, the maid proved coy,
And firm refused to be his joy ;
Her virgin heart no man could gain,
'Twas clear a maid she must remain.

And so he had his way to wend,
With hopes the maid might still unbend ;
His bosom burned with Love's true fire,
In truth, she was his heart's desire.

And many suitors came and went,
But unto none the maiden meant
To plight her troth, to give her hand,
For that which she did most demand,

These lovers had not to bestow ;
However much their hearts might glow
With honest love ; she little cares
If gold and riches are not theirs.

' Oh, back to the New World, I'll hie ! '
Cried she with disappointed sigh.
' The boasted beauties of your isle
I guess, my fancy can't beguile.'

There was a something in that voice
Which one would hardly like from choice ;
A tone peculiar to that land
Which by Atlantic winds is fanned.

At length a period to her stay
Was fixed upon, and soon the day
Of her departure drew full near,
Which scarcely brought one single tear,

And scarce she felt one small regret
At leaving the kind friends she'd met ;
Her visit here 'twas plain to see
Was sorry failure as could be,

When another, and a better lover
Around her path began to hover ;
He told her that his heart was hers ;
And now no longer she demurs,

For he lays before her glist'ning eyes
Vast piles of shining gold which lies,
In rich profusion at her feet,
Where he has taken lowly seat.

' All—all, my darling, to be thine
If only thou wilt be but mine ! '
Cried he with fervour and delight,
While love made his dim eyes grow bright.

His grizzly beard, and scanty hair
Had seen full many a passing year,
Old age had touched him on the shoulder,
But that was naught, since oft he told her,

That without doubt all he possessed
Should sure be hers, if he were blest
With her as his own darling wife,
Tho' albeit his span of life,

Was somewhat narrow and confined,
But wealth and love, these two combined,
Would cover any want so small,
As that of youth, which after all,

Is merely an imagination
Compared to money and high station.
What woman would such good refuse !
'Twere tempting Fate such luck to lose !

And so the maid was quite convinced,
The matter now no longer minced,
Accepted him who thus had wooed her,
And took the money and the suitor.

Her lot since then, I dare not say ;
I only know that every day
She wishes either she, or he,
Were gone to bliss eternally.

A LETTER

(WRITTEN IN A DRAUGHTY ROOM)

WITHOUT the snow lies on the ground ;
  Within the wind doth play
Upon my back, and all around
  (Thou know'st its little way).

My fingers stiffen as I write
  In this too airy place,
For sundry draughts now take their flight,
  And rise from feet to face.

They settle on my shoulders chill ;
  They run adown my spine,
Ah, how can I this letter fill
  Or make another sign ?

Thou know'st full well the truth of this,
    For often thou didst swear,
When zephyrs bold thy cheek would kiss,
    And take thee unaware.

And then, perchance, an ugly sneeze,
    Would screw thy visage fair,
And almost bring thee on thy knees ;
    (A posture now so rare.)

Now write me, write me, son of mine,
    The pages long and sweet,
And let each goodly, newsy line
    Be ample, full, complete.

The overflowing measure mete
    Beyond what thou dost owe ;
Then I'll peruse each covered sheet,
    Recounting how things go.

Skimp not the herald mute, that speaks
    Of all that comes to thee ;
That tells the doings of past weeks
    So truthfully to me.

And when thou sittest down to think
  In calm and quiet mood,
Just take the handy pen and ink,
  And chronicle what's good.

And on the virgin paper pour
  The fruit of thoughtful mind ;
Something that we may ponder o'er,
  With sense and love combined.

The utterance of the soul is thus
  Embalmed, and ever near,
It is thyself who speaks to us,
  Although no longer here.

A VALENTINE

The Fate of The Flatterer

There is a sure unerring law—
  A part of Nature's plan,
That what man giveth unto maids,
  Maids render back to man.

For men's duplicity they yield
  Their mighty scorn in full,
And with severity tenfold
  His character they pull,

Remorselessly to pieces small,
  Until the very shreds,
Would take full countless pairs of hands,
  To gather up the threads.

The man who tells each girl he meets
   ' She's fairest of her sex,'
In course of time will surely find,
   He flatters but to vex.

What is the worth of honeyed phrase,
   That's given to all around ?
It bears no meaning when 'tis known
   To be but empty sound.

But retribution comes at length,
   No woman wants his praise,
There's not a maid in all the world
   Believes a word he says.

REFLECTIONS OF A STUDENT

WHEN queerest problems rack my brain,
And give me infinite of pain,
That sure I feel I'm near insane
                    As madman.

I sit, and think, and read, and pore,
And go on wondering more and more
While conning ' methods ' o'er and o'er,
                    Till heart-sick.

I wonder if my genius rare
Will ever the round circle square,
And make my work beyond compare
                    Of mortal.

T

My mind disturbed and ill at ease,
Sweet satisfaction none it sees,
For all prove vain soliloquies,
          And worthless.

At length my temper grows quite hot,
For I declare the thing ' all rot,'
And to my dear tobacco-pot
          I turn me.

My pipe, what consolation kind
I ever in thy incense find !
It soothes and cheers my troubled mind
          Most sweetly.

Ah, what care I for love and kisses ?
My heart such transport never misses
Nor ever seeks those tender blisses,
          To cheer it.

When sober, thoughtful, walking through
The green fields decked with diamond dew,
I take my one companion true,
          And love it.

Yes, to my lips I press the shank
As seated on a sloping bank
I smoke amidst its grasses rank
                        Quite happy.

Now, I'll be wedded by-and-by,
But not to woman—no—not I ;
'Twill be to pipe and brown birdseye.
                        I'm mated.

LINES ON A LADY'S PORTRAIT PAINTED ON AN ASH-TRAY

(ADDRESSED TO ITS OWNER)

I

SAY canst thou on this brow so rare
So beauteous, pure, and smooth, and fair ;
Or on this cheek of damask rose
The ashes from thy weed dispose ?

II

Though fragrant it may seem to thee ;
Delightful to the senses be,
Yet couldst thou to so base a use
Put this sweet face, if thou mightst choose ?

III

While balancing thy cigarette
Like any little vain coquette ;
Methinks I see thee gazing now
Upon that white, and spotless brow,

IV

And wishing that its owner were
Ensconced not too far from thy chair ;
And in her sunny eyes of brown
Watch the reflection of thine own.

V

But what's the use of speculation,
Or making this vain calculation,
Upon a piece of painted china
Which represents the face of Nina ?

VI

Now cover o'er those features bright,
With veil of ashes thin and white,
And put that sweet face out of sight,
While wishing it a fond ' Good-night ! '

PRINTED BY
SPOTTISWOODE AND CO., NEW-STREET SQUARE
LONDON

A LIST OF

KEGAN PAUL, TRENCH, TRÜBNER & CO.'S
(LIMITED)

PUBLICATIONS.

7.90.

57 and 59, Ludgate Hill; and 1, Paternoster Square,

London.

A LIST OF

KEGAN PAUL, TRENCH, TRÜBNER & CO.'S
(LIMITED)

PUBLICATIONS.

CONTENTS.

GENERAL LITERATURE.

Actors, Eminent. Edited by WILLIAM ARCHER. Crown 8vo, 2s. 6d. each.

    I. **William Charles Macready.** By WILLIAM ARCHER.

    II. **Thomas Betterton.** By. R. W. LOWE.

ADAMS, W. H. Davenport.—**The White King**; or, Charles the First, and Men and Women, Life and Manners, etc., in the First Half of the Seventeenth Century. 2 vols. Demy 8vo, 21s.

AGASSIZ, Louis.—**An Essay on Classification.** 8vo, 12s.

ALLIBONE, S. A.—**A Critical Dictionary of English Literature and British and American Authors.** From the Earliest Accounts to the latter half of the Nineteenth Century. 3 vols. Royal 8vo, £5 8s.

Amateur Mechanic's Workshop (The). A Treatise containing Plain and Concise Directions for the Manipulation of Wood and Metals. By the Author of "The Lathe and its Uses." Sixth Edition. Numerous Woodcuts. Demy 8vo, 6s.

American Almanac and Treasury of Facts, Statistical, Financial, and Political. Edited by AINSWORTH R. SPOFFORD. Published Yearly. Crown 8vo, 7s. 6d. each.

AMOS, Professor Sheldon.—**The History and Principles of the Civil Law of Rome.** An aid to the Study of Scientific and Comparative Jurisprudence. Demy 8vo, 16s.

ANDERSON, William.—**Practical Mercantile Correspondence.** A Collection of Modern Letters of Business, with Notes, Critical and Explanatory, and an Appendix. Thirtieth Edition. Crown 8vo, 3s. 6d.

ANDERSON, W., and TUGMAN, J. E.—**Mercantile Correspondence.** A Collection of Letters in Portuguese and English, treating of the system of Business in the principal Cities of the World. With Introduction and Notes. 12mo, 6s.

Antiquarian Magazine and Bibliographer (The). Edited by EDWARD WALFORD, M.A., and G. W. REDWAY, F.R.H.S. Complete in 12 vols. £3 nett.

ARISTOTLE.—**The Nicomachean Ethics of Aristotle.** Translated by F. H. PETERS, M.A. Third Edition. Crown 8vo, 6s.

ARMITAGE, Edward, R.A.—**Lectures on Painting:** Delivered to the Students of the Royal Academy. Crown 8vo, 7s. 6d.

AUBERTIN, J. J.—**A Flight to Mexico.** With 7 full-page Illustrations and a Railway Map of Mexico. Crown 8vo, 7s. 6d.

    Six Months in Cape Colony and Natal. With Illustrations and Map. Crown 8vo, 6s.

    A Fight with Distances. Illustrations and Maps. Crown 8vo, 7s. 6d.

Australia, The Year-Book of, for 1889. Published under the auspices of the Governments of the Australian Colonies. With Maps. Demy 8vo, 10s. 6d.

AXON, W. E. A.—**The Mechanic's Friend.** A Collection of Receipts and Practical Suggestions relating to Aquaria, Bronzing, Cements, Drawing, Dyes, Electricity, Gilding, Glass-working, etc. Numerous Woodcuts. Edited by W. E. A. AXON. Crown 8vo, 3s. 6d.

Bacon-Shakespeare Question Answered (The). By C. STOPES. Second Edition. Demy 8vo, 6s.

BAGEHOT, Walter.—**The English Constitution.** Fifth Edition. Crown 8vo, 7s. 6d.

    Lombard Street. A Description of the Money Market. Ninth Edition. Crown 8vo, 7s. 6d.

    Essays on Parliamentary Reform. Crown 8vo, 5s.

    Some Articles on the Depreciation of Silver, and Topics connected with it. Demy 8vo, 5s.

BALL, V.—The Diamonds, Coal, and Gold of India. Their Mode of Occurrence and Distribution. Fcap. 8vo, 5*s*.

A Manual of the Geology of India. Part III. Economic Geology. Royal 8vo, 10*s*.

BARNES, William.—A Glossary of the Dorset Dialect. With a Grammar of its Word-Shapening and Wording. Demy 8vo, sewed, 6*s*.

BARTLETT, J. R.—Dictionary of Americanisms. A Glossary of Words and Phrases colloquially used in the United States. Fourth Edition. 8vo, 21*s*.

BARTON, G. B.—The History of New South Wales. From the Records. Vol. I. Illustrated with Maps, Portraits, and Sketches. Demy 8vo, cloth, 15*s*. ; half-morocco, 20*s*.

BAUGHAN, Rosa.—The Influence of the Stars. A Treatise on Astrology, Chiromancy, and Physiognomy. Demy 8vo, 5*s*.

BEARD, Charles, LL.D.—Martin Luther and the Reformation in Germany until the Close of the Diet of Worms. Demy 8vo, 16*s*.

Becket, Thomas, Martyr-Patriot. By R. A. Thompson, M.A. Crown 8vo, 6*s*.

BENSON, A. C.—William Laud, sometime Archbishop of Canterbury. A Study. With Portrait. Crown 8vo, 6*s*.

BEVAN, Theodore F., F.R.G.S.—Toil, Travel, and Discovery in British New Guinea. With Maps. Large crown 8vo, 7*s*. 6*d*.

BLACKET, W. S.—Researches into the Lost Histories of America. Illustrated by numerous Engravings. 8vo, 10*s*. 6*d*.

BLADES, W.—The Biography and Typography of William Caxton, England's First Printer. Demy 8vo, hand-made paper, imitation old bevelled binding, £1 1*s*. Cheap Edition. Crown 8vo, 5*s*.

BLEEK, W. H. I.—Reynard the Fox in South Africa ; or, Hottentot Fables and Tales. From Original Manuscripts. Post 8vo, 3*s*. 6*d*.

A Brief Account of Bushman Folk-Lore, and Other Texts. Folio, 2*s*. 6*d*.

BOTTRELL, William.—Stories and Folk-Lore of West Cornwall. With Illustrations by Joseph Blight. Second and Third Series. 8vo, 6*s*. each.

BRADLEY, F. H.—The Principles of Logic. Demy 8vo, 16*s*.

BRADSHAW.—Dictionary of Bathing-Places and Climatic Health Resorts. With Map. New Edition. Crown 8vo, 2*s*. 6*d*.

BRADSHAW—continued.

A B C Dictionary of the United States, Canada, and Mexico. Showing the most important Towns and Points of Interest. With Maps, Routes, etc. New Edition, Revised. Fcap. 8vo, 2*s.* 6*d.*

Bradshaw, Henry: Memoir. By G. W. PROTHERO. With Portrait and Fac-simile. Demy 8vo, 16*s.*

BRENTANO, Lujo.—On the History and Development of Gilds, and the Origin of Trade-Unions. 8vo, 3*s.* 6*d.*

BRERETON, C. S. H.—The Last Days of Olympus. A Modern Myth. Crown 8vo, 3*s.* 6*d.*

BRIDGETT, Rev. T. E.—Blunders and Forgeries. Historical Essays. Crown 8vo, 6*s.*

BROWN, Horatio F.—Life on the Lagoons. With 2 Illustrations and Map. Crown 8vo, 6*s.*

Venetian Studies. Crown 8vo, 7*s.* 6*d.*

BROWN, Marie A.—The Icelandic Discoverers of America; or, Honour to whom Honour is due. With 8 Plates. Crown 8vo, 7*s.* 6*d.*

BROWNE, Hugh Junor.—The Grand Reality. Being Experiences in Spirit-Life of a Celebrated Dramatist, received through a Trance Medium. Edited by HUGH JUNOR BROWNE. Large post 8vo, 7*s.* 6*d.*

Browning Society's Papers.—Demy 8vo, 1881-84. Part I., 10*s.* Part II., 10*s.* Part III., 10*s.* Part IV., 10*s.* Part V., 10*s.* Part VII., 10*s.* Part VIII., 10*s.* Part IX., 10*s.* Part X., 10*s.*

BROWNING. — Bibliography of Robert Browning from 1833-81. 12*s.*

Poems of, Illustrations to. Parts I. and II. 4to, 10*s.* each.

BRUGMANN, Karl.—Elements of a Comparative Grammar of the Indo-Germanic Languages. Translated by JOSEPH WRIGHT. Vol. I. Introduction and Phonetics. 8vo, 18*s.*

BRYANT, Sophie, D.Sc.—Celtic Ireland. With 3 Maps. Crown 8vo, 5*s.*

BURKE, The Late Very Rev. T. N.—His Life. By W. J. FITZPATRICK. 2 vols. With Portrait. Demy 8vo, 30*s.*

Burma.—The British Burma Gazetteer. Compiled by Major H. R. SPEARMAN, under the direction of the Government of India. 2 vols. With 11 Photographs. 8vo, £2 10*s.*

BURTON, Lady.—The Inner Life of Syria, Palestine, and the Holy Land. Post 8vo, 6*s.*

BURY, Richard de.—Philobiblon. Edited by E. C. THOMAS. Crown 8vo, 10*s.* 6*d.*

CAMPBELL, Wm.—An Account of Missionary Success in the Island of Formosa. Published in London in 1650, and now reprinted with copious Appendices. 2 vols. With 6 Illustrations and Map of Formosa. Crown 8vo, 10*s.*

The Gospel of St. Matthew in Formosan (Sinkang Dialect). With Corresponding Versions in Dutch and English. Edited from Gravius's Edition of 1661. Fcap. 4to, 10*s.* 6*d.*

CATLIN, George.—O-Kee-Pa. A Religious Ceremony; and other Customs of the Mandans. With 13 Coloured Illustrations. Small 4to, 14*s.*

The Lifted and Subsided Rocks of America, with their Influence on the Oceanic, Atmospheric, and Land Currents, and the Distribution of Races. With 2 Maps. Crown 8vo, 6*s.* 6*d.*

Shut your Mouth and Save your Life. With 29 Illustrations. Eighth Edition. Crown 8vo, 2*s.* 6*d.*

CHAMBERS, John David.—The Theological and Philosophical Works of Hermes Trismegistus, Christian Neoplatonist. Translated from the Greek. Demy 8vo, 7*s.* 6*d.*

CHARNOCK, Richard Stephen.—A Glossary of the Essex Dialect. Fcap., 3*s.* 6*d.*

Nuces Etymologicæ. Crown 8vo, 10*s.*

Prœnomina; or, The Etymology of the Principal Christian Names of Great Britain and Ireland. Crown 8vo, 6*s.*

Chaucer Society.—Subscription, two guineas per annum. List of Publications on application.

CLAPPERTON, Jane Hume.—Scientific Meliorism and the Evolution of Happiness. Large crown 8vo, 8*s.* 6*d.*

CLARKE, Henry W.—The History of Tithes, from Abraham to Queen Victoria. Crown 8vo, 5*s.*

CLAUSEWITZ, General Carl von.—On War. Translated by Colonel J. J. GRAHAM. Fcap. 4to, 10*s.* 6*d.*

CLEMENT, C. E., and HUTTON, L.—Artists of the Nineteenth Century and their Works. Two Thousand and Fifty Biographical Sketches. Third, Revised Edition. Crown 8vo, 15*s.*

CLODD, Edward, F.R.A.S.—The Childhood of the World: a Simple Account of Man in Early Times. Eighth Edition. Crown 8vo, 3*s.*
A Special Edition for Schools. 1*s.*

The Childhood of Religions. Including a Simple Account of the Birth and Growth of Myths and Legends. Eighth Thousand. Crown 8vo, 5*s.*
A Special Edition for Schools. 1*s.* 6*d.*

CLODD, *Edward, F.R.A.S.—continued.*
Jesus of Nazareth. With a brief sketch of Jewish History to the Time of His Birth. Second Edition. Small crown 8vo, 6*s.*
A Special Edition for Schools. In 2 parts. Each 1*s.* 6*d.*

COLEBROOKE, *Henry Thomas.*—Life and Miscellaneous Essays of. The Biography by his Son, Sir T. E. COLEBROOKE, Bart., M.P. 3 vols. Demy 8vo, 42*s.*

COLLETTE, *Charles Hastings.*—The Life, Times, and Writings of Thomas Cranmer, D.D., the First Reforming Archbishop of Canterbury. Demy 8vo, 7*s.* 6*d.*

Pope Joan. An Historical Study. Translated from the Greek, with Preface. 12mo, 2*s.* 6*d.*

COLLINS, *Mabel.*—Through the Gates of Gold. A Fragment of Thought. Small 8vo, 4*s.* 6*d.*

CONWAY, *Moncure D.*—Travels in South Kensington. Illustrated. 8vo, 12*s.*

COOK, *Louisa S.*—Geometrical Psychology ; or, The Science of Representation. An Abstract of the Theories and Diagrams of B. W. Betts. 16 Plates, coloured and plain. Demy 8vo, 7*s.* 6*d.*

COTTON, *H. J. S.*—New India, or India in Transition. Third Edition. Crown 8vo, 4*s.* 6*d.* ; Cheap Edition, paper covers, 1*s.*

COTTON, *Louise.*—Palmistry and its Practical Uses. 12 Plates. Crown 8vo, 2*s.* 6*d.*

COX, *Rev. Sir George W., M.A., Bart.*—The Mythology of the Aryan Nations. New Edition. Demy 8vo, 16*s.*

Tales of Ancient Greece. New Edition. Small crown 8vo, 6*s.*

A Manual of Mythology in the form of Question and Answer. New Edition. Fcap. 8vo, 3*s.*

An Introduction to the Science of Comparative Mythology and Folk-Lore. Second Edition. Crown 8vo, 7*s.* 6*d.*

COX, *Rev. Sir G. W., M.A., Bart., and JONES, Eustace Hinton.*—Popular Romances of the Middle Ages. Third Edition, in 1 vol. Crown 8vo, 6*s.*

CURR, *Edward M.*—The Australian Race : Its Origin, Languages, Customs, Place of Landing in Australia, and the Routes by which it spread itself over that Continent. In 4 vols. With Map and Illustrations. £2 2*s.*

CUST, *R. N.*—The Shrines of Lourdes, Zaragossa, the Holy Stairs at Rome, the Holy House of Loretto and Nazareth, and St. Ann at Jerusalem. With 4 Autotypes. Fcap. 8vo, 2*s.*

Davis, Thomas: The Memoirs of an Irish Patriot, 1840–46. By Sir CHARLES GAVAN DUFFY, K.C.M.G. Demy 8vo, 12*s*.

DAVITT, Michael.—**Speech before the Special Commission.** Crown 8vo, 5*s*.

DAWSON, Geo.—**Biographical Lectures.** Edited by GEORGE ST. CLAIR, F.G.S. Third Edition. Large crown 8vo, 7*s*. 6*d*.

    Shakespeare, and other Lectures. Edited by GEORGE ST. CLAIR, F.G.S. Large crown 8vo, 7*s*. 6*d*.

DEAN, Teresa H.—**How to be Beautiful.** Nature Unmasked. A Book for Every Woman. Fcap. 8vo, 2*s*. 6*d*.

DEATH, J.—**The Beer of the Bible: one of the hitherto Unknown Leavens of Exodus.** With a Visit to an Arab Brewery, and Map of the Routes of the Exodus, etc. Crown 8vo, 6*s*.

DE JONCOURT, Madame Marie.—**Wholesome Cookery.** Fifth Edition. Crown 8vo, cloth, 1*s*. 6*d*. ; paper covers, 1*s*.

DENMAN, Hon. G.—**The Story of the Kings of Rome.** In Verse. 16mo, parchment, 1*s*. 6*d*.

DONOVAN, J.—**Music and Action** ; or, The Elective Affinity between Rhythm and Pitch. Crown 8vo, 3*s*. 6*d*.

DOWDEN, Edward, LL.D.—**Shakspere :** a Critical Study of his Mind and Art. Ninth Edition. Post 8vo, 12*s*.

    Shakspere's Sonnets. With Introduction and Notes. Large post 8vo, 7*s*. 6*d*.

    Studies in Literature, 1789–1877. Fourth Edition. Large post 8vo, 6*s*.

    Transcripts and Studies. Large post 8vo, 12*s*.

DOWSETT, F. C.—**Striking Events in Irish History.** Crown 8vo, 2*s*. 6*d*.

Dreamland and Ghostland. An Original Collection of Tales and Warnings from the Borderland of Substance and Shadow. 3 vols. 6*s*. per vol., sold separately.

Drummond, Thomas, Under Secretary in Ireland, 1835–40. Life and Letters. By R. BARRY O'BRIEN. Demy 8vo, 14*s*.

DU PREL, Carl.—**The Philosophy of Mysticism.** Translated from the German by C. C. MASSEY. 2 vols. Demy 8vo, cloth, 25*s*.

Early English Text Society.—Subscription, one guinea per annum. *Extra Series.* Subscriptions—Small paper, one guinea per annum. List of Publications on application.

EDMUNDSON, George.—**Milton and Vondel.** A Curiosity of Literature. Crown 8vo, 6*s*.

EDWARDS, Edward.—**Memoirs of Libraries**, together with a Practical Handbook of Library Economy. Numerous Illustrations. 2 vols. Royal 8vo, £2 8s. Large paper Edition. Imperial 8vo, £4 4s.

Libraries and Founders of Libraries. 8vo, 18s. Large paper Edition. Imperial 8vo, £1 10s.

Free Town Libraries, their Formation, Management, and History in Britain, France, Germany, and America. Together with Brief Notices of Book Collectors, and of the respective Places of Deposit of their Surviving Collections. 8vo, 21s.

Eighteenth Century Essays. Selected and Edited by AUSTIN DOBSON. Cheap Edition. Cloth, 1s. 6d.

Ellis, William (Founder of the Birkbeck Schools). Life, with Account of his Writings. By E. KELL BLYTH. Demy 8vo, 14s.

Emerson's (Ralph Waldo) Life. By OLIVER WENDELL HOLMES. English Copyright Edition. With Portrait. Crown 8vo, 6s.

Emerson (Ralph Waldo), Talks with. By CHARLES J. WOODBURY. Crown 8vo, 5s.

English Dialect Society.—Subscription, 10s. 6d. per annum. List of Publications on application.

FIELD, David Dudley.—**Outlines of an International Code.** Second Edition. Royal 8vo, £2 2s.

Five o'clock Tea. Containing Receipts for Cakes, Savoury Sandwiches, etc. Eighth Thousand. Fcap. 8vo, cloth, 1s. 6d.; paper covers, 1s.

Forbes, Bishop. A Memoir. By the Rev. DONALD J. MACKAY. With Portrait and Map. Crown 8vo, 7s. 6d.

FOTHERINGHAM, James.—**Studies in the Poetry of Robert Browning.** Second Edition. Crown 8vo, 6s.

FOX, Charles.—**The Pilgrims.** An Allegory of the Soul's Progress from the Earthly to the Heavenly State. Crown 8vo, 5s.

FOX, J. A.—**A Key to the Irish Question.** Crown 8vo, 7s. 6d.

FRANKLYN, Henry Bowles.—**The Great Battles of 1870, and Blockade of Metz.** With Large Map, Sketch Map, and Frontispiece. 8vo, 15s.

FREEBOROUGH, E., and RANKEN, C. E.—**Chess Openings,** Ancient and Modern. Revised and Corrected up to the Present Time from the best Authorities. Large post 8vo, 7s. 6d.; interleaved, 9s.

FREEMAN, E. A.—**Lectures to American Audiences.** I. The English People in its Three Homes. II. Practical Bearings of General European History. Post 8vo, 8s. 6d

FRITH, I.—Life of Giordano Bruno, the Nolan. Revised by Prof. MORIZ CARRIERE. With Portrait. Post 8vo, 14*s*.

Froebel's Ethical Teaching. Two Essays by M. J. LYSCHINSKA and THERESE G. MONTEFIORE. Fcap., 2*s*. 6*d*.

From World to Cloister ; or, My Novitiate. By BERNARD. Crown 8vo, 5*s*.

Garfield, The Life and Public Service of James A., Twentieth President of the United States. A Biographical Sketch. By Captain F. H. MASON. With a Preface by BRET HARTE. With Portrait. Crown 8vo, 2*s*. 6*d*.

GASTER, M.—Greeko-Slavonic Literature and its Relation to the Folk-Lore of Europe during the Middle Ages. Large post 8vo, 7*s*. 6*d*.

GEORGE, Henry.—Progress and Poverty. An Inquiry into the Causes of Industrial Depressions, and of Increase of Want with Increase of Wealth. The Remedy. Fifth Library Edition. Post 8vo, 7*s*. 6*d*. Cabinet Edition. Crown 8vo, 2*s*. 6*d*. Also a Cheap Edition. Limp cloth, 1*s*. 6*d*. ; paper covers, 1*s*.

Protection, or Free Trade. An Examination of the Tariff Question, with especial regard to the Interests of Labour. Second Edition. Crown 8vo, 5*s*. Cheap Edition. Limp cloth, 1*s*. 6*d*. ; paper covers, 1*s*.

Social Problems. Fourth Thousand. Crown 8vo, 5*s*. Cheap Edition. Limp cloth, 1*s*. 6*d*. ; paper covers, 1*s*.

GIBB, E. J. W.—The History of the Forty Vezirs ; or, The Story of the Forty Morns and Eves. Translated from the Turkish. Crown 8vo, 10*s*. 6*d*.

GILBERT, Mrs.—Autobiography, and other Memorials. Edited by JOSIAH GILBERT. Fifth Edition. Crown 8vo, 7*s*. 6*d*.

Glossary of Terms and Phrases. Edited by the Rev. H. PERCY SMITH and others. Second and Cheaper Edition. Medium 8vo, 3*s*. 6*d*.

Goethe's Faust. Translated from the German by JOHN ANSTER, LL.D. With an Introduction by BURDETT MASON. Illustrated by FRANK M. GREGORY. Folio, £3 3*s*.

GORDON, Major-General C. G.—His Journals at Kartoum. Printed from the original MS. With Introduction and Notes by A. EGMONT HAKE. Portrait, 2 Maps, and 30 Illustrations. Two vols., demy 8vo, 21*s*. Also a Cheap Edition in 1 vol., 6*s*.

Gordon's (General) Last Journal. A Facsimile of the last Journal received in England from GENERAL GORDON. Reproduced by Photo-lithography. Imperial 4to, £3 3*s*.

GORDON, Major-General C. G.—continued.
> **Events in his Life.** From the Day of his Birth to the Day of his Death. By Sir H. W. GORDON. With Maps and Illustrations. Second Edition. Demy 8vo, 7s. 6d.

GOSSE, Edmund.—**Seventeenth Century Studies.** A Contribution to the History of English Poetry. Demy 8vo, 10s. 6d.

GOSSIP, G. H. D.—**The Chess-Player's Text-Book.** An Elementary Treatise on the Game of Chess. Illustrated by numerous Diagrams for Beginners and Advanced Students. Medium 16mo, 2s.

GOULD, Rev. S. Baring, M.A.—**Germany, Present and Past.** New and Cheaper Edition. Large crown 8vo, 7s. 6d.

GOWER, Lord Ronald.—**My Reminiscences.** MINIATURE EDITION, printed on hand-made paper, limp parchment antique, 10s. 6d.

> **Bric-à-Brac.** Being some Photoprints illustrating art objects at Gower Lodge, Windsor. With descriptions. Super royal 8vo, 15s. ; extra binding, 21s.

> **Last Days of Mary Antoinette.** An Historical Sketch. With Portrait and Facsimiles. Fcap. 4to, 10s. 6d.

> **Notes of a Tour from Brindisi to Yokohama, 1883–1884.** Fcap. 8vo, 2s. 6d.

> **Rupert of the Rhine :** A Biographical Sketch of the Life of Prince Rupert. With 3 Portraits. Crown 8vo, buckram, 6s.

GRAHAM, William, M.A.—**The Creed of Science,** Religious, Moral, and Social. Second Edition, Revised. Crown 8vo, 6s.

> **The Social Problem, in its Economic, Moral, and Political Aspects.** Demy 8vo, 14s.

GUBERNATIS, Angelo de.—**Zoological Mythology ;** or, The Legends of Animals. 2 vols. 8vo, £1 8s.

GURNEY, Rev. Alfred.—**Wagner's Parsifal.** A Study. Fcap. 8vo, 1s. 6d.

HADDON, Caroline.—**The Larger Life : Studies in Hinton's Ethics.** Crown 8vo, 5s.

HAGGARD, H. Rider.—**Cetywayo and his White Neighbours ;** or, Remarks on Recent Events in Zululand, Natal, and the Transvaal. Third Edition. Crown 8vo, 6s.

HALDEMAN, S. S.—**Pennsylvania Dutch : A Dialect of South Germany** with an Infusion of English. 8vo, 3s. 6d.

HALL, F. T.—**The Pedigree of the Devil.** With 7 Autotype Illustrations from Designs by the Author. Demy 8vo, 7s. 6d.

HALLOCK, Charles.—**The Sportsman's Gazetteer and General Guide.** The Game Animals, Birds, and Fishes of North America. Maps and Portrait. Crown 8vo, 15s.

Hamilton, Memoirs of Arthur, B.A., of Trinity College, Cambridge. Crown 8vo, 6*s.*

Handbook of Home Rule, being Articles on the Irish Question by Various Writers. Edited by JAMES BRYCE, M.P. Second Edition. Crown 8vo, 1*s.* sewed, or 1*s.* 6*d.* cloth.

HARRIS, Emily Marion.—**The Narrative of the Holy Bible.** Crown 8vo, 5*s.*

HARTMANN, Franz.—**Magic, White and Black;** or, The Science of Finite and Infinite Life. Crown 8vo, 7*s.* 6*d.*

 The Life of Paracelsus, and the Substance of his Teachings. Post 8vo, 10*s.* 6*d.*

 Life and Doctrines of Jacob Behmen. Post 8vo, 10*s.* 6*d.*

HAWTHORNE, Nathaniel.—**Works.** Complete in Twelve Volumes. Large post 8vo, 7*s.* 6*d.* each volume.

HECKER, J. F. C.—**The Epidemics of the Middle Ages.** Translated by G. B. BABINGTON, M.D., F.R.S. Third Edition. 8vo, 9*s.* 6*d.*

HENDRIK, Hans.—**Memoirs of Hans Hendrik, the Arctic Traveller;** serving under Kane, Hayes, Hall, and Nares, 1853-76. Translated from the Eskimo Language by Dr. HENRY RINK. Crown 8vo, 3*s.* 6*d.*

HENDRIKS, Dom Lawrence.—**The London Charterhouse:** its Monks and its Martyrs. Illustrated. Demy 8vo, 14*s.*

HERZEN, Alexander.—**Du Developpement des Idées Revolutionnaires en Russie.** 12mo, 2*s.* 6*d.*

 A separate list of A. Herzen's works in Russian may be had on application.

HILL, Alfred.—**The History of the Reform Movement** in the Dental Profession in Great Britain during the last twenty years. Crown 8vo, 10*s.* 6*d.*

HILLEBRAND, Karl.—**France and the French in the Second Half of the Nineteenth Century.** Translated from the Third German Edition. Post 8vo, 10*s.* 6*d.*

HINTON, J.—**Life and Letters.** With an Introduction by Sir W. W. GULL, Bart., and Portrait engraved on Steel by C. H. Jeens. Sixth Edition. Crown 8vo, 8*s.* 6*d.*

 Philosophy and Religion. Selections from the Manuscripts of the late James Hinton. Edited by CAROLINE HADDON. Second Edition. Crown 8vo, 5*s.*

 The Law Breaker, and The Coming of the Law. Edited by MARGARET HINTON. Crown 8vo, 6*s.*

 The Mystery of Pain. New Edition. Fcap. 8vo, 1*s.*

HODGSON, J. E.—**Academy Lectures.** Crown 8vo, 7*s.* 6*d.*

Holbein Society.—Subscription, one guinea per annum. List of Publications on application.

HOLMES-FORBES, Avary W.—**The Science of Beauty.** An Analytical Inquiry into the Laws of Æsthetics. Second Edition. Post 8vo, 3*s.* 6*d.*

HOLYOAKE, G. J.—**The History of Co-operation in England :** Its Literature and its Advocates. 2 vols. Crown 8vo, 14*s.*

Self-Help by the People. Thirty-three Years of Co-operation in Rochdale. Ninth Edition. Crown 8vo, 2*s.* 6*d.*

HOME, Mme. Dunglas.—**D. D. Home : His Life and Mission.** With Portrait. Demy 8vo, 12*s.* 6*d.*

Gift of D. D. Home. Demy 8vo, 10*s.*

Homer's Iliad. Greek Text with Translation. By J. G. CORDERY, C.S.I. Two vols. Demy 8vo, 14*s.* Cheap Edition, Translation only. One vol. Crown 8vo, 5*s.*

HOOLE, Henry.—**The Science and Art of Training.** A Handbook for Athletes. Demy 8vo, 3*s.* 6*d.*

HOOPER, Mary.—**Little Dinners : How to Serve them with Elegance and Economy.** Twenty-first Edition. Crown 8vo, 2*s.* 6*d.*

Cookery for Invalids, Persons of Delicate Digestion, and Children. Fifth Edition. Crown 8vo, 2*s.* 6*d.*

Every-day Meals. Being Economical and Wholesome Recipes for Breakfast, Luncheon, and Supper. Seventh Edition. Crown 8vo, 2*s.* 6*d.*

HOPKINS, Ellice.—**Work amongst Working Men.** Sixth Edition. Crown 8vo, 3*s.* 6*d.*

HORNADAY, W. T.—**Two Years in a Jungle.** With Illustrations. Demy 8vo, 21*s.*

HOWELLS, W. D.—**A Little Girl among the Old Masters.** With Introduction and Comment. 54 Plates. Oblong crown 8vo, 10*s.*

HUMBOLDT, Baron Wilhelm Von.—**The Sphere and Duties of Government.** Translated from the German by JOSEPH COULTHARD, Jun. Post 8vo, 5*s.*

HYNDMAN, H. M.—**The Historical Basis of Socialism in England.** Large crown 8vo, 8*s.* 6*d.*

IM THURN, Everard F.—**Among the Indians of Guiana.** Being Sketches, chiefly anthropologic, from the Interior of British Guiana. With 53 Illustrations and a Map. Demy 8vo, 18*s.*

INGLEBY, the late Clement M.—**Essays.** Edited by his Son. Crown 8vo, 7*s.* 6*d.*

Irresponsibility and its Recognition. By a Graduate of Oxford.
Crown 8vo, 3s. 6d.

JAGIELSKI, V.—Modern Massage Treatment in Combination with the Electric Bath. 8vo, 1s. 6d.

JAPP, Alexander H.—Days with Industrials. Adventures and Experiences among Curious Industries. With Illustrations. Crown 8vo, 6s.

JENKINS, E., and RAYMOND, J.—The Architect's Legal Handbook. Fourth Edition, Revised. Crown 8vo, 6s.

JENKINS, E.—A Modern Paladin. Contemporary Manners. Crown 8vo, 5s.

JENKINS, Jabez.—Vest-Pocket Lexicon. An English Dictionary of all except familiar Words, including the principal Scientific and Technical Terms, and Foreign Moneys, Weights, and Measures. 64mo, 1s.

JENKINS, Rev. Canon R. C.—Heraldry : English and Foreign. With a Dictionary of Heraldic Terms and 156 Illustrations. Small crown 8vo, 3s. 6d.

Jesus the Carpenter of Nazareth. By a Layman. Crown 8vo, 7s. 6d.

JOHNSON, C. P.—Hints to Collectors of Original Editions of the Works of Charles Dickens. Crown 8vo, vellum, 6s.

Hints to Collectors of Original Editions of the Works of William Makepeace Thackeray. Crown 8vo, vellum, 6s.

JOHNSTON, H. H., F.Z.S.—The Kilima-njaro Expedition. A Record of Scientific Exploration in Eastern Equatorial Africa, and a General Description of the Natural History, Languages, and Commerce of the Kilima-njaro District. With 6 Maps, and over 80 Illustrations by the Author. Demy 8vo, 21s.

The History of a Slave. With 47 Illustrations. Square 8vo, 6s.

Juvenalis Satiræ. With a Literal English Prose Translation and Notes. By J. D. Lewis. Second Edition. 2 vols. 8vo, 12s.

KARDEC, Allen.—The Spirit's Book. The Principles of Spiritist Doctrine on the Immortality of the Soul, etc. Transmitted through various mediums. Translated by Anna Blackwell. Crown 8vo, 7s. 6d.

The Medium's Book ; or, Guide for Mediums and for Evocations. Translated by Anna Blackwell. Crown 8vo, 7s. 6d.

Heaven and Hell ; or, The Divine Justice Vindicated in the Plurality of Existences. Translated by Anna Blackwell. Crown 8vo, 7s. 6d.

KAUFMANN, Rev. M., M.A.—Socialism : its Nature, its Dangers, and its Remedies considered. Crown 8vo, 7*s*. 6*d*.

Utopias ; or, Schemes of Social Improvement, from Sir Thomas More to Karl Marx. Crown 8vo, 5*s*.

Christian Socialism. Crown 8vo, 4*s*. 6*d*.

KERRISON, Lady Caroline.—A Commonplace Book of the Fifteenth Century. Containing a Religious Play and Poetry, Legal Forms, and Local Accounts. From the Original MS. at Brome Hall, Suffolk. Edited by LUCY TOULMIN SMITH. With 2 Facsimiles. Demy 8vo, 7*s*. 6*d*.

KINGSFORD, Anna, M.D.—The Perfect Way in Diet. A Treatise advocating a Return to the Natural and Ancient Food of our Race. Third Edition. Small crown 8vo, 2*s*.

The Spiritual Hermeneutics of Astrology and Holy Writ. Illustrated. 4to, parchment, 10*s*. 6*d*.

KINGSFORD, Anna, and MAITLAND, Edward.—The Virgin of the World of Hermes Mercurius Trismegistus. Rendered into English. 4to, parchment, 10*s*. 6*d*.

The Perfect Way ; or, The Finding of Christ. Third Edition, Revised. Square 16mo, 7*s*. 6*d*.

KINGSFORD, William.—History of Canada. 3 vols. 8vo, £2 5*s*.

KITTON, Fred. G.—John Leech, Artist and Humourist. A Biographical Sketch. Demy 18mo, 1*s*.

KRAUS, J.—Carlsbad and its Natural Healing Agents. With Notes, Introductory, by the Rev. JOHN T. WALLERS. Third Edition. Crown 8vo, 6*s*. 6*d*.

LAMB, Charles.—Beauty and the Beast ; or, A Rough Outside with a Gentle Heart. A Poem. Fcap. 8vo, vellum, 10*s*. 6*d*.

LANG, Andrew.—Lost Leaders. Crown 8vo, 5*s*.

Lathe (The) and its Uses ; or, Instruction in the Art of Turning Wood and Metal. Sixth Edition. Illustrated. 8vo, 10*s*. 6*d*.

LEE, Frederick Geo.—A Manual of Politics. In three Chapters. With Footnotes and Appendices. Small crown 8vo, 2*s*. 6*d*.

LEFEVRE, Right Hon. G. Shaw.—Peel and O'Connell. Demy 8vo, 10*s*. 6*d*.

Incidents of Coercion. A Journal of Visits to Ireland. Third Edition. Crown 8vo, limp cloth, 1*s*. 6*d*. ; paper covers, 1*s*.

Irish Members and English Gaolers. Crown 8vo, limp cloth, 1*s*. 6*d*. ; paper covers, 1*s*.

Combination and Coercion in Ireland. A Sequel to "Incidents of Coercion." Crown 8vo, cloth, 1*s*. 6*d*. ; paper covers, 1*s*.

LELAND, Charles G.—The Breitmann Ballads. The only authorized Edition. Complete in 1 vol., including Nineteen Ballads, illustrating his Travels in Europe (never before printed). Crown 8vo, 6s.

Gaudeamus. Humorous Poems translated from the German of Joseph Victor Scheffel and others. 16mo, 3s. 6d.

The English Gipsies and their Language. Second Edition. Crown 8vo, 7s. 6d.

Fu-Sang; or, The Discovery of America by Chinese Buddhist Priests in the Fifth Century. Crown 8vo, 7s. 6d.

Pidgin-English Sing-Song; or, Songs and Stories in the China-English Dialect. With a Vocabulary. Second Edition. Crown 8vo, 5s.

The Gypsies. Crown 8vo, 10s. 6d.

Light on the Path. For the Personal Use of those who are Ignorant of the Eastern Wisdom. Written down by M. C. Fcap. 8vo, 1s. 6d.

LOCHER, Carl.—An Explanation of Organ Stops, with Hints for Effective Combinations. Demy 8vo, 5s.

LONGFELLOW, H. Wadsworth.—Life. By his Brother, Samuel Longfellow. With Portraits and Illustrations. 3 vols. Demy 8vo, 42s.

LONSDALE, Margaret.—Sister Dora: a Biography. With Portrait. Thirtieth Edition. Small crown 8vo, 2s. 6d.

George Eliot: Thoughts upon her Life, her Books, and Herself. Second Edition. Small crown 8vo, 1s. 6d.

Lotos Series (The). Pot 8vo, bound in two styles: (1) cloth, gilt back and edges; (2) half-parchment, cloth sides, gilt top, uncut, 3s. 6d. each.

The Original Travels and Surprising Adventures of Baron Munchausen. Illustrated by Alfred Crowquill.

The Breitmann Ballads. By Charles G. Leland. Author's Copyright Edition, with a New Preface and Additional Poems.

Essays on Men and Books Selected from the Earlier Writings of Lord Macaulay. Vol. 1. Introductory— Lord Clive—Milton—Earl Chatham—Lord Byron. With Critical Introduction and Notes by Alexander H. Japp, LL.D. With Portraits.

The Light of Asia; or, The Great Renunciation. Being the Life and Teaching of Gautama, Prince of India and Founder of Buddhism. Told in Verse by an Indian Buddhist. By Sir Edwin Arnold, K.C.I.E., C.S.I. With Illustrations and a Portrait of the Author.

Lotos Series (The)—*continued.*

The Marvellous and Rare Conceits of Master Tyll Owlglass. Newly Collected, Chronicled, and set forth in an English Tongue. By KENNETH H. R. MACKENZIE. Adorned with many most Diverting and Cunning Devices by ALFRED CROWQUILL.

A Lover's Litanies, and other Poems. By ERIC MACKAY. With Portrait of the Author.

The Large Paper Edition of these Volumes will be limited to 101 numbered copies for sale in England, price 12s. 6d. each, net.

Lowder, Charles: A Biography. By the Author of "St. Teresa." Twelfth Edition. With Portrait. Crown 8vo, 3s. 6d.

LOWELL, James Russell.—**The Biglow Papers.** Edited by THOMAS HUGHES, Q.C. First and Second Series in 1 vol. Fcap., 2s. 6d.

LOWSLEY, Major B.—**A Glossary of Berkshire Words and Phrases.** Crown 8vo, half-calf, gilt edges, interleaved, 12s. 6d.

LÜCKES, Eva C. E.—**Lectures on General Nursing,** delivered to the Probationers of the London Hospital Training School for Nurses. Third Edition. Crown 8vo, 2s. 6d.

LUDEWIG, Hermann E.—**The Literature of American Aboriginal Languages.** Edited by NICOLAS TRÜBNER. 8vo, 10s. 6d.

LUKIN, J.—**Amongst Machines.** A Description of Various Mechanical Appliances used in the Manufacture of Wood, Metal, etc. A Book for Boys. Second Edition. 64 Engravings. Crown 8vo, 3s. 6d.

The Young Mechanic. Containing Directions for the Use of all Kinds of Tools, and for the Construction of Steam-Engines, etc. A Book for Boys. Second Edition. With 70 Engravings. Crown 8vo, 3s. 6d.

The Boy Engineers: What they Did, and How they Did it. A Book for Boys. 30 Engravings. Imperial 16mo, 3s. 6d.

LUMLEY, E.—**The Art of Judging the Character of Individuals from their Handwriting and Style.** With 35 Plates. Square 16mo, 5s.

LYTTON, Edward Bulwer, Lord.—**Life, Letters and Literary Remains.** By his Son, the EARL OF LYTTON. With Portraits, Illustrations and Facsimiles. Demy 8vo. Vols. I. and II., 32s.

MACDONALD, W. A.—**Humanitism:** The Scientific Solution of the Social Problem. Large post 8vo, 7s. 6d.

MACHIAVELLI, Niccolò.

Discourses on the First Decade of Titus Livius. Translated from the Italian by NINIAN HILL THOMSON, M.A. Large crown 8vo, 12*s.*

The Prince. Translated from the Italian by N. H. T. Small crown 8vo, printed on hand-made paper, bevelled boards, 6*s.*

MAIDEN, J. H.—**The Useful Native Plants of Australia** (including Tasmania). Demy 8vo, 12*s.* 6*d.*

Maintenon, Madame de. By EMILY BOWLES. With Portrait. Large crown 8vo, 7*s.* 6*d.*

MARCHANT, W. T.—**In Praise of Ale.** Songs, Ballads, Epigrams, and Anecdotes. Crown 8vo, 10*s.* 6*d.*

MARKHAM, Capt. Albert Hastings, R.N.—**The Great Frozen Sea :** A Personal Narrative of the Voyage of the *Alert* during the Arctic Expedition of 1875-6. With 6 full-page Illustrations, 2 Maps, and 27 Woodcuts. Sixth and Cheaper Edition. Crown 8vo, 6*s.*

Marriage and Divorce. Including Religious, Practical, and Political Aspects of the Question. By AP RICHARD. Crown 8vo, 5*s.*

MARTIN, G. A.—**The Family Horse :** Its Stabling, Care, and Feeding. Crown 8vo, 3*s.* 6*d.*

MATHERS, S. L. M.—**The Key of Solomon the King.** Translated from Ancient MSS. in the British Museum. With Plates. Crown 4to, 25*s.*

The Kabbalah Unveiled. Containing the Three Books of the Zohar. Translated into English. With Plates. Post 8vo, 10*s.* 6*d.*

The Tarot : its Occult Signification, Use in Fortune-Telling, and Method of Play. 32mo, 1*s.* 6*d.* ; with pack of 78 Tarot Cards, 5*s.*

MAUDSLEY, H., M.D.—**Body and Will.** Being an Essay concerning Will, in its Metaphysical, Physiological, and Pathological Aspects. 8vo, 12*s.*

Natural Causes and Supernatural Seemings. Second Edition. Crown 8vo, 6*s.*

Mechanic, The Young. A Book for Boys. Containing Directions for the Use of all Kinds of Tools, and for the Construction of Steam-Engines and Mechanical Models. By the Rev. J. LUKIN. Sixth Edition. With 70 Engravings. Crown 8vo, 3*s.* 6*d.*

Mechanic's Workshop, Amateur. Plain and Concise Directions for the Manipulation of Wood and Metals. By the Author of "The Lathe and its Uses." Sixth Edition. Illustrated. Demy 8vo, 6*s.*

Mendelssohn's Letters to Ignaz and Charlotte Moscheles. Translated by FELIX MOSCHELLES. Numerous Illustrations and Facsimiles. 8vo, 12*s.*

METCALFE, Frederick.—**The Englishman and the Scandinavian.** Post 8vo, 18*s.*

MINTON, Rev. Francis.—**Capital and Wages.** 8vo, 15*s.*

  The Welfare of the Millions. Crown 8vo, limp cloth, 1*s.* 6*d.* ; paper covers, 1*s.*

Mitchel, John, Life. By WILLIAM DILLON. 2 vols. With Portrait. 8vo, 21*s.*

MITCHELL, Lucy M.—**A History of Ancient Sculpture.** With numerous Illustrations, including 6 Plates in Phototype. Super-royal 8vo, 42*s.*

Mohl, Julius and Mary, Letters and Recollections of. By M. C. M. SIMPSON. With Portraits and 2 Illustrations. Demy 8vo, 15*s.*

MOODIE, D. C. F.—**The History of the Battles and Adventures of the British, the Boers, the Zulus, etc., in Southern Africa,** from the Time of Pharaoh Necho to 1880. With Illustrations and Coloured Maps. 2 vols. Crown 8vo, 36*s.*

MORFIT, Campbell.—**A Practical Treatise on the Manufacture of Soaps.** With Illustrations. Demy 8vo, £2 12*s.* 6*d.*

  A Practical Treatise on Pure Fertilizers, and the Chemical Conversion of Rock Guanos, etc., into various valuable Products. With 28 Plates. 8vo, £4 4*s.*

MOORE, Aubrey L.—**Science and the Faith :** Essays on Apologetic Subjects. Crown 8vo, 6*s.*

MORISON, J. Cotter.—**The Service of Man :** an Essay towards the Religion of the Future. Crown 8vo, 5*s.*

MORRIS, Charles.—**Aryan Sun-Myths the Origin of Religions.** With an Introduction by CHARLES MORRIS. Crown 8vo, 6*s.*

MORRIS, Gouverneur, U.S. Minister to France.—**Diary and Letters.** 2 vols. Demy 8vo, 30*s.*

MOSENTHAL, J. de, and HARTING, James E.—**Ostriches and Ostrich Farming.** Second Edition. With 8 full-page Illustrations and 20 Woodcuts. Royal 8vo, 10*s.* 6*d.*

Motley, John Lothrop. A Memoir. By OLIVER WENDELL HOLMES. Crown 8vo, 6*s.*

MULHALL, M. G. and E. T.—**Handbook of the River Plate,** comprising the Argentine Republic, Uruguay, and Paraguay. With Six Maps. Fifth Edition. Crown 8vo, 7*s.* 6*d.*

Munro, Major-Gen. Sir Thomas. A Memoir. By Sir A. J. ARBUTHNOT. Crown 8vo, 3*s.* 6*d.*

Natural History. "Riverside" Edition. Edited by J. S. KINGSLEY. 6 vols. 2200 Illustrations. 4to, £6 6s.

NEVILL, J. H. N.—**The Biology of Daily Life.** Post 8vo, 3s. 6d.

NEWMAN, Cardinal.—**Characteristics from the Writings of.** Being Selections from his various Works. Arranged with the Author's personal Approval. Eighth Edition. **With Portrait.** Crown 8vo, 6s.

> *** A Portrait of Cardinal Newman, mounted for framing, can be had, 2s. 6d.

NEWMAN, Francis William.—**Essays on Diet.** Small crown 8vo, cloth limp, 2s.

> **Miscellanies.** Vol. II., III., and IV. Essays, Tracts, and Addresses, Moral and Religious. Demy 8vo. Vols. II. and III., 12s. Vol. IV., 10s. 6d.

> **Reminiscences of Two Exiles and Two Wars.** Crown 8vo, 3s. 6d.

> **Phases of Faith ;** or, Passages from the History of my Creed. Crown 8vo, 3s. 6d.

> **The Soul : Her Sorrows and her Aspirations.** Tenth Edition. Post 8vo, 3s. 6d.

> **Hebrew Theism.** Royal 8vo, 4s. 6d.

> **Anglo-Saxon Abolition of Negro Slavery.** Demy 8vo, 5s.

New South Wales, Journal and Proceedings of the Royal Society of. Published annually. Price 10s. 6d.

New South Wales, Publications of the Government of. List on application.

New Zealand Institute Publications :—

> I. **Transactions and Proceedings of the** New Zealand Institute. Vols. I. to XX., 1868 to 1887. Demy 8vo, stitched, £1 1s. each.

> II. **An Index to the Transactions and Proceedings of** the New Zealand Institute. Edited by JAMES HECTOR, M.D., F.R.S. Vols. I. to VIII. Demy 8vo, 2s. 6d.

New Zealand : Geological Survey. List of Publications on application.

OATES, Frank, F.R.G.S.—**Matabele Land and the Victoria Falls.** A Naturalist's Wanderings in the Interior of South Africa. Edited by C. G. OATES, B.A. With numerous Illustrations and 4 Maps. Demy 8vo, 21s.

O'BRIEN, R. Barry.—**Irish Wrongs and English Remedies,** with other Essays. Crown 8vo, 5s.

O'BRIEN, R. Barry.—continued.

The Home Ruler's Manual. Crown 8vo, cloth, 1s. 6d. ;
paper covers, 1s.

OLCOTT, Henry S.—**Theosophy, Religion, and Occult Science.**
With Glossary of Eastern Words. Crown 8vo, 7s. 6d.

Posthumous Humanity. A Study of Phantoms. By ADOLPHE
D'ASSIER. Translated and Annotated by HENRY S. OLCOTT.
Crown 8vo, 7s. 6d.

**Our Public Schools—Eton, Harrow, Winchester, Rugby,
Westminster, Marlborough, The Charterhouse.**
Crown 8vo, 6s.

OWEN, Robert Dale.—**Footfalls on the Boundary of Another
World.** With Narrative Illustrations. Post 8vo, 7s. 6d.

The Debatable Land between this World and the Next.
With Illustrative Narrations. Second Edition. Crown 8vo,
7s. 6d.

Threading my Way. Twenty-Seven Years of Autobiography.
Crown 8vo, 7s. 6d.

OXLEY, William.—**Modern Messiahs and Wonder-Workers.**
A History of the Various Messianic Claimants to Special Divine
Prerogatives. Post 8vo, 5s.

Parchment Library. Choicely Printed on hand-made paper, limp
parchment antique or cloth, 6s. ; vellum, 7s. 6d. each volume.

Selected Poems of Matthew Prior. With an Introduction
and Notes by AUSTIN DOBSON.

Sartor Resartus. By THOMAS CARLYLE.

The Poetical Works of John Milton. 2 vols.

Chaucer's Canterbury Tales. Edited by A. W. POLLARD,
2 vols.

Letters and Journals of Jonathan Swift. Selected and
edited, with a Commentary and Notes, by STANLEY LANE-POOLE.

De Quincey's Confessions of an English Opium Eater.
Reprinted from the First Edition. Edited by RICHARD GARNETT.

The Gospel according to Matthew, Mark, and Luke.

Selections from the Prose Writings of Jonathan Swift.
With a Preface and Notes by STANLEY LANE-POOLE and
Portrait.

English Sacred Lyrics.

Sir Joshua Reynolds's Discourses. Edited by EDMUND
GOSSE.

Parchment Library—*continued.*

Selections from Milton's Prose Writings. Edited by ERNEST MYERS.

The Book of Psalms. Translated by the Rev. Canon T. K. CHEYNE, M.A., D.D.

The Vicar of Wakefield. With Preface and Notes by AUSTIN DOBSON.

English Comic Dramatists. Edited by OSWALD CRAWFURD.

English Lyrics.

The Sonnets of John Milton. Edited by MARK PATTISON. With Portrait after Vertue.

French Lyrics. Selected and Annotated by GEORGE SAINTSBURY. With a Miniature Frontispiece designed and etched by H. G. Glindoni.

Fables by Mr. John Gay. With Memoir by AUSTIN DOBSON, and an Etched Portrait from an unfinished Oil Sketch by Sir Godfrey Kneller.

Select Letters of Percy Bysshe Shelley. Edited, with an Introduction, by RICHARD GARNETT.

The Christian Year. Thoughts in Verse for the Sundays and Holy Days throughout the Year. With Miniature Portrait of the Rev. J. Keble, after a Drawing by G. Richmond, R.A.

Shakspere's Works. Complete in Twelve Volumes.

Eighteenth Century Essays. Selected and Edited by AUSTIN DOBSON. With a Miniature Frontispiece by R. Caldecott.

Q. Horati Flacci Opera. Edited by F. A. CORNISH, Assistant Master at Eton. With a Frontispiece after a design by L. Alma Tadema, etched by Leopold Lowenstam.

Edgar Allan Poe's Poems. With an Essay on his Poetry by ANDREW LANG, and a Frontispiece by Linley Sambourne.

Shakspere's Sonnets. Edited by EDWARD DOWDEN. With a Frontispiece etched by Leopold Lowenstam, after the Death Mask.

English Odes. Selected by EDMUND GOSSE. With Frontispiece on India paper by Hamo Thornycroft, A.R.A.

Of the Imitation of Christ. By THOMAS À KEMPIS. A revised Translation. With Frontispiece on India paper, from a Design by W. B. Richmond.

Poems: Selected from PERCY BYSSHE SHELLEY. Dedicated to Lady Shelley. With a Preface by RICHARD GARNETT and a Miniature Frontispiece.

PARSLOE, Joseph.—Our Railways. Sketches, Historical and Descriptive. With Practical Information as to Fares and Rates, etc., and a Chapter on Railway Reform. Crown 8vo, 6s.

PATON, A. A.—A History of the Egyptian Revolution, from the Period of the Mamelukes to the Death of Mohammed Ali. Second Edition. 2 vols. Demy 8vo, 7s. 6d.

PAULI, Reinhold.—Simon de Montfort, Earl of Leicester, the Creator of the House of Commons. Crown 8vo, 6s.

Paul of Tarsus. By the Author of "Rabbi Jeshua." Crown 8vo, 4s. 6d.

PEMBERTON, T. Edgar.—Charles Dickens and the Stage. A Record of his Connection with the Drama. Crown 8vo, 6s.

PEZZI, Domenico.—Aryan Philology, according to the most recent researches (Glottologia Aria Recentissima). Translated by E. S. ROBERTS. Crown 8vo, 6s.

PFEIFFER, Emily.—Women and Work. An Essay on the Relation to Health and Physical Development of the Higher Education of Girls. Crown 8vo, 6s.

Phantasms of the Living. By EDMUND GURNEY, FREDERIC W. H. MYERS, M.A., and FRANK PODMORE, M.A. 2 vols. Demy 8vo, 21s.

Philological Society, Transactions of. Published irregularly. List of Publications on application.

PICCIOTTO, James.—Sketches of Anglo-Jewish History. Demy 8vo, 12s.

Pierce Gambit: Chess Papers and Problems. By JAMES PIERCE, M.A., and W. TIMBRELL PIERCE. Crown 8vo, 6s. 6d.

PIESSE, Charles H.—Chemistry in the Brewing-Room. Being the substance of a Course of Lessons to Practical Brewers. Fcap., 5s.

PLINY.—The Letters of Pliny the Younger. Translated by J. D. LEWIS. Post 8vo, 5s.

PLUMPTRE, Charles John.—King's College Lectures on Elocution. Fourth Edition. Post 8vo, 15s.

POOLE, W. F.—An Index to Periodical Literature. Third Edition. Royal 8vo, £3 13s. 6d.

POOLE, W. F., and FLETCHER, W. I.—Index to Periodical Literature. First Supplement. 1882 to 1887. Royal 8vo, £1 16s.

Practical Guides.—France, Belgium, Holland, and the Rhine. 1s. Italian Lakes. 1s. Wintering Places of the South. 2s. Switzerland, Savoy, and North Italy. 2s. 6d. General Continental Guide. 5s. Geneva. 1s. Paris. 1s. Bernese Oberland. 1s. Italy. 4s.

Psychical Research, Proceedings of the Society for. Published irregularly. Post 8vo. Vol. I. to III. 10*s.* each. Vol. IV. 8*s.* Vol. V. 10*s.*

PURITZ, Ludwig.—**Code-Book of Gymnastic Exercises.** Translated by O. KNOFE and J. W. MACQUEEN. 32mo, 1*s.* 6*d.*

RAPSON, Edward J.—**The Struggle between England and France for Supremacy in India.** Crown 8vo, 4*s.* 6*d.*

RAVENSTEIN, E. G., and HULLEY, John.—**The Gymnasium and its Fittings.** With 14 Plates of Illustrations. 8vo, 2*s.* 6*d.*

READE, Winwood.—**The Martyrdom of Man.** Thirteenth Edition. 8vo, 7*s.* 6*d.*

RENDELL, J. M.—**Concise Handbook of the Island of Madeira.** With Plan of Funchal and Map of the Island. Second Edition. Fcap. 8vo, 1*s.* 6*d.*

RHYS, John.—**Lectures on Welsh Philology.** Second Edition. Crown 8vo, 15*s.*

RIDEAL, C. F.—**Wellerisms, from "Pickwick" and "Master Humphrey's Clock."** 18mo, 2*s.*

RIPPER, William.—**Machine Drawing and Design,** for Engineering Students and Practical Engineers. Illustrated by 55 Plates and numerous Explanatory Notes. Royal 4to, 25*s.*

ROBINSON, A. Mary F.—**The Fortunate Lovers.** Twenty-seven Novels of the Queen of Navarre. Large crown 8vo, 10*s.* 6*d.*

ROLFE, Eustace Neville, and INGLEBY, Holcombe.—**Naples in 1888.** With Illustrations. Crown 8vo, 6*s.*

ROSMINI SERBATI, Antonio.—**Life.** By the Rev. W. LOCKHART. 2 vols. With Portraits. Crown 8vo, 12*s.*

ROSS, Percy.—**A Professor of Alchemy.** Crown 8vo, 3*s.* 6*d.*

ROUTLEDGE, James.—**English Rule and Native Opinion in India.** 8vo, 10*s.* 6*d.*

RULE, Martin, M.A.—**The Life and Times of St. Anselm, Archbishop of Canterbury and Primate of the Britains.** 2 vols. Demy 8vo, 32*s.*

RUTHERFORD, Mark.—**The Autobiography of Mark Rutherford and Mark Rutherford's Deliverance.** Edited by REUBEN SHAPCOTT. Third Edition. Crown 8vo, 7*s.* 6*d.*

The Revolution in Tanner's Lane. Edited by REUBEN SHAPCOTT. Crown 8vo, 7*s.* 6*d.*

Miriam's Schooling: and other Papers. Edited by REUBEN SHAPCOTT. Crown 8vo, 6*s.*

SAMUELSON, James.—**India, Past and Present:** Historical, Social, and Political. With a Map, Explanatory Woodcuts and Collotype Views, Portraits, etc., from 36 Photographs. 8vo, 21*s.*

SAMUELSON, James—continued.

> **History of Drink.** A Review, Social, Scientific, and Political. Second Edition. 8vo, 6s.
>
> **Bulgaria, Past and Present:** Historical, Political, and Descriptive. With Map and numerous Illustrations. Demy 8vo, 10s. 6d.

SANDWITH, F. M.—**Egypt as a Winter Resort.** Crown 8vo, 3s. 6d.

SANTIAGOE, Daniel.—**The Curry Cook's Assistant.** Fcap. 8vo, cloth. 1s. 6d. ; paper covers, 1s.

SAYCE, Rev. Archibald Henry.—**Introduction to the Science of Language.** New and Cheaper Edition. 2 vols. Crown 8vo, 9s.

SAYWELL, J. L.—**New Popular Handbook of County Dialects.** Crown 8vo, 5s.

SCHAIBLE, C. H.—**An Essay on the Systematic Training of the Body.** Crown 8vo, 5s.

SCHLEICHER, August.—**A Compendium of the Comparative Grammar of the Indo-European, Sanskrit, Greek, and Latin Languages.** Translated from the Third German Edition by HERBERT BENDALL. 2 parts. 8vo, 13s. 6d.

SCOONES, W. Baptiste.—**Four Centuries of English Letters:** A Selection of 350 Letters by 150 Writers, from the Period of the Paston Letters to the Present Time. Third Edition. Large crown 8vo, 6s.

SCOTT, Benjamin.—**A State Iniquity: Its Rise, Extension, and Overthrow.** Demy 8vo, plain cloth, 3s. 6d. ; gilt, 5s.

SELBY, H. M.—**The Shakespeare Classical Dictionary ;** or, Mythological Allusions in the Plays of Shakespeare Explained. Fcap. 8vo, 1s.

Selwyn, Bishop, *of New Zealand and of Lichfield.* A Sketch of his Life and Work, with Further Gleanings from his Letters, Sermons, and Speeches. By the Rev. Canon CURTEIS. Large crown 8vo, 7s. 6d.

SERJEANT, W. C. Eldon.—**The Astrologer's Guide (Anima Astrologiæ).** Demy 8vo, 7s. 6d.

Shakspere's Works. The Avon Edition, 12 vols., fcap. 8vo, cloth, 18s. ; in cloth box, 21s. ; bound in 6 vols., cloth, 15s.

Shakspere's Works, an Index to. By EVANGELINE O'CONNOR. Crown 8vo, 5s.

SHAKESPEARE.—**The Bankside Shakespeare.** The Comedies, Histories, and Tragedies of Mr. William Shakespeare, as presented at the Globe and Blackfriars Theatres, *circa* 1591-1623. Being the Text furnished the Players, in parallel pages with the first revised folio text, with Critical Introductions. 8vo.

[In preparation.

SHAKESPEARE—continued.

A **New Study of Shakespeare.** An Inquiry into the Connection of the Plays and Poems, with the Origins of the Classical Drama, and with the Platonic Philosophy, through the Mysteries. Demy 8vo, 10s. 6d.

Shakespeare's Cymbeline. Edited, with Notes, by C. M. INGLEBY. Crown 8vo, 1s. 6d.

A **New Variorum Edition of Shakespeare.** Edited by HORACE HOWARD FURNESS. Royal 8vo. Vol. I. Romeo and Juliet. 18s. Vol. II. Macbeth. 18s. Vols. III. and IV. Hamlet. 2 vols. 36s. Vol. V. King Lear. 18s. Vol. VI. Othello. 18s.

Shakspere Society (The New).—Subscription, one guinea per annum. List of Publications on application.

SHELLEY, Percy Bysshe.—**Life.** By EDWARD DOWDEN, LL.D. 2 vols. With Portraits. Demy 8vo, 36s.

SIBREE, James, Jun.—**The Great African Island.** Chapters on Madagascar. A Popular Account of the Physical Geography, etc., of the Country. With Physical and Ethnological Maps and 4 Illustrations. 8vo, 10s. 6d.

SIGERSON, George, M.D.—**Political Prisoners at Home and Abroad.** With Appendix on Dietaries. Crown 8vo, 2s. 6d.

SIMCOX, Edith.—**Episodes in the Lives of Men, Women, and Lovers.** Crown 8vo, 7s. 6d.

SINCLAIR, Thomas.—**Essays: in Three Kinds.** Crown 8vo, 1s. 6d. ; wrappers, 1s.

Sinclairs of England (The). Crown 8vo, 12s.

SINNETT, A. P.—**The Occult World.** Fourth Edition. Crown 8vo, 3s. 6d.

Incidents in the Life of Madame Blavatsky. Demy 8vo, 10s. 6d.

Skinner, James: A Memoir. By the Author of "Charles Lowder." With a Preface by the Rev. Canon CARTER, and Portrait. Large crown, 7s. 6d.

** Also a cheap Edition. With Portrait. Fourth Edition. Crown 8vo, 3s. 6d.

SMITH, Huntington.—**A Century of American Literature:** Benjamin Franklin to James Russell Lowell. Crown 8vo, 6s.

SMITH, S.—**The Divine Government.** Fifth Edition. Crown 8vo, 6s.

SMYTH, R. Brough.—The Aborigines of Victoria. Compiled for the Government of Victoria. With Maps, Plates, and Wood-cuts. 2 vols. Royal 8vo, £3 3*s.*

Sophocles: The Seven Plays in English Verse. Translated by LEWIS CAMPBELL. Crown 8vo, 7*s.* 6*d.*

Specimens of English Prose Style from Malory to Macaulay. Selected and Annotated, with an Introductory Essay, by GEORGE SAINTSBURY. Large crown 8vo, printed on hand-made paper, parchment antique or cloth, 12*s.* ; vellum, 15*s.*

SPEDDING, James.—The Life and Times of Francis Bacon. 2 vols. Post 8vo, 21*s.*

Spinoza, Benedict de : His Life, Correspondence, and Ethics. By R. WILLIS, M.D. 8vo, 21*s.*

SPRAGUE, Charles E.—Handbook of Volapük : The International Language. Second Edition. Crown 8vo, 5*s.*

ST. HILL, Katharine.—The Grammar of Palmistry. With 18 Illustrations. 12mo, 1*s.*

STOKES, Whitley.—Goidelica : Old and Early-Middle Irish Glosses. Prose and Verse. Second Edition. Med. 8vo, 18*s.*

STRACHEY, Sir John, G.C.S.I.—India. With Map. Demy 8vo, 15*s.*

STREET, J. C.—The Hidden Way across the Threshold ; or, The Mystery which hath been hidden for Ages and from Genera-tions. With Plates. Large 8vo, 15*s.*

SUMNER, W. G.—What Social Classes owe to Each Other. 18mo, 3*s.* 6*d.*

SWINBURNE, Algernon Charles. — A Word for the Navy. Imperial 16mo, 5*s.*

The Bibliography of Swinburne, 1857-1887. Crown 8vo, vellum gilt, 6*s.*

Sylva, Carmen (Queen of Roumania), The Life of. Translated by Baroness DEICHMANN. With 4 Portraits and 1 Illustration. 8vo, 12*s.*

TAYLER, J. J.—A Retrospect of the Religious Life of England ; or, Church, Puritanism, and Free Inquiry. Second Edition. Post 8vo, 7*s.* 6*d.*

TAYLOR, Rev. Canon Isaac, LL.D.—The Alphabet. An Account of the Origin and Development of Letters. With numerous Tables and Facsimiles. 2 vols. Demy 8vo, 36*s.*

Leaves from an Egyptian Note-book. Crown 8vo, 5*s.*

TAYLOR, Sir Henry.—The Statesman. Fcap. 8vo, 3*s.* 6*d.*

Taylor, Reynell, C.B., C.S.I. : A Biography. By E. GAMBIER PARRY. With Portait and Map. Demy 8vo, 14*s.*

Technological Dictionary of the Terms employed in the Arts and Sciences; Architecture; Engineering; Mechanics; Shipbuilding and Navigation; Metallurgy; Mathematics, etc. Second Edition. 3 vols. 8vo.

Vol. I.   German-English-French.   12*s*.
Vol. II.   English-German-French.   12*s*.
Vol. III.   French-German-English.   15*s*.

THACKERAY, Rev. S. W., LL.D—The Land and the Community.   Crown 8vo, 3*s*. 6*d*.

THACKERAY, William Makepeace.—An Essay on the Genius of George Cruikshank.   Reprinted verbatim from the *Westminster Review.*   40 Illustrations.   Large paper Edition.   Royal 8vo, 7*s*. 6*d*.

Sultan Stork ; and other Stories and Sketches.   1829–1844. Now First Collected.   To which is added the Bibliography of Thackeray, Revised and Considerably Enlarged.   Large demy 8vo, 10*s*. 6*d*.

THOMPSON, Sir H.—Diet in Relation to Age and Activity.   Fcap. 8vo, cloth, 1*s*. 6*d*. ; paper covers, 1*s*.

Modern Cremation.   Crown 8vo, 2*s*. 6*d*.

Tobacco Talk and Smokers' Gossip.   16mo, 2*s*.

TRANT, William.—Trade Unions: Their Origin, Objects, and Efficacy.   Small crown 8vo, 1*s*. 6*d*. ; paper covers, 1*s*.

TRENCH, The late R. C., Archbishop.—Letters and Memorials. By the Author of "Charles Lowder."   With two Portraits. 2 vols.   8vo, 21*s*.

A Household Book of English Poetry.   Selected and Arranged, with Notes.   Fourth Edition, Revised.   Extra fcap. 8vo, 5*s*.

An Essay on the Life and Genius of Calderon.   With Translations from his "Life's a Dream" and "Great Theatre of the World."   Second Edition, Revised and Improved.   Extra fcap. 8vo, 5*s*. 6*d*.

Gustavus Adolphus in Germany, and other Lectures on the Thirty Years' War.   Third Edition, Enlarged. Fcap. 8vo, 4*s*.

Plutarch : his Life, his Lives, and his Morals.   Second Edition, Enlarged.   Fcap. 8vo, 3*s*. 6*d*.

Remains of the late Mrs. Richard Trench.   Being Selections from her Journals, Letters, and other Papers.   New and Cheaper Issue.   With Portrait. 8vo, 6*s*.

Lectures on Mediæval Church History.   Being the Substance of Lectures delivered at Queen's College, London.   Second Edition. 8vo, 12*s*.

TRENCH, The late R. C., Archbishop—continued.

English, Past and Present. Thirteenth Edition, Revised and Improved. Fcap. 8vo, 5s.

On the Study of Words. Twentieth Edition, Revised. Fcap. 8vo, 5s.

Select Glossary of English Words used Formerly in Senses Different from the Present. Seventh Edition, Revised and Enlarged. Fcap. 8vo, 5s.

Proverbs and Their Lessons. Seventh Edition, Enlarged. Fcap. 8vo, 4s.

TRIMEN, Roland.—**South-African Butterflies.** A Monograph of the Extra-Tropical Species. With 12 Coloured Plates. 3 vols. Demy 8vo, £2 12s. 6d.

Trübner's Bibliographical Guide to American Literature. A Classed List of Books published in the United States of America, from 1817 to 1857. Edited by NICOLAS TRÜBNER. 8vo, half-bound, 18s.

TRUMBULL, H. Clay.—**The Blood-Covenant, a Primitive Rite, and its Bearings on Scripture.** Post 8vo, 7s. 6d.

TURNER, Charles Edward.—**Count Tolstoï, as Novelist and Thinker.** Lectures delivered at the Royal Institution. Crown 8vo, 3s. 6d.

The Modern Novelists of Russia. Lectures delivered at the Taylor Institution, Oxford. Crown 8vo, 3s. 6d.

TWEEDIE, Mrs. Alec.—**The Ober-Ammergau Passion Play, 1890.** Small crown 8vo, 2s. 6d.

VAUGHAN, H. H.—**British Reason in English Rhyme.** Crown 8vo, 6s.

VESCELIUS-SHELDON, Louise.—**An I. D. B. in South Africa.** Illustrated by G. E. GRAVES and AL. HENCKE. Crown 8vo, 7s. 6d.

Yankee Girls in Zulu-Land. Illustrated by G. E. GRAVES. Crown 8vo, 5s.

Victoria Government, Publications of the. [*List in preparation.*

VINCENT, Frank.—**Around and about South America.** Twenty Months of Quest and Query. With Maps, Plans, and 54 Illustrations. Medium 8vo, 21s.

WAITE, A. E.—**Lives of Alchemystical Philosophers.** Demy 8vo, 10s. 6d.

The Magical Writings of Thomas Vaughan. Small 4to, 10s. 6d.

The Real History of the Rosicrucians. With Illustrations. Crown 8vo, 7s. 6d.

WAITE, A. E.—continued.

    The Mysteries of Magic. A Digest of the Writings of Éliphas Lévi. With Illustrations. Demy 8vo, 10*s*. 6*d*.

WAKE, C. Staniland.—**Serpent-Worship, and other Essays, with a Chapter on Totemism.** Demy 8vo, 10*s*. 6*d*.

    The Development of Marriage and Kinship. Demy 8vo, 18*s*.

Wales.—**Through North Wales with a Knapsack.** By Four Schoolmistresses. With a Sketch Map. Small crown 8vo, 2*s*. 6*d*.

WALL, George.—**The Natural History of Thought in its Practical Aspect, from its Origin in Infancy.** Demy 8vo, 12*s*. 6*d*.

WALLACE, Alfred Russel.—**On Miracles and Modern Spiritualism.** Second Edition. Crown 8vo, 5*s*.

WALPOLE, Chas. George.—**A Short History of Ireland from the Earliest Times to the Union with Great Britain.** With 5 Maps and Appendices. Third Edition. Crown 8vo, 6*s*.

WALTERS, J. Cuming.—**In Tennyson Land.** Being a Brief Account of the Home and Early Surroundings of the Poet-Laureate. With Illustrations. Demy 8vo, 5*s*.

WARTER, J. W.—**An Old Shropshire Oak.** 2 vols. Demy 8vo, 28*s*.

WATSON, R. G.—**Spanish and Portuguese South America during the Colonial Period.** 2 vols. Post 8vo, 21*s*.

WEDGWOOD, H.—**A Dictionary of English Etymology.** Fourth Edition, Revised and Enlarged. With Introduction on the Origin of Language. 8vo, £1 1*s*.

    Contested Etymologies in the Dictionary of the Rev. W. W. Skeat. Crown 8vo, 5*s*.

WEDGWOOD, Julia.—**The Moral Ideal.** An Historic Study. Second Edition. Demy 8vo, 9*s*.

WEISBACH, Julius.—**Theoretical Mechanics.** A Manual of the Mechanics of Engineering. Designed as a Text-book for Technical Schools, and for the Use of Engineers. Translated from the German by ECKLEY B. COXE. With 902 Woodcuts. Demy 8vo, 31*s*. 6*d*.

WESTROPP, Hodder M.—**Primitive Symbolism as Illustrated in Phallic Worship;** or, The Reproductive Principle. With an Introduction by Major-Gen. FORLONG. Demy 8vo, parchment, 7*s*. 6*d*.

WHEELDON, J. P. — **Angling Resorts near London.** The Thames and the Lea. Crown 8vo, paper, 1*s*. 6*d*.

WHIBLEY, Chas.—In Cap and Gown : Three Centuries of Cambridge Wit. Crown 8vo, 7s. 6d.

WHITMAN, Sidney.—Imperial Germany. A Critical Study of Fact and Character. Crown 8vo, 7s. 6d.

WIGSTON, W. F. C.—Hermes Stella ; or, Notes and Jottings on the Bacon Cipher. 8vo, 6s.

Wilberforce, Bishop, *of Oxford and Winchester,* Life. By his Son REGINALD WILBERFORCE. Crown 8vo, 6s.

WILDRIDGE, T. Tyndall.—The Dance of Death, in Painting and in Print. With Woodcuts. 4to, 3s. 6d ; the Woodcuts coloured by hand, 5s.

WOLTMANN, Dr. Alfred, and WOERMANN, Dr. Karl.—History of Painting. With numerous Illustrations. Medium 8vo. Vol. I. Painting in Antiquity and the Middle Ages. 28s. ; bevelled boards, gilt leaves, 30s. Vol. II. The Painting of the Renascence. 42s. ; bevelled boards, gilt leaves, 45s.

WOOD, M. W.—Dictionary of Volapük. Volapük-English and English-Volapük. Volapükatidel e cif. Crown 8vo, 10s. 6d.

WORTHY, Charles.—Practical Heraldry ; or, An Epitome of English Armory. 124 Illustrations. Crown 8vo, 7s. 6d.

WRIGHT, Thomas.—The Homes of Other Days. A History of Domestic Manners and Sentiments during the Middle Ages. With Illustrations from the Illuminations in Contemporary Manuscripts and other Sources. Drawn and Engraved by F. W. FAIRHOLT, F.S.A. 350 Woodcuts. Medium 8vo, 21s.

Anglo-Saxon and Old English Vocabularies. Second Edition. Edited by RICHARD PAUL WULCKER. 2 vols. Demy 8vo, 28s.

The Celt, the Roman, and the Saxon. A History of the Early Inhabitants of Britain down to the Conversion of the Anglo-Saxons to Christianity. Illustrated by the Ancient Remains brought to light by Recent Research. Corrected and Enlarged Edition. With nearly 300 Engravings. Crown 8vo, 9s.

YELVERTON, Christopher.—Oneiros ; or, Some Questions of the Day. Crown 8vo, 5s.

THEOLOGY AND PHILOSOPHY.

ALEXANDER, William, D.D., Bishop of Derry.—The Great Question, and other Sermons. Crown 8vo, 6s.

AMBERLEY, Viscount.—An Analysis of Religious Belief. 2 vols. Demy 8vo, 30s.

Antiqua Mater: A Study of Christian Origins. Crown 8vo, 7s. 6d.

BELANY, Rev. K.—The Bible and the Papacy. Crown 8vo, 2s.

BENTHAM, Jeremy.—Theory of Legislation. Translated from the French of Etienne Dumont by R. HILDRETH. Fifth Edition. Post 8vo, 7s. 6d.

BEST, George Payne.—Morality and Utility. A Natural Science of Ethics. Crown 8vo, 5s.

BROOKE, Rev. Stopford A.—The Fight of Faith. Sermons preached on various occasions. Fifth Edition. Crown 8vo, 7s. 6d.

The Spirit of the Christian Life. Third Edition. Crown 8vo, 5s.

Theology in the English Poets. Cowper, Coleridge, Wordsworth, and Burns. Sixth Edition. Post 8vo, 5s.

Christ in Modern Life. Seventeenth Edition. Crown 8vo, 5s.

Sermons. First Series. Thirteenth Edition. Crown 8vo, 5s.

Sermons. Second Series. Sixth Edition. Crown 8vo, 5s.

BROWN, Rev. J. Baldwin.—The Higher Life. Its Reality, Experience, and Destiny. Seventh Edition. Crown 8vo, 5s.

Doctrine of Annihilation in the Light of the Gospel of Love. Five Discourses. Fourth Edition. Crown 8vo, 2s. 6d.

The Christian Policy of Life. A Book for Young Men of Business. Third Edition. Crown 8vo, 3s. 6d.

BUNSEN, Ernest de.—Islam ; or, True Christianity. Crown 8vo, 5s.

Catholic Dictionary. Containing some Account of the Doctrine, Discipline, Rites, Ceremonies, Councils, and Religious Orders of the Catholic Church. Edited by THOMAS ARNOLD, M.A. Third Edition. Demy 8vo, 21s.

CHEYNE, Canon.—The Prophecies of Isaiah. Translated with Critical Notes and Dissertations. 2 vols. Fifth Edition. Demy 8vo, 25s.

Job and Solomon ; or, The Wisdom of the Old Testament. Demy 8vo, 12s. 6d.

The Psalms ; or, Book of The Praises of Israel. Translated with Commentary. Demy 8vo. 16s.

CLARKE, James Freeman.—Ten Great Religions. An Essay in Comparative Theology. Demy 8vo, 10s. 6d.

Ten Great Religions. Part II. A Comparison of all Religions. Demy 8vo, 10s. 6d.

COKE, Henry.—Creeds of the Day ; or, Collated Opinions of Reputable Thinkers. 2 vols. Demy 8vo, 21s.

COMTE, *Auguste.*—The Catechism of Positive Religion. Translated from the French by RICHARD CONGREVE. Second Edition. Crown 8vo, 2s. 6d.

The Eight Circulars of Auguste Comte. Translated from the French. Fcap. 8vo, 1s. 6d.

Appeal to Conservatives. Crown 8vo, 2s. 6d.

The Positive Philosophy of Auguste Comte. Translated and condensed by HARRIET MARTINEAU. 2 vols. Second Edition. 8vo, 25s.

CONWAY, *Moncure D.*—The Sacred Anthology. A Book of Ethnical Scriptures. Edited by MONCURE D. CONWAY. New Edition. Crown 8vo, 5s.

Idols and Ideals. With an Essay on Christianity. Crown 8vo, 4s.

COX, *Rev. Samuel, D.D.*—A Commentary on the Book of Job. With a Translation. Second Edition. Demy 8vo, 15s.

Salvator Mundi; or, Is Christ the Saviour of all Men? Twelfth Edition. Crown 8vo, 2s. 6d.

The Larger Hope. A Sequel to "Salvator Mundi." Second Edition. 16mo, 1s.

The Genesis of Evil, and other Sermons, mainly expository. Third Edition. Crown 8vo, 6s.

Balaam. An Exposition and a Study. Crown 8vo, 5s.

Miracles. An Argument and a Challenge. Crown 8vo, 2s. 6d.

CRANBROOK, *James.*—Credibilia; or, Discourses on Questions of Christian Faith. Post 8vo, 3s. 6d.

The Founders of Christianity; or, Discourses upon the Origin of the Christian Religion. Post 8vo, 6s.

DAWSON, *Geo., M.A.*—Prayers, with a Discourse on Prayer. Edited by his Wife. First Series. Tenth Edition. Small Crown 8vo, 3s. 6d.

Prayers, with a Discourse on Prayer. Edited by GEORGE ST. CLAIR, F.G.S. Second Series. Small Crown 8vo, 3s. 6d.

Sermons on Disputed Points and Special Occasions. Edited by his Wife. Fourth Edition. Crown 8vo, 3s. 6d.

Sermons on Daily Life and Duty. Edited by his Wife. Fifth Edition. Small crown 8vo, 3s. 6d.

The Authentic Gospel, and other Sermons. Edited by GEORGE ST. CLAIR, F.G.S. Third Edition. Crown 8vo, 6s.

Every-day Counsels. Edited by GEORGE ST. CLAIR, F.G.S. Crown 8vo, 6s.

DELEPIERRE, Octave.—L'Enfer : Essai Philosophique et Historique sur les Légendes de la Vie Future. Only 250 copies printed. Crown 8vo, 6s.

Doubter's Doubt about Science and Religion. Crown 8vo, 3s. 6d.

FICHTE, Johann Gottlieb.—Characteristics of the Present Age. Translated by WILLIAM SMITH. Post 8vo, 6s.

Memoir of Johann Gottlieb Fichte. By WILLIAM SMITH. Second Edition. Post 8vo, 4s.

On the Nature of the Scholar, and its Manifestations. Translated by WILLIAM SMITH. Second Edition. Post 8vo, 3s.

New Exposition of the Science of Knowledge. Translated by A. E. KROEGER. 8vo, 6s.

FITZ-GERALD, Mrs. P. F.—A Protest against Agnosticism : Introduction to a New Theory of Idealism. Demy 8vo.

An Essay on the Philosophy of Self-Consciousness. Comprising an Analysis of Reason and the Rationale of Love. Demy 8vo, 5s.

A Treatise on the Principle of Sufficient Reason. A Psychological Theory of Reasoning, showing the Relativity of Thought to the Thinker, of Recognition to Cognition, the Identity of Presentation and Representation, of Perception and Apperception. Demy 8vo, 6s.

GALLWEY, Rev. P.—Apostolic Succession. A Handbook. Demy 8vo, 1s.

GOUGH, Edward.—The Bible True from the Beginning. A Commentary on all those Portions of Scripture that are most Questioned and Assailed. Vols. I., II., and III. Demy 8vo, 16s. each.

GREG, W. R.—Literary and Social Judgments. Fourth Edition. 2 vols. Crown 8vo, 15s.

The Creed of Christendom. Eighth Edition. 2 vols. Post 8vo, 15s.

Enigmas of Life. Seventeenth Edition. Post 8vo, 10s. 6d.

Political Problems for our Age and Country. Demy 8vo, 10s. 6d.

Miscellaneous Essays. 2 Series. Crown 8vo, 7s. 6d. each.

GRIMLEY, Rev. H. N., M.A.—Tremadoc Sermons, chiefly on the Spiritual Body, the Unseen World, and the Divine Humanity. Fourth Edition. Crown 8vo, 6s.

The Temple of Humanity, and other Sermons. Crown 8vo, 6s.

GURNEY, Alfred.—Our Catholic Inheritance in the Larger Hope. Crown 8vo, 1s. 6d.

HAINES, C. R.—Christianity and Islam in Spain, A.D. 756-1031. Crown 8vo, 2s. 6d.

HAWEIS, Rev. H. R., M.A.—Current Coin. Materialism—The Devil—Crime—Drunkenness—Pauperism—Emotion—Recreation—The Sabbath. Fifth Edition. Crown 8vo, 5s.

Arrows in the Air. Fifth Edition. Crown 8vo, 5s.

Speech in Season. Sixth Edition. Crown 8vo, 5s.

Thoughts for the Times. Fourteenth Edition. Crown 8vo, 5s.

Unsectarian Family Prayers. New Edition. Fcap. 8vo, 1s. 6d.

HUGHES, Rev. H., M.A.—Principles of Natural and Supernatural Morals. Vol. I. Natural Morals. Demy 8vo, 12s.

JOSEPH, N. S.—Religion, Natural and Revealed. A Series of Progressive Lessons for Jewish Youth. Crown 8vo, 3s.

KEMPIS, Thomas à.—Of the Imitation of Christ. Parchment Library Edition.—Parchment or cloth, 6s. ; vellum, 7s. 6d. The Red Line Edition, fcap. 8vo, cloth extra, 2s. 6d. The Cabinet Edition, small 8vo, cloth limp, 1s. ; cloth boards, 1s. 6d. The Miniature Edition, cloth limp, 32mo, 1s. ; or with red lines, 1s. 6d.

Of the Imitation of Christ. A Metrical Version. By HENRY CARRINGTON. Crown 8vo, 5s.

Notes of a Visit to the Scenes in which his Life was spent. With numerous Illustrations. By F. R. CRUISE, M.D. Demy 8vo, 12s.

Keys of the Creeds (The). Third Revised · Edition. Crown 8vo, 2s. 6d.

LEWES, George Henry.—Problems of Life and Mind. Demy 8vo. First Series : The Foundations of a Creed. 2 vols. 28s. Second Series : The Physical Basis of Mind. With Illustrations. 16s. Third Series. 2 vols. 22s. 6d.

LEWIS, Harry S.—Targum on Isaiah i.-v. With Commentary. Demy 8vo, 5s.

MANNING, Cardinal.—Towards Evening. Selections from his Writings. Third Edition. 16mo, 2s.

MARTINEAU, James.—Essays, Philosophical and Theological. 2 vols. Crown 8vo, £1 4s.

MEAD, C. M., D.D.—Supernatural Revelation. An Essay concerning the Basis of the Christian Faith. Royal 8vo, 14s.

Meditations on Death and Eternity. Translated from the German by FREDERICA ROWAN. Published by Her Majesty's gracious permission. Crown 8vo, 6s.

Meditations on Life and its Religious Duties. Translated from the German by FREDERICA ROWAN. Published by Her Majesty's gracious permission. Being the Companion Volume to "Meditations on Death and Eternity." Crown 8vo, 6s.

NEVILL, F.—Retrogression or Development. Crown 8vo, 3s. 6d.

NICHOLS, J. Broadhurst, and DYMOND, Charles William.—Practical Value of Christianity. Two Prize Essays. Crown 8vo, 3s. 6d.

PARKER, Theodore. — Discourse on Matters pertaining to Religion. People's Edition. Crown 8vo, 1s. 6d. ; cloth, 2s.

The Collected Works of Theodore Parker, Minister of the Twenty-eighth Congregational Society at Boston, U.S. In 14 vols. 8vo, 6s. each.

Vol. I. Discourse on Matters pertaining to Religion. II. Ten Sermons and Prayers. III. Discourses on Theology. IV. Discourses on Politics. V. and VI. Discourses on Slavery. VII. Discourses on Social Science. VIII. Miscellaneous Discourses. IX. and X. Critical Writings. XI. Sermons on Theism, Atheism, and Popular Theology. XII. Autobiographical and Miscellaneous Pieces. XIII. Historic Americans. XIV. Lessons from the World of Matter and the World of Man.

Plea for Truth in Religion. Crown 8vo, 2s. 6d

Psalms of the West. Small crown 8vo, 5s.

Pulpit Commentary, The. (*Old Testament Series.*) Edited by the Rev. J. S. EXELL, M.A., and the Very Rev. Dean H. D. M. SPENCE, M.A., D.D.

Genesis. By the Rev. T. WHITELAW, D.D. With Homilies by the Very Rev. J. F. MONTGOMERY, D.D., Rev. Prof. R. A. REDFORD, M.A., LL.B., Rev. F. HASTINGS, Rev. W. ROBERTS, M.A. An Introduction to the Study of the Old Testament by the Venerable Archdeacon FARRAR, D.D., F.R.S. ; and Introductions to the Pentateuch by the Right Rev. H. COTTERILL, D.D., and Rev. T. WHITELAW, D.D. Ninth Edition. 1 vol., 15s.

Exodus. By the Rev. Canon RAWLINSON. With Homilies by the Rev. J. ORR, D.D., Rev. D. YOUNG, B.A., Rev. C. A. GOODHART, Rev. J. URQUHART, and the Rev. H. T. ROBJOHNS. Fourth Edition. 2 vols., 9s. each.

Leviticus. By the Rev. Prebendary MEYRICK, M.A. With Introductions by the Rev. R. COLLINS, Rev. Professor A. CAVE, and Homilies by the Rev. Prof. REDFORD, LL.B., Rev. J. A. MACDONALD, Rev. W. CLARKSON, B.A., Rev. S. R. ALDRIDGE, LL.B., and Rev. McCHEYNE EDGAR. Fourth Edition. 15s.

Pulpit Commentary, The—*continued*.

Numbers. By the Rev. R. WINTERBOTHAM, LL.B. With Homilies by the Rev. Professor W. BINNIE, D.D., Rev. E. S. PROUT, M.A., Rev. D. YOUNG, B.A., Rev. J. WAITE, B.A., and an Introduction by the Rev. THOMAS WHITELAW, D.D. Fifth Edition. 15*s*.

Deuteronomy. By the Rev. W. L. ALEXANDER, D.D. With Homilies by the Rev. C. CLEMANCE, D.D., Rev. J. ORR, D.D., Rev. R. M. EDGAR, M.A., Rev. D. DAVIES, M.A. Fourth edition. 15*s*.

Joshua. By the Rev. J. J. LIAS, M.A. With Homilies by the Rev. S. R. ALDRIDGE, LL.B., Rev. R. GLOVER, Rev. E. DE PRESSENSÉ, D.D., Rev. J. WAITE, B.A., Rev. W. F. ADENEY, M.A.; and an Introduction by the Rev. A. PLUMMER, D.D. Fifth Edition. 12*s*. 6*d*.

Judges and Ruth. By the Bishop of BATH and WELLS, and Rev. J. MORISON, D.D. With Homilies by the Rev. A. F. MUIR, M.A., Rev. W. F. ADENEY, M.A., Rev. W. M. STATHAM, and Rev. Professor J. THOMSON, M.A. Fifth Edition. 10*s*. 6*d*.

1 and 2 Samuel. By the Very Rev. R. P. SMITH, D.D. With Homilies by the Rev. DONALD FRASER, D.D., Rev. Prof. CHAPMAN, Rev. B. DALE, and Rev. G. WOOD, B.A. Seventh Edition. 15*s*. each.

1 Kings. By the Rev. JOSEPH HAMMOND, LL.B. With Homilies by the Rev. E. DE PRESSENSÉ, D.D., Rev. J. WAITE, B.A., Rev. A. ROWLAND, LL.B., Rev. J. A. MACDONALD, and Rev. J. URQUHART. Fifth Edition. 15*s*.

2 Kings. By the Rev. Canon RAWLINSON. With Homilies by the Rev. J. ORR, D.D., Rev. D. THOMAS, D.D., and Rev. C. H. IRWIN, M.A. 15*s*.

1 Chronicles. By the Rev. Prof. P. C. BARKER, M.A., LL.B. With Homilies by the Rev. Prof. J. R. THOMSON, M.A., Rev. R. TUCK, B.A., Rev. W. CLARKSON, B.A., Rev. F. WHITFIELD, M.A., and Rev. RICHARD GLOVER. 15*s*.

Ezra, Nehemiah, and Esther. By the Rev. Canon G. RAWLINSON, M.A. With Homilies by the Rev. Prof. J. R. THOMSON, M.A., Rev. Prof. R. A. REDFORD, LL.B., M.A., Rev. W. S. LEWIS, M.A., Rev. J. A. MACDONALD, Rev. A. MACKENNAL, B.A., Rev. W. CLARKSON, B.A., Rev. F. HASTINGS, Rev. W. DINWIDDIE, LL.B., Rev. Prof. ROWLANDS, B.A., Rev. G. WOOD, B.A., Rev. Prof. P. C. BARKER, M.A., LL.B., and the Rev. J. S. EXELL, M.A. Seventh Edition. 1 vol., 12*s*. 6*d*.

Isaiah. By the Rev. Canon G. RAWLINSON, M.A. With Homilies by the Rev. Prof. E. JOHNSON, M.A., Rev. W. CLARKSON, B.A., Rev. W. M. STATHAM, and Rev. R. TUCK, B.A. Second Edition. 2 vols., 15*s*. each.

Pulpit Commentary, The—*continued.*

Jeremiah. (Vol. I.) By the Rev. Canon T. K. CHEYNE, D.D. With Homilies by the Rev. W. F. ADENEY, M.A., Rev. A. F. MUIR, M.A., Rev. S. CONWAY, B.A., Rev. J. WAITE, B.A., and Rev. D. YOUNG, B.A. Third Edition. 15*s*.

Jeremiah (Vol. II.) and Lamentations. By the Rev. Canon T. K. CHEYNE, D.D. With Homilies by the Rev. Prof. J. R. THOMSON, M.A., Rev. W. F. ADENEY, M.A., Rev. A. F. MUIR, M.A., Rev. S. CONWAY, B.A., Rev. D. YOUNG, B.A. 15*s*.

Hosea and Joel. By the Rev. Prof. J. J. GIVEN, Ph.D., D.D. With Homilies by the Rev. Prof. J. R. THOMSON, M.A., Rev. A. ROWLAND, B.A., LL.B., Rev. C. JERDAN, M.A., LL.B., Rev. J. ORR, D.D., and Rev. D. THOMAS, D.D. 15*s*.

Pulpit Commentary, The. (*New Testament Series.*)

St. Mark. By the Very Rev. E. BICKERSTETH, D.D., Dean of Lichfield. With Homilies by the Rev. Prof. THOMSON, M.A., Rev. Prof. J. J. GIVEN, Ph.D., D.D., Rev. Prof. JOHNSON, M.A., Rev. A. ROWLAND, B.A., LL.B., Rev. A. MUIR, and Rev. R. GREEN. Fifth Edition. 2 vols., 10*s*. 6*d*. each.

St. Luke. By the Very Rev. H. D. M. SPENCE. With Homilies by the Rev. J. MARSHALL LANG, D.D., Rev. W. CLARKSON, B.A., and Rev. R. M. EDGAR, M.A. 2 vols., 10*s*. 6*d*. each.

St. John. By the Rev. Prof. H. R. REYNOLDS, D.D. With Homilies by the Rev. Prof. T. CROSKERY, D.D., Rev. Prof. J. R. THOMSON, M.A., Rev. D. YOUNG, B.A., Rev. B. THOMAS, Rev. G. BROWN. Second Edition. 2 vols., 15*s*. each.

The Acts of the Apostles. By the Bishop of BATH and WELLS. With Homilies by the Rev. Prof. P. C. BARKER, M.A., LL.B., Rev. Prof. E. JOHNSON, M.A., Rev. Prof. R. A. REDFORD, LL.B., Rev. R. TUCK, B.A., Rev. W. CLARKSON, B.A. Fourth Edition. 2 vols., 10*s*. 6*d*. each.

1 Corinthians. By the Ven. Archdeacon FARRAR, D.D. With Homilies by the Rev. Ex-Chancellor LIPSCOMB, LL.D., Rev. DAVID THOMAS, D.D., Rev. D. FRASER, D.D., Rev. Prof. J. R. THOMSON, M.A., Rev. J. WAITE, B.A., Rev. R. TUCK, B.A., Rev. E. HURNDALL, M.A., and Rev. H. BREMNER, B.D. Fourth Edition. 15*s*.

2 Corinthians and Galatians. By the Ven. Archdeacon FARRAR, D.D., and Rev. Prebendary E. HUXTABLE. With Homilies by the Rev. Ex-Chancellor LIPSCOMB, LL.D., Rev. DAVID THOMAS, D.D., Rev. DONALD FRASER, D.D., Rev. R. TUCK, B.A., Rev. E. HURNDALL, M.A., Rev. Prof. J. R. THOMSON, M.A., Rev. R. FINLAYSON, B.A., Rev. W. F. ADENEY, M.A., Rev. R. M. EDGAR, M.A., and Rev. T. CROSKERY, D.D. Second Edition. 21*s*.

Pulpit Commentary, The—*continued.*

> **Ephesians, Philippians, and Colossians.** By the Rev. Prof. W. G. BLAIKIE, D.D., Rev. B. C. CAFFIN, M.A., and Rev. G. G. FINDLAY, B.A. With Homilies by the Rev. D. THOMAS, D.D., Rev. R. M. EDGAR, M.A., Rev. R. FINLAYSON, B.A., Rev. W. F. ADENEY, M.A., Rev. Prof. T. CROSKERY, D.D., Rev. E. S. PROUT, M.A., Rev. Canon VERNON HUTTON, and Rev. U. R. THOMAS, D.D. Second Edition. 21*s.*

> **Thessalonians, Timothy, Titus, and Philemon.** By the Bishop of BATH and WELLS, Rev. Dr. GLOAG, and Rev. Dr. EALES. With Homilies by the Rev. B. C. GAFFIN, M.A., Rev. R. FINLAYSON, B.A., Rev. Prof. T. CROSKERY, D.D., Rev. W. F. ADENEY, M.A., Rev. W. M. STATHAM, and Rev. D. THOMAS, D.D. 15*s.*

> **Hebrews and James.** By the Rev. J. BARMBY, D.D., and Rev. Prebendary E. C. S. GIBSON, M.A. With Homileties by the Rev. C. JERDAN, M.A., LL.B., and Rev. Prebendary E. C. S. GIBSON. And Homilies by the Rev. W. JONES, Rev. C. NEW, Rev. D. YOUNG, B.A., Rev. J. S. BRIGHT, Rev. T. F. LOCKYER, B.A., and Rev. C. JERDAN, M.A., LL.B. Second Edition. 15*s.*

> **Peter, John, and Jude.** By the Rev. B. C. CAFFIN, M.A., Rev. A. PLUMMER, D.D., and Rev. S. D. F. SALMOND, D.D. With Homilies by the Rev. A. MACLAREN, D.D., Rev. C. CLEMANCE, D.D., Rev. Prof. J. R. THOMSON, M.A., Rev. C. NEW, Rev. U. R. THOMAS, Rev. R. FINLAYSON, B.A., Rev. W. JONES, Rev. Prof. T. CROSKERY, D.D., and Rev. J. S. BRIGHT, D.D. 15*s.*

> **Revelation.** Introduction by the Rev. T. RANDELL, B.D., Principal of Bede College, Durham ; and Exposition by the Rev. T. RANDELL, assisted by the Rev. A. PLUMMER, M.A., D.D., Principal of University College, Durham, and A. T. BOTT, M.A. With Homilies by the Rev. C. CLEMANCE, D.D., Rev. S. CONWAY, B.A., Rev. R. GREEN, and Rev. D. THOMAS, D.D.

PUSEY, Dr.—**Sermons for the Church's Seasons from Advent to Trinity.** Selected from the Published Sermons of the late EDWARD BOUVERIE PUSEY, D.D. Crown 8vo, 5*s.*

RENAN, Ernest.—**Philosophical Dialogues and Fragments.** From the French. Post 8vo, 7*s. 6d.*

> **An Essay on the Age and Antiquity of the Book of Nabathæan Agriculture.** Crown 8vo, 3*s. 6d.*

> **The Life of Jesus.** Crown 8vo, cloth, 1*s. 6d.* ; paper covers, 1*s.*

> **The Apostles.** Crown 8vo, cloth, 1*s. 6d.* ; paper covers, 1*s.*

REYNOLDS, Rev. J. W.—**The Supernatural in Nature.** A Verification by Free Use of Science. Third Edition, Revised and Enlarged. Demy 8vo, 14*s.*

REYNOLDS, Rev. J. W.—continued.

The Mystery of Miracles. Third and Enlarged Edition. Crown 8vo, 6s.

The Mystery of the Universe our Common Faith. Demy 8vo, 14s.

The World to Come: Immortality a Physical Fact. Crown 8vo, 6s.

RICHARDSON, Austin.—"What are the Catholic Claims?" With Introduction by Rev. LUKE RIVINGTON. Crown 8vo, 3s. 6d.

RIVINGTON, Luke.—Authority, or a Plain Reason for joining the Church of Rome. Fifth Edition. Crown 8vo, 3s. 6d.

Dependence; or, The Insecurity of the Anglican Position. Crown 8vo, 5s.

ROBERTSON, The late Rev. F. W., M.A.—Life and Letters of. Edited by the Rev. STOPFORD BROOKE, M.A.

 I. Two vols., uniform with the Sermons. With Steel Portrait. Crown 8vo, 7s. 6d.
 II. Library Edition, in Demy 8vo, with Portrait. 12s.
 III. A Popular Edition, in 1 vol. Crown 8vo, 6s.

Sermons. Five Series. Small crown 8vo, 3s. 6d. each.

Notes on Genesis. New and Cheaper Edition. Small crown 8vo, 3s. 6d.

Expository Lectures on St. Paul's Epistles to the Corinthians. A New Edition. Small crown 8vo, 5s.

Lectures and Addresses, with other Literary Remains. A New Edition. Small crown 8vo, 5s.

An Analysis of Tennyson's "In Memoriam." (Dedicated by Permission to the Poet-Laureate.) Fcap. 8vo, 2s.

The Education of the Human Race. Translated from the German of GOTTHOLD EPHRAIM LESSING. Fcap. 8vo, 2s. 6d.

*** A Portrait of the late Rev. F. W. Robertson, mounted for framing, can be had, 2s. 6d.

SCANNELL, Thomas B., B.D., and WILHELM, Joseph, D.D.—A Manual of Catholic Theology. Based on SCHEEBEN'S "Dogmatik." 2 vols. Demy 8vo. Vol. I., 15s.

SHEEPSHANKS, Rev. J.—Confirmation and Unction of the Sick. Small crown 8vo, 3s. 6d.

STEPHEN, Caroline E.—Quaker Strongholds. Crown 8vo, 5s.

Theology and Piety alike Free; from the Point of View of Manchester New College, Oxford. A Contribution to its effort offered by an old Student. Demy 8vo, 9s.

TRENCH, Archbishop.—Notes on the Parables of Our Lord. 8vo, 12*s.* Cheap Edition. Fifty-sixth Thousand. 7*s.* 6*d.*

Notes on the Miracles of Our Lord. 8vo, 12*s.* Cheap Edition. Forty-eighth Thousand. 7*s.* 6*d.*

Studies in the Gospels. Fifth Edition, Revised. 8vo, 10*s.* 6*d.*

Brief Thoughts and Meditations on Some Passages in Holy Scripture. Third Edition. Crown 8vo, 3*s.* 6*d.*

Synonyms of the New Testament. Tenth Edition, Enlarged. 8vo, 12*s.*

Sermons New and Old. Crown 8vo, 6*s.*

Westminster and other Sermons. Crown 8vo, 6*s.*

On the Authorized Version of the New Testament. Second Edition. 8vo, 7*s.*

Commentary on the Epistles to the Seven Churches in Asia. Fourth Edition, Revised. 8vo, 8*s.* 6*d.*

The Sermon on the Mount. An Exposition drawn from the Writings of St. Augustine, with an Essay on his Merits as an Interpreter of Holy Scripture. Fourth Edition, Enlarged. 8vo, 10*s.* 6*d.*

Shipwrecks of Faith. Three Sermons preached before the University of Cambridge in May, 1867. Fcap. 8vo, 2*s.* 6*d.*

TRINDER, Rev. D.—The Worship of Heaven, and other Sermons. Crown 8vo, 5*s.*

WARD, Wilfrid.—The Wish to Believe. A Discussion Concerning the Temper of Mind in which a reasonable Man should undertake Religious Inquiry. Small crown 8vo, 5*s.*

WARD, William George, Ph.D.—Essays on the Philosophy of Theism. Edited, with an Introduction, by WILFRID WARD. 2 vols. Demy 8vo, 21*s.*

What is Truth? A Consideration of the Doubts as to the Efficacy of Prayer, raised by Evolutionists, Materialists, and others. By "Nemo."

WILHELM, Joseph, D.D., and SCANNELL, Thomas B., B.D.—A Manual of Catholic Theology. Based on SCHEEBEN'S "Dogmatik." 2 vols. Demy 8vo. Vol. I., 15*s.*

WYNELL-MAYOW, S. S.—The Light of Reason. Crown 8vo, 5*s.*

ENGLISH AND FOREIGN PHILOSOPHICAL LIBRARY.

Auguste Comte and Positivism. By the late JOHN STUART MILL. Third Edition. 3s. 6d.

Candid Examination of Theism (A). By PHYSICUS. Second Edition. 7s. 6d.

Colour-Sense (The): Its Origin and Development. An Essay in Comparative Psychology. By GRANT ALLEN. 10s. 6d.

Contributions to the History of the Development of the Human Race. Lectures and Dissertations. By LAZARUS GEIGER. Translated from the German by D. ASHER. 6s.

Creed of Christendom (The). Its Foundations contrasted with its Superstructure. By W. R. GREG. Eighth Edition. 2 vols. 15s.

Dr. Appleton: His Life and Literary Relics. By J. H. APPLETON and A. H. SAYCE. 10s. 6d.

Edgar Quinet: His Early Life and Writings. By RICHARD HEATH. With Portraits, Illustrations, and an Autograph Letter. 12s. 6d.

Emerson at Home and Abroad. By M. D. CONWAY. With Portrait. 10s. 6d.

Enigmas of Life. By W. R. GREG. Seventeenth Edition. 10s. 6d.

Essays and Dialogues of Giacomo Leopardi. Translated by CHARLES EDWARDES. With Biographical Sketch. 7s. 6d.

Essence of Christianity (The). By L. FEUERBACH. Translated from the German by MARIAN EVANS. Second Edition. 7s. 6d.

Ethic Demonstrated in Geometrical Order and Divided into Five Parts, which treat (1) Of God, (2) Of the Nature and Origin of the Mind, (3) Of the Origin and Nature of the Affects, (4) Of Human Bondage, or of the Strength of the Affects, (5) Of the Power of the Intellect, or of Human Liberty. By BENEDICT DE SPINOZA. Translated from the Latin by WILLIAM HALE WHITE. 10s. 6d.

Guide of the Perplexed of Maimonides (The). Translated from the Original Text and Annotated by M. FRIEDLANDER. 3 vols. 31s. 6d.

History of Materialism (A), and Criticism of its present Importance. By Prof. F. A. LANGE. Authorized Translation from the German by ERNEST C. THOMAS. In 3 vols. 10s. 6d. each.

Johann Gottlieb Fichte's Popular Works. The Nature of the Scholar; The Vocation of the Scholar; The Vocation of Man; The Doctrine of Religion; Characteristics of the Present Age; Outlines of the Doctrine of Knowledge. With a Memoir by WILLIAM SMITH, LL.D. 2 vols. 21s.

Moral Order and Progress. An Analysis of Ethical Conceptions. By S. ALEXANDER. 14*s.*

Natural Law. An Essay in Ethics. By EDITH SIMCOX. Second Edition. 10*s.* 6*d.*

Outlines of the History of Religion to the Spread of the Universal Religions. By Prof. C. P. TIELE. Translated from the Dutch by J. ESTLIN CARPENTER. Fourth Edition. 7*s.* 6*d.*

Philosophy of Law (The). By Prof. DIODATO LIOY. Translated by W. HASTIE.

Philosophy of Music (The). Lectures delivered at the Royal Institution of Great Britain. By WILLIAM POLE, F.R.S. Second Edition. 7*s.* 6*d.*

Philosophy of the Unconscious (The). By EDUARD VON HARTMANN. Translated by WILLIAM C. COUPLAND. 3 vols. 31*s.* 6*d.*

Religion and Philosophy in Germany. A Fragment. By HEINRICH HEINE. Translated by J. SNODGRASS. 6*s.*

Religion in China. Containing a brief Account of the Three Religions of the Chinese ; with Observations on the Prospects of Christian Conversion amongst that People. By JOSEPH EDKINS, D.D. Third Edition. 7*s.* 6*d.*

Science of Knowledge (The). By J. G. FICHTE. Translated from the German by A. E. KROEGER. With an Introduction by Prof. W. T. HARRIS. 10*s.* 6*d.*

Science of Rights (The). By J. G. FICHTE. Translated from the German by A. E. KROEGER. With an Introduction by Prof. W. T. HARRIS. 12*s.* 6*d.*

World as Will and Idea (The). By ARTHUR SCHOPENHAUER. Translated from the German by R. B. HALDANE and JOHN KEMP. 3 vols. £2 10*s.*

Extra Series.

An Account of the Polynesian Race : Its Origin and Migrations, and the Ancient History of the Hawaiian People. By ABRAHAM FORNANDER. 3 vols. 27*s.*

Lessing : His Life and Writings. By JAMES SIME. Second Edition. 2 vols. With Portraits. 21*s.*

Oriental Religions, and their Relation to Universal Religion—India. By SAMUEL JOHNSON. 2 vols. 21*s.*

SCIENCE.

BADER, C.—The Natural and Morbid Changes of the Human Eye, and their Treatment. Medium 8vo, 16*s.*

Plates illustrating the Natural and Morbid Changes of the Human Eye. With Explanatory Text. Medium 8vo, in a portfolio, 21*s.* Price for Text and Atlas taken together, £1 12*s.*

BICKNELL, C.—Flowering Plants and Ferns of the Riviera and Neighbouring Mountains. Drawn and described by C. BICKNELL. With 82 full-page Plates, containing Illustrations of 350 Specimens. Imperial 8vo, half-roan, gilt edges, £3 3*s.*

BLATER, Joseph.—Table of Quarter-Squares of all Whole Numbers from 1 to 200,000. For Simplifying Multiplication, Squaring, and Extraction of the Square Root. Royal 4to, half-bound, 21*s.*

Table of Napier. Giving the Nine Multiples of all Numbers. Cloth case, 1*s.* 3*d.*

BROWNE, Edgar A.—How to use the Ophthalmoscope. Being Elementary Instruction in Ophthalmoscopy. Third Edition. Crown 8vo, 3*s.* 6*d.*

BUNGE, G.—Text-Book of Physiological and Pathological Chemistry. For Physicians and Students. Translated from the German by L. C. WOODBRIDGE, M.D. Demy 8vo, 16*s.*

CALLEJA, Camilo, M.D.—Principles of Universal Physiology. Crown 8vo, 3*s.* 6*d.*

CANDLER, C.—The Prevention of Consumption : A New Theory of the Nature of the Tubercle-Bacillus. Demy 8vo, 10*s.* 6*d.*

The Prevention of Measles. Crown 8vo, 5*s.*

CARPENTER, W. B.—The Principles of Mental Physiology. With their Applications to the Training and Discipline of the Mind, and the Study of its Morbid Conditions. Illustrated. Sixth Edition. 8vo, 12*s.*

Nature and Man. With a Memorial Sketch by the Rev. J. ESTLIN CARPENTER. Portrait. Large crown 8vo, 8*s.* 6*d.*

COTTA, B. von.—Geology and History. A Popular Exposition of all that is known of the Earth and its Inhabitants in Pre-historic Times. 12mo, 2*s.*

DANA, James D.—A Text-Book of Geology, designed for Schools and Academies. Illustrated. Crown 8vo, 10*s.*

Manual of Geology. Illustrated by a Chart of the World, and over 1000 Figures. 8vo, 21*s.*

DANA, James D.—continued.

The Geological Story Briefly Told. Illustrated. 12mo, 7s. 6d.

A System of Mineralogy. By J. D. DANA, aided by G. J. BRUSH. Fifth Edition. Royal 8vo, £2 2s.

Manual of Mineralogy and Petrography. Fourth Edition. Numerous Woodcuts. Crown 8vo, 8s. 6d.

*DANA, E. S.—*A Text-Book of Mineralogy. With Treatise on Crystallography and Physical Mineralogy. Third Edition. 800 Woodcuts and 1 Coloured Plate. 8vo, 15s.

*DU MONCEL, Count.—*The Telephone, the Microphone, and the Phonograph. With 74 Illustrations. Third Edition. Small crown 8vo, 5s.

*DYMOCK, W.—*The Vegetable Materia Medica of Western India. 4 Parts. 8vo, 5s. each.

*FEATHERMAN, A.—*The Social History of the Races of Mankind. Demy 8vo. Div. I. The Nigritians. £1 11s. 6d. Div. II.-I. Papuo and Malayo Melanesians. £1 5s. Div. II.-II. Oceano-Melanesians. £1 5s. Div. III.-I. Aoneo-Maranonians. 25s. Div. III.-II. Chiapo and Guazano Maranonians. 28s. Div. V. The Aramæans. £1 1s.

*FITZGERALD, R. D.—*Australian Orchids. Folio. Part I. 7 Plates. Part II. 10 Plates. Part III. 10 Plates. Part IV. 10 Plates. Part V. 10 Plates. Part VI. 10 Plates. Each Part, coloured, 21s.; plain, 10s. 6d. Part VII. 10 Plates. Vol. II., Part I. 10 Plates. Each, coloured, 25s.

*GALLOWAY, Robert.—*A Treatise on Fuel. Scientific and Practical. With Illustrations. Post 8vo, 6s.

Education : Scientific and Technical ; or, How the Inductive Sciences are Taught, and How they Ought to be Taught. 8vo, 10s. 6d.

*HAECKEL, Prof. Ernst.—*The History of Creation. Translation revised by Professor E. RAY LANKESTER, M.A., F.R.S. With Coloured Plates and Genealogical Trees of the various groups of both Plants and Animals. 2 vols. Third Edition. Post 8vo, 32s.

The History of the Evolution of Man. With numerous Illustrations. 2 vols. Post 8vo, 32s.

A Visit to Ceylon. Post 8vo, 7s. 6d.

Freedom in Science and Teaching. With a Prefatory Note by T. H. HUXLEY, F.R.S. Crown 8vo, 5s.

*HEIDENHAIN, Rudolph, M.D.—*Hypnotism, or Animal Magnetism. With Preface by G. J. ROMANES. Second Edition. Small crown 8vo, 2s. 6d.

HENWOOD, William Jory.—The Metalliferous Deposits of Cornwall and Devon. With Appendices on Subterranean Temperature; the Electricity of Rocks and Veins; the Quantities of Water in the Cornish Mines; and Mining Statistics. With 113 Tables, and 12 Plates, half-bound. 8vo, £2 2*s.*

Observations on Metalliferous Deposits, and on Subterranean Temperature. In 2 Parts. With 38 Tables, 31 Engravings on Wood, and 6 Plates. 8vo, £1 16*s.*

HOSPITALIER, E.—The Modern Applications of Electricity. Translated and Enlarged by JULIUS MAIER, Ph.D. 2 vols. Second Edition, Revised, with many additions and numerous Illustrations. Demy 8vo, 25*s.*

HULME, F. Edward.—Mathematical Drawing Instruments, and How to Use Them. With Illustrations. Third Edition. Imperial 16mo, 3*s.* 6*d.*

INMAN, James.—Nautical Tables. Designed for the Use of British Seamen. New Edition, Revised and Enlarged. Demy 8vo, 16*s.*

KINAHAN, G. H.—Valleys and their Relation to Fissures, Fractures, and Faults. Crown 8vo, 7*s.* 6*d.*

KLEIN, Felix.—Lectures on the Ikosahedron, and the Solution of Equations of the Fifth Degree. Translated by G. G. MORRICE. Demy 8vo, 10*s.* 6*d.*

LENDENFELD, R. von.—Monograph of the Horny Sponges. With 50 Plates. Issued by direction of the Royal Society. 4to, £3.

LESLEY, J. P.—Man's Origin and Destiny. Sketched from the Platform of the Physical Sciences. Second Edition. Crown 8vo, 7*s.* 6*d.*

LIVERSIDGE, A.—The Minerals of New South Wales, etc. With large Coloured Map. Royal 8vo, 18*s.*

MIVART, St. George.—On Truth. Demy 8vo, 16*s.*

The Origin of Human Reason. Demy 8vo, 10*s.* 6*d.*

NICOLS, Arthur, F.G.S., F.R.G.S.—Chapters from the Physical History of the Earth. An Introduction to Geology and Palæontology. With numerous Illustrations. Crown 8vo, 5*s.*

PYE, Walter.—Surgical Handicraft. A Manual of Surgical Manipulations. With 233 Illustrations on Wood. Second Edition. Crown 8vo, 10*s.* 6*d.*

Elementary Bandaging and Surgical Dressing. For the Use of Dressers and Nurses. 18mo, 2*s.*

RAMSAY, E. P.—Tabular List of all the Australian Birds at present known to the Author. Crown 4to, 12*s.* 6*d.*

RIBOT, Prof. Th.—Heredity: A Psychological Study of its Phenomena, its Laws, its Causes, and its Consequences. Second Edition. Large crown 8vo, 9s.

English Psychology. Crown 8vo, 7s. 6d.

RODD, Edward Hearle.—The Birds of Cornwall and the Scilly Islands. Edited by J. E. HARTING. With Portrait and Map. 8vo, 14s.

ROMANES, G. J.—Mental Evolution in Animals. With a Posthumous Essay on Instinct by CHARLES DARWIN, F.R.S. Demy 8vo, 12s. '

Mental Evolution in Man : Origin of Human Faculty. Demy 8vo, 14s.

ROSS, Lieut.-Colonel W. A.—Alphabetical Manual of Blow-pipe Analysis. Crown 8vo, 5s.

Pyrology, or Fire Chemistry. Small 4to, 36s.

SCHWENDLER, Louis.—Instructions for Testing Telegraph Lines, and the Technical Arrangements in Offices. 2 vols. Demy 8vo, 21s.

SMITH, Hamilton, Jun.—Hydraulics. The Flow of Water through Orifices, over Weirs, and through Open Conduits and Pipes. With 17 Plates. Royal 4to, 30s.

STRECKER-WISLICENUS.—Organic Chemistry. Translated and Edited, with Extensive Additions, by W. R. HODGKINSON, Ph.D., and A. J. GREENAWAY, F.I.C. Second and cheaper Edition. Demy 8vo, 12s. 6d.

SYMONS, G. J.—The Eruption of Krakatoa, and Subsequent Phenomena. Report of the Krakatoa Committee of the Royal Society. Edited by G. J. SYMONS, F.R.S. With 6 Chromolithographs of the Remarkable Sunsets of 1883, and 40 Maps and Diagrams. 4to, £1 10s.

WANKLYN, J. A.—Milk Analysis. A Practical Treatise on the Examination of Milk and its Derivatives, Cream, Butter, and Cheese. Second Edition. Crown 8vo, 5s.

Tea, Coffee, and Cocoa. A Practical Treatise on the Analysis of Tea, Coffee, Cocoa, Chocolate, Maté (Paraguay Tea). Crown 8vo, 5s.

WANKLYN, J. A., and COOPER, W. J.—Bread Analysis. A Practical Treatise on the Examination of Flour and Bread. Crown 8vo, 5s.

WANKLYN, J. A., and CHAPMAN, E. T.—Water Analysis. A Treatise on the Examination of Potable Water. Seventh Edition. Entirely rewritten. Crown 8vo, 5s.

WRIGHT, G. Frederick, D.D.—The Ice Age in North America, and its bearing upon the Antiquity of Man. With Maps and Illustrations. 8vo, 21*s*.

THE INTERNATIONAL SCIENTIFIC SERIES.

I. **Forms of Water in Clouds and Rivers, Ice and Glaciers.** By J. Tyndall, LL.D., F.R.S. With 25 Illustrations. Ninth Edition. 5*s*.

II. **Physics and Politics;** or, Thoughts on the Application of the Principles of "Natural Selection" and "Inheritance" to Political Society. By Walter Bagehot. Eighth Edition. 5*s*.

III. **Foods.** By Edward Smith, M.D., LL.B., F.R.S. With numerous Illustrations. Ninth Edition. 5*s*.

IV. **Mind and Body: the Theories of their Relation.** By Alexander Bain, LL.D. With Four Illustrations. Eighth Edition. 5*s*.

V. **The Study of Sociology.** By Herbert Spencer. Fourteenth Edition. 5*s*.

VI. **The Conservation of Energy.** By Balfour Stewart, M.A., LL.D., F.R.S. With 14 Illustrations. Seventh Edition. 5*s*.

VII. **Animal Locomotion;** or, Walking, Swimming, and Flying. By J. B. Pettigrew, M.D., F.R.S., etc. With 130 Illustrations. Third Edition. 5*s*.

VIII. **Responsibility in Mental Disease.** By Henry Maudsley, M.D. Fourth Edition. 5*s*.

IX. **The New Chemistry.** By Professor J. P. Cooke. With 31 Illustrations. Ninth Edition. 5*s*.

X. **The Science of Law.** By Professor Sheldon Amos. Sixth Edition. 5*s*.

XI. **Animal Mechanism:** a Treatise on Terrestrial and Aerial Locomotion. By Professor E. J. Marey. With 117 Illustrations. Third Edition. 5*s*.

XII. **The Doctrine of Descent and Darwinism.** By Professor Oscar Schmidt. With 26 Illustrations. Seventh Edition. 5*s*.

XIII. **The History of the Conflict between Religion and Science.** By J. W. Draper, M.D., LL.D. Twentieth Edition. 5*s*.

XIV. **Fungi: their Nature, Influences, and Uses.** By M. C. Cooke, M.A., LL.D. Edited by the Rev. M. J. Berkeley, M.A., F.L.S. With numerous Illustrations. Fourth Edition. 5*s*.

XV. **The Chemistry of Light and Photography.** By Dr. Hermann Vogel. With 100 Illustrations. Fifth Edition. 5s.

XVI. **The Life and Growth of Language.** By Professor William Dwight Whitney. Fifth Edition. 5s.

XVII. **Money and the Mechanism of Exchange.** By W. Stanley Jevons, M.A., F.R.S. Eighth Edition. 5s.

XVIII. **The Nature of Light.** With a General Account of Physical Optics. By Dr. Eugene Lommel. With 188 Illustrations and a Table of Spectra in Chromo-lithography. Fifth Edition. 5s.

XIX. **Animal Parasites and Messmates.** By P. J. Van Beneden. With 83 Illustrations. Third Edition. 5s.

XX. **On Fermentation.** By Professor Schützenberger. With 28 Illustrations. Fourth Edition. 5s.

XXI. **The Five Senses of Man.** By Professor Bernstein. With 91 Illustrations. Fifth Edition. 5s.

XXII. **The Theory of Sound in its Relation to Music.** By Professor Pietro Blaserna. With numerous Illustrations. Third Edition. 5s.

XXIII. **Studies in Spectrum Analysis.** By J. Norman Lockyer, F.R.S. With 6 Photographic Illustrations of Spectra, and numerous engravings on Wood. Fourth Edition. 6s. 6d.

XXIV. **A History of the Growth of the Steam Engine.** By Professor R. H. Thurston. With numerous Illustrations. Fourth Edition. 5s.

XXV. **Education as a Science.** By Alexander Bain, LL.D. Seventh Edition. 5s.

XXVI. **The Human Species.** By Professor A. de Quatrefages. Fifth Edition. 5s.

XXVII. **Modern Chromatics.** With Applications to Art and Industry. By Ogden N. Rood. With 130 original Illustrations. Second Edition. 5s.

XXVIII. **The Crayfish:** an Introduction to the Study of Zoology. By Professor T. H. Huxley. With 82 Illustrations. Fifth Edition, 5s.

XXIX. **The Brain as an Organ of Mind.** By H. Charlton Bastian, M.D. With numerous Illustrations. Third Edition. 5s.

XXX. **The Atomic Theory.** By Professor Wurtz. Translated by E. Cleminshaw, F.C.S. Fifth Edition. 5s.

XXXI. **The Natural Conditions of Existence as they affect Animal Life.** By Karl Semper. With 2 Maps and 106 Woodcuts. Third Edition. 5s.

XXXII. **General Physiology of Muscles and Nerves.** By Professor J. Rosenthal. Third Edition. With 75 Illustrations. 5s.

XXXIII. **Sight:** an Exposition of the Principles of Monocular and Binocular Vision. By Joseph le Conte, LL.D. Second Edition. With 132 Illustrations. 5*s*.

XXXIV. **Illusions:** a Psychological Study. By James Sully. Third Edition. 5*s*.

XXXV. **Volcanoes: what they are and what they teach.** By Professor J. W. Judd, F.R.S. With 96 Illustrations on Wood. Fourth Edition. 5*s*.

XXXVI. **Suicide:** an Essay on Comparative Moral Statistics. By Professor H. Morselli. Second Edition. With Diagrams. 5*s*.

XXXVII. **The Brain and its Functions.** By J. Luys. With Illustrations. Second Edition. 5*s*.

XXXVIII. **Myth and Science:** an Essay. By Tito Vignoli. Third Edition. With Supplementary Note. 5*s*.

XXXIX. **The Sun.** By Professor Young. With Illustrations. Third Edition. 5*s*.

XL. **Ants, Bees, and Wasps:** a Record of Observations on the Habits of the Social Hymenoptera. By Sir John Lubbock, Bart., M.P. With 5 Chromo-lithographic Illustrations. Ninth Edition. 5*s*.

XLI. **Animal Intelligence.** By G. J. Romanes, LL.D., F.R.S. Fourth Edition. 5*s*.

XLII. **The Concepts and Theories of Modern Physics.** By J. B. Stallo. Third Edition. 5*s*.

XLIII. **Diseases of Memory:** an Essay in the Positive Psychology. By Professor Th. Ribot. Third Edition. 5*s*.

XLIV. **Man before Metals.** By N. Joly. With 148 Illustrations. Fourth Edition. 5*s*.

XLV. **The Science of Politics.** By Professor Sheldon Amos. Third Edition. 5*s*.

XLVI. **Elementary Meteorology.** By Robert H. Scott. Fourth Edition. With numerous Illustrations. 5*s*.

XLVII. **The Organs of Speech and their Application in the Formation of Articulate Sounds.** By Georg Hermann Von Meyer. With 47 Woodcuts. 5*s*.

XLVIII. **Fallacies.** A View of Logic from the Practical Side. By Alfred Sidgwick. Second Edition. 5*s*.

XLIX. **Origin of Cultivated Plants.** By Alphonse de Candolle. Second Edition. 5*s*.

L. **Jelly-Fish, Star-Fish, and Sea-Urchins.** Being a Research on Primitive Nervous Systems. By G. J. Romanes. With Illustrations. 5*s*.

LI. **The Common Sense of the Exact Sciences.** By the late William Kingdon Clifford. Second Edition. With 100 Figures. 5*s.*

LII. **Physical Expression : Its Modes and Principles.** By Francis Warner, M.D., F.R.C.P., Hunterian Professor of Comparative Anatomy and Physiology, R.C.S.E. With 50 Illustrations. 5*s.*

LIII. **Anthropoid Apes.** By Robert Hartmann. With 63 Illustrations. 5*s.*

LIV. **The Mammalia in their Relation to Primeval Times.** By Oscar Schmidt. With 51 Woodcuts. 5*s.*

LV. **Comparative Literature.** By H. Macaulay Posnett, LL.D. 5*s.*

LVI. **Earthquakes and other Earth Movements.** By Professor John Milne. With 38 Figures. Second Edition. 5*s.*

LVII. **Microbes, Ferments, and Moulds.** By E. L. Trouessart. With 107 Illustrations. 5*s.*

LVIII. **Geographical and Geological Distribution of Animals.** By Professor A. Heilprin. With Frontispiece. 5*s.*

LIX. **Weather.** A Popular Exposition of the Nature of Weather Changes from Day to Day. By the Hon. Ralph Abercromby. Second Edition. With 96 Illustrations. 5*s.*

LX. **Animal Magnetism.** By Alfred Binet and Charles Féré. Second Edition. 5*s.*

LXI. **Manual of British Discomycetes,** with descriptions of all the Species of Fungi hitherto found in Britain included in the Family, and Illustrations of the Genera. By William Phillips, F.L.S. 5*s.*

LXII. **International Law.** With Materials for a Code of International Law. By Professor Leone Levi. 5*s.*

LXIII. **The Geological History of Plants.** By Sir J. William Dawson. With 80 Figures. 5*s.*

LXIV. **The Origin of Floral Structures through Insect and other Agencies.** By Rev. Professor G. Henslow. With 88 Illustrations. 5*s.*

LXV. **On the Senses, Instincts, and Intelligence of Animals.** With special Reference to Insects. By Sir John Lubbock, Bart., M.P. 100 Illustrations. Second Edition. 5*s.*

LXVI. **The Primitive Family : Its Origin and Development.** By C. N. Starcke. 5*s.*

LXVII. **Physiology of Bodily Exercise.** By Fernand Lagrange, M.D. 5*s.*

LXVIII. The Colours of Animals: their Meaning and Use, especially considered in the Case of Insects. By E. B. Poulton, F.R.S. With Coloured Frontispiece and 66 Illustrations in Text. 5*s.*

LXIX. Introduction to Fresh-Water Algæ. With an Enumeration of all the British Species. By M. C. Cooke. 13 Plates. 5*s.*

ORIENTAL, EGYPTIAN, ETC.

AHLWARDT, W.—The Divans of the Six Ancient Arabic Poets, Ennābiga, 'Antara, Tharafa, Zuhair, 'Alquama, and Imruulquais. Edited by W. AHLWARDT. Demy 8vo, 12*s.*

ALABASTER, Henry.—The Wheel of the Law : Buddhism illustrated from Siamese Sources. Demy 8vo, 14*s.*

ALI, Moulaví Cherágh.—The Proposed Political, Legal, and Social Reforms in the Ottoman Empire and other Mohammedan States. Demy 8vo, 8*s.*

ARNOLD, Sir Edwin, C.S.I.—With Sa'di in the Garden ; or, The Book of Love. Being the "Ishk," or Third Chapter of the "Bostân" of the Persian Poet Sa'di. Embodied in a Dialogue held in the Garden of the Taj Mahal, at Agra. Crown 8vo, 7*s.* 6*d.*

Lotus and Jewel. Containing "In an Indian Temple," "A Casket of Gems," "A Queen's Revenge," with Other Poems. Second Edition. Crown 8vo, 7*s.* 6*d.*

Death—and Afterwards. Reprinted from the *Fortnightly Review* of August, 1885. With a Supplement. Ninth Edition. Crown 8vo, 1*s.* 6*d.* ; paper, 1*s.*

India Revisited. With 32 Full-page Illustrations. From Photographs selected by the Author. Crown 8vo, 7*s.* 6*d.*

The Light of Asia ; or, The Great Renunciation. Being the Life and Teaching of Gautama, Prince of India, and Founder of Buddhism. With Illustrations and a Portrait of the Author. Post 8vo, cloth, gilt back and edges ; or half-parchment, cloth sides, 3*s.* 6*d.* Library Edition. Crown 8vo, 7*s.* 6*d.* Illustrated Edition. Small 4to, 21*s.*

Indian Poetry. Containing "The Indian Song of Songs," from the Sanskrit of the Gîta Govinda of Jayadeva ; Two Books from "The Iliad of India ; " and other Oriental Poems. Fifth Edition. 7*s.* 6*d*

ARNOLD, Sir Edwin, C.S.I.—continued.

> **Pearls of the Faith** ; or, Islam's Rosary : being the Ninety-nine beautiful names of Allah. With Comments in Verse from various Oriental sources. Fourth Edition. Crown 8vo, 7*s.* 6*d.*

> **Indian Idylls.** From the Sanskrit of the Mahâbhârata. Crown 8vo, 7*s.* 6*d.*

> **The Secret of Death.** Being a Version of the Katha Upanishad, from the Sanskrit. Third Edition. Crown 8vo, 7*s.* 6*d.*

> **The Song Celestial** ; or, Bhagavad-Gîtâ. Translated from the Sanskrit Text. Second Edition. Crown 8vo, 5*s.*

> **Poetical Works.** Uniform Edition, comprising "The Light of Asia," "Indian Poetry," "Pearls of the Faith," "Indian Idylls," "The Secret of Death," "The Song Celestial," and "With Sa'di in the Garden." In 8 vols. Crown 8vo, cloth, 48*s.*

> **The Iliad and Odyssey of India.** Fcap. 8vo, 1*s.*

> **A Simple Transliteral Grammar of the Turkish Language.** Post 8vo, 2*s.* 6*d.*

Asiatic Society.—Journal of the Royal Asiatic Society of Great Britain and Ireland, from the Commencement to 1863. First Series, complete in 20 vols. 8vo, with many Plates, £10, or in parts from 4*s.* to 6*s.* each.

> Journal of the Royal Asiatic Society of Great Britain and Ireland. New Series. 8vo. Stitched in wrapper. 1864–88.

> Vol. I., 2 Parts, pp. iv. and 490, 16*s.*—Vol. II., 2 Parts, pp. 522, 16*s.*—Vol. III., 2 Parts, pp. 516, with Photograph, 22*s.*—Vol. IV., 2 Parts, pp. 521, 16*s.*—Vol. V., 2 Parts, pp. 463, with 10 full-page and folding Plates, 18*s.* 6*d.*—Vol. VI., Part 1, pp. 212, with 2 Plates and a Map, 8*s.*—Vol. VI., Part 2, pp. 272, with Plate and a Map, 8*s.*—Vol. VII., Part 1, pp. 194, with a Plate, 8*s.*—Vol. VII., Part 2, pp. 204, with 7 Plates and a Map, 8*s.*—Vol. VIII., Part 1, pp. 156, with 3 Plates and a Plan, 8*s.*—Vol. VIII., Part 2, pp. 152, 8*s.*—Vol. IX., Part 1, pp. 154, with a Plate, 8*s.*—Vol. IX., Part 2, pp. 292, with 3 Plates, 10*s.* 6*d.*—Vol. X., Part 1, pp. 156, with 2 Plates and a Map, 8*s.*—Vol. X., Part 2, pp. 146, 6*s.*—Vol. X., Part 3, pp. 204, 8*s.*—Vol. XI., Part 1, pp. 128, 5*s.*—Vol. XI., Part 2, pp. 158, with 2 Plates, 7*s.* 6*d.*—Vol. XI., Part 3, pp. 250, 8*s.*—Vol. XII., Part 1, pp. 152, 5*s.*—Vol. XII., Part 2, pp. 182, with 2 Plates and a Map, 6*s.*—Vol. XII., Part 3, pp. 100, 4*s.*—Vol. XII., Part 4, pp. x., 152, cxx., 16, 8*s.*—Vol. XIII., Part 1, pp. 120, 5*s.*—Vol. XIII., Part 2, pp. 170, with a Map, 8*s.*—Vol. XIII., Part 3, pp. 178, with a Table, 7*s.* 6*d.*—Vol. XIII., Part 4, pp. 282, with a Plate and Table, 10*s.* 6*d.*—Vol. XIV., Part 1, pp. 124, with a Table and 2 Plates, 5*s.*—Vol. XIV., Part 2, pp. 164, with 1 Table, 7*s.* 6*d.*—Vol. XIV., Part 3, pp. 206, with 6 Plates, 8*s.*—Vol. XIV., Part 4, pp. 492, with 1 Plate, 14*s.*—Vol. XV., Part 1, pp. 136, 6*s.*—Vol. XV., Part 2, pp. 158, with 3 Tables, 5*s.*—Vol. XV., Part 3, pp. 192, 6*s.*—Vol. XV., Part 4, pp.

Asiatic Society—*continued.*

140, 5*s*.—Vol. XVI., Part 1, pp. 138, with 2 Plates, 7*s*.—Vol. XVI., Part 2, pp. 184, with 1 Plate, 9*s*.—Vol. XVI., Part 3, July, 1884, pp. 74-clx., 10*s*. 6*d*.—Vol. XVI., Part 4, pp. 132, 8*s*.—Vol. XVII., Part 1, pp. 144, with 6 Plates, 10*s*. 6*d*.—Vol. XVII., Part 2, pp. 194, with a Map, 9*s*.—Vol. XVII., Part 3, pp. 342, with 3 Plates, 10*s*. 6*d*.—Vol. XVIII., Part 1, pp. 126, with 2 Plates, 5*s*.—Vol. XVIII., Part 2, pp. 196, with 2 Plates, 6*s*.—Vol. XVIII., Part 3, pp. 130, with 11 Plates, 10*s*. 6*d*.—Vol. XVIII., Part 4, pp. 314, with 8 Plates, 7*s*. 6*d*.—Vol. XIX., Part 1, pp. 100, with 3 Plates, 10*s*.—Vol. XIX., Part 2, pp. 156, with 6 Plates, 10*s*.—Vol. XIX., Part 3, pp. 216, with 6 Plates, 10*s*.—Vol. XIX., Part 4, pp. 216, with 1 Plate, 10*s*.—Vol. XX., Part 1, pp. 163, 10*s*.—Vol. XX., Part 2, pp. 155, 10*s*.—Vol. XX., Part 3, pp. 143, with 3 Plates and a Map, 10*s*.—Vol. XX., Part 4, pp. 318, 10*s*.

ASTON, W. G.—**A Short Grammar of the Japanese Spoken Language.** Fourth Edition. Crown 8vo, 12*s*.

A Grammar of the Japanese Written Language. Second Edition. 8vo, 28*s*.

Auctores Sanscriti :—

Vol. I. **The Jaiminîya-Nyâya-Mâlâ-Vistara.** Edited under the supervision of THEODOR GOLDSTÜCKER. Large 4to, £3 13*s*. 6*d*.

Vol. II. **The Institutes of Gautama.** Edited, with an Index of Words, by A. F. STENZLER, Ph.D., Prof. of Oriental Languages in the University of Breslau. 8vo, cloth, 4*s*. 6*d*. ; stitched, 3*s*. 6*d*.

Vol. III. **Vaitâna Sutra : The Ritual of the Atharva Veda.** Edited, with Critical Notes and Indices, by Dr. R. GARBE. 8vo, 5*s*.

Vols. IV. and V. **Vardhamana's Ganaratnamahodadhi,** with the Author's Commentary. Edited, with Critical Notes and Indices, by JULIUS EGGELING. Part I. 8vo, 6*s*. Part II. 8vo, 6*s*.

BABA, Tatui.—**An Elementary Grammar of the Japanese Language.** With Easy Progressive Exercises. Second Edition. Crown 8vo, 5*s*.

BADGER, George Percy, D.C.L.—**An English-Arabic Lexicon.** In which the equivalent for English Words and Idiomatic Sentences are rendered into literary and colloquial Arabic. Royal 4to, 80*s*.

BALFOUR, F. H.—**The Divine Classic of Nan-Hua.** Being the Works of Chuang Tsze, Taoist Philosopher. 8vo, 14*s*.

Taoist Texts, Ethical, Political, and Speculative. Imperial 8vo, 10*s*. 6*d*.

Leaves from my Chinese Scrap-Book. Post 8vo, 7*s*. 6*d*.

BALLANTYNE, J. R.—Elements of Hindi and Braj Bhakha Grammar. Compiled for the use of the East India College at Haileybury. Second Edition. Crown 8vo, 5*s.*

First Lessons in Sanskrit Grammar; together with an Introduction to the Hitopadeśa. Fourth Edition. 8vo, 3*s.* 6*d.*

BEAL, S.—A Catena of Buddhist Scriptures from the Chinese. 8vo, 15*s.*

The Romantic Legend of Sakya Buddha. From the Chinese-Sanskrit. Crown 8vo, 12*s.*

Buddhist Literature in China. Four Lectures. Demy 8vo, 10*s.* 6*d.*

BEAMES, John.—Outlines of Indian Philology. With a Map showing the Distribution of Indian Languages. Second enlarged Edition. Crown 8vo, 5*s.*

A Comparative Grammar of the Modern Aryan Languages of India : Hindi, Panjabi, Sindhi, Gujarati, Marathi, Oriya, and Bengali. 3 vols. 16*s.* each.

BELLEW, Deputy-Surgeon-General H. W.—The History of Cholera in India from 1862 to 1881. With Maps and Diagrams. Demy 8vo, £2 2*s.*

A Short Practical Treatise on the Nature, Causes, and Treatment of Cholera. Demy 8vo, 7*s.* 6*d.*

From the Indus to the Tigris. A Narrative of a Journey through Balochistan, Afghanistan, Khorassan, and Iran, in 1872. 8vo, 10*s.* 6*d.*

Kashmir and Kashghar. A Narrative of the Journey of the Embassy to Kashghar in 1873–74. Demy 8vo, 10*s.* 6*d.*

The Races of Afghanistan. Being a Brief Account of the Principal Nations inhabiting that Country. 8vo, 7*s.* 6*d.*

BELLOWS, John.—English Outline Vocabulary, for the Use of Students of the Chinese, Japanese, and other Languages. Crown 8vo, 6*s.*

BENFEY, Theodor.—A Practical Grammar of the Sanskrit Language, for the Use of Early Students. Second Edition. Royal 8vo, 10*s.* 6*d.*

BENTLEY, W. Holman.—Dictionary and Grammar of the Kongo Language, as spoken at San Salvador, the Ancient Capital of the Old Kongo Empire, West Africa. Demy 8vo, 21*s.*

BEVERIDGE, H.—The District of Bakarganj : Its History and Statistics. 8vo, 21*s.*

Buddhist Catechism (A) ; or, Outline of the Doctrine of the Buddha Gotama. By SUBHADRA BHIKSHU. 12mo, 2*s.*

BUDGE, Ernest A.—Archaic Classics. Assyrian Texts ; being Extracts from the Annals of Shalmaneser II., Sennacherib, and Assur-Bani-Pal. With Philological Notes. Small 4to, 7s. 6d.

BURGESS, James.—ARCHÆOLOGICAL SURVEY OF WESTERN INDIA :—

Reports—

The Belgâm and Kaladi Districts. With 56 Photographs and Lithographic Plates. Royal 4to, half-bound, £2 2s.

The Antiquities of Kâthiâwâd and Kachh. Royal 4to, with 74 Plates. Half-bound, £3 3s.

The Antiquities in the Bidar and Aurangabad Districts, in the Territories of His Highness the Nizam of Haiderabad. With 63 Photographic Plates. Royal 4to, half-bound, £2 2s.

The Buddhist Cave-Temples and their Inscriptions. Containing Views, Plans, Sections, and Elevation of Façades of Cave-Temples ; Drawings of Architectural and Mythological Sculptures ; Facsimiles of Inscriptions, etc. ; with Descriptive and Explanatory Text, and Translations of Inscriptions. With 86 Plates and Woodcuts. Royal 4to, half-bound, £3 3s.

Elura Cave-Temples, and the Brahmanical and Jaina Caves in Western India. With 66 Plates and Woodcuts. Royal 4to, half-bound, £3 3s.

ARCHÆOLOGICAL SURVEY OF SOUTHERN INDIA :—

Reports of the Amaravati and Jaggaypyaeta Buddhist Stupas. Containing numerous Collotype and other Illustrations of Buddhist Sculpture and Architecture, etc., in South-Eastern India ; Facsimiles of Inscriptions, etc. ; with Descriptive and Explanatory Text. Together with Transcriptions, Translations, and Elucidations of the Dhauli and Jaugada Inscriptions of Asoka, by Professor G. BUHLER, LL.D. Vol. I. With numerous Plates and Woodcuts. Royal 4to, half-bound, £4 4s.

BURGESS, James.—Epigraphia Indica and Record of the Archæological Survey of India. Edited by JAS. BURGESS, LL.D. Parts I., II., and III. Royal 4to, wrappers, 7s. each.

BURNELL, A. C.—Elements of South Indian Palæography, from the Fourth to the Seventeenth Century A.D. Being an Introduction to the Study of South Indian Inscriptions and MSS. Second enlarged and improved Edition. Map and 35 Plates. 4to, £2 12s. 6d.

A Classified Index to the Sanskrit MSS. in the Palace at Tanjore. Prepared for the Madras Government. 3 Parts. 4to, 10s. each.

CALDWELL, Bishop R.—A Comparative Grammar of the Dravidian or South Indian Family of Languages. A second, corrected, and enlarged Edition. Demy 8vo, 28s.

CAPPELLER, Carl.—A Sanskrit-English Dictionary. Based upon the St. Petersburg Lexicons. Royal 8vo. [*In preparation.*

CHALMERS, J.—Structure of Chinese Characters, under 300 Primary Forms, after the Shwoh-wan, 100 A.D. Demy 8vo, 12s. 6d.

CHAMBERLAIN, B. H.—A Romanised Japanese Reader. Consisting of Japanese Anecdotes, Maxims, with English Translation and Notes. 12mo, 6s.

The Classical Poetry of the Japanese. Post 8vo, 7s. 6d.

Handbook of Colloquial Japanese. 8vo, 12s. 6d.

CHATTERJI, Mohini M.—The Bhagavad Gîtâ ; or, The Lord's Lay. With Commentary and Notes. Translated from the Sanskrit. Second Edition. Royal 8vo, 10s. 6d.

CHILDERS, R. C.—A Pali-English Dictionary, with Sanskrit Equivalents. Imperial 8vo, £3 3s.

The Mahaparinibbanasutta of the Sutta Pitaka. The Pali Text. Edited by R. C. CHILDERS. 8vo, 5s.

CHINTAMON, H.—A Commentary on the Text of the Bhagavad-Gítá ; or, The Discourse between Khrishna and Arjuna of Divine Matters. Post 8vo, 6s.

COOMARA SWAMY, Mutu.—The Dathavansa ; or, The History of the Tooth Relic of Gotama Buddha, in Pali Verse. Edited by MUTU COOMARA SWAMY. Demy 8vo, 10s. 6d. English Translation. With Notes. 6s.

Sutta Nipata ; or, Dialogues and Discourses of Gotama Buddha. Translated from the original Pali. Crown 8vo, 6s.

COWELL, E. B.—A Short Introduction to the Ordinary Prakrit of the Sanskrit Dramas. Crown 8vo, 3s. 6d.

Prakrita-Prakasa ; or, The Prakrit Grammar of Vararuchi, with the Commentary (Manorama) of Bhamaha. 8vo, 14s.

CRAVEN, T.—English-Hindustani and Hindustani-English Dictionary. 18mo, 3s. 6d.

CUNNINGHAM, Major-General Alexander.—The Ancient Geography of India. I. The Buddhist Period, including the Campaigns of Alexander and the Travels of Hwen-Thsang. With 13 Maps. 8vo, £1 8s.

Archæological Survey of India, Reports. With numerous Plates. Vols. I. to XXIII. Royal 8vo, 10s. and 12s. each. General Index to Vols. I. to XXIII. Royal 8vo, 12s.

CUST, R. N.—Pictures of Indian Life, Sketched with the Pen from 1852 to 1881. With Maps. Crown 8vo, 7s. 6d.

DENNYS, N. B.—The Folk-Lore of China, and its Affinities with that of the Aryan and Semitic Races. 8vo, 10s. 6d.

DOUGLAS, R. K.—Chinese Language and Literature. Two Lectures. Crown 8vo, 5s.

The Life of Jenghiz Khan. Translated from the Chinese. Crown 8vo, 5s.

DOWSON, John.—A Grammar of the Urdū or Hindūstānī Language. Second Edition. Crown 8vo, 10s. 6d.

A Hindūstānī Exercise Book. Containing a Series of Passages and Extracts adapted for Translation into Hindūstānī. Crown 8vo, 2s. 6d.

DUKA, Theodore.—An Essay on the Brāhūī Grammar. Demy 8vo, 3s. 6d.

DUTT, Romesh Chunder.—A History of Civilization in Ancient India. Based on Sanscrit Literature. 3 vols. Crown 8vo. Vol. I. Vedic and Epic Ages. 8s. Vol. II. Rationalistic Age. 8s. Vol. III.   [*In preparation.*

EDKINS, Joseph.—China's Place in Philology. An Attempt to show that the Languages of Europe and Asia have a common origin. Crown 8vo, 10s. 6d.

The Evolution of the Chinese Language. As Exemplifying the Origin and Growth of Human Speech. Demy 8vo, 4s. 6d.

The Evolution of the Hebrew Language. Demy 8vo, 5s.

Introduction to the Study of the Chinese Characters. Royal 8vo, 18s.

Egypt Exploration Fund :—

The Store-City of Pithom, and the Route of the Exodus. By EDOUARD NAVILLE. Third Edition. With 13 Plates and 2 Maps. Royal 4to, 25s.

Tanis. Part I., 1883–84. By W. M. FLINDERS PETRIE. With 19 Plates and Plans. Royal 4to, 25s.

Tanis. Part II. Nebesha, Daphnæ (Tahpenes). By W. M. FLINDERS PETRIE and F. LL. GRIFFITH. 64 Plates. Royal 4to, 25s.

Naukratis. Part I. By W. M. FLINDERS PETRIE, CECIL SMITH, E. A. GARDNER, and B. V. HEAD. With 45 Plates. Royal 4to, 25s.

Naukratis. Part II. By ERNEST A. GARDNER. With an Appendix by F. LL. GRIFFITH. With 24 Plates. Royal 4to, 25s.

Goshen. By E. NAVILLE. With 11 Plates. Royal 4to, 25s.

EITEL, E. J.—**Buddhism :** Its Historical, Theoretical, and Popular Aspects. Third, Revised Edition. Demy 8vo, 5s.

Handbook for the Student of Chinese Buddhism. Second Edition. Crown 8vo, 18s.

ELLIOT, Sir H. M.—**Memoirs on the History, Folk-Lore, and Distribution of the Races of the North-Western Provinces of India.** Edited by J. BEAMES. 2 vols. With 3 Coloured Maps. Demy 8vo, £1 16s.

The History of India, as told by its own Historians. The Muhammadan Period. Edited from the Posthumous Papers of the late Sir H. M. ELLIOT. Revised and continued by Professor JOHN DOWSON. 8 vols. 8vo, £8 8s.

EMERSON, Ellen Russell.—**Indian Myths ;** or, Legends, Traditions, and Symbols of the Aborigines of America. Illustrated. Post 8vo, £1 1s.

FERGUSSON, T.—**Chinese Researches.** First Part. Chinese Chronology and Cycles. Crown 8vo, 10s. 6d.

FINN, Alexander.—**Persian for Travellers.** Oblong 32mo, 5s.

FRYER, Major G. E.—**The Khyeng People of the Sandoway District, Arakan.** With 2 Plates. 8vo, 3s. 6d.

Páli Studies. No. I. Analysis, and Páli Text of the Subodhálankara, or Easy Rhetoric, by Sangharakkhita Thera. 8vo, 3s. 6d.

GHOSE, Loke N.—**The Modern History of the Indian Chiefs, Rajas, etc.** 2 vols. Post 8vo, 21s.

GILES, Herbert A.—**Chinese Sketches.** 8vo, 10s. 6d.

A Dictionary of Colloquial Idioms in the Mandarin Dialect. 4to, 28s.

Synoptical Studies in Chinese Character. 8vo, 15s.

Chinese without a Teacher. Being a Collection of Easy and Useful Sentences in the Mandarin Dialect. With a Vocabulary. 12mo, 5s.

The San Tzu Ching ; or, Three Character Classic ; and the Ch'Jen Tsu Wen ; or, Thousand Character Essay. Metrically translated by HERBERT A. GILES. 12mo, 2s. 6d.

GOVER, C. E.—**The Folk-Songs of Southern India.** Containing Canarese, Badaga, Coorg, Tamil, Malayalam, and Telugu Songs. The Cural. 8vo, 10s. 6d.

GRIFFIN, L. H.—**The Rajas of the Punjab.** History of the Principal States in the Punjab, and their Political Relations with the British Government. Royal 8vo, 21s.

GRIFFITH, F. L.—**The Inscriptions of Siut and Der Rifeh.** With 21 Plates. 4to, 10s.

GRIFFIS, W. E.—**The Mikado's Empire.** Book I. History of Japan, from B.C. 660 to A.D. 1872. Book II. Personal Experiences, Observations, and Studies in Japan, 1870–1874. Second Edition. Illustrated. 8vo, 20*s.*

Japanese Fairy World. Stories from the Wonder-Lore of Japan. With 12 Plates. Square 16mo, 7*s.* 6*d.*

HAFIZ OF SHIRAZ.—**Selections from his Poems.** Translated from the Persian by HERMANN BICKNELL. With Oriental Bordering in gold and colour, and Illustrations by J. R. HERBERT, R.A. Demy 4to, £2 2*s.*

HAGGARD, W. H., and LE STRANGE, G.—**The Vazir of Lankuran.** A Persian Play. Edited, with a Grammatical Introduction, a Translation, Notes, and a Vocabulary, giving the Pronunciation. Crown 8vo, 10*s.* 6*d.*

HALL, John Carey.—**A General View of Chinese Civilization,** and of the Relations of the West with China. From the French of M. PIERRE LAFFITTE. Demy 8vo, 3*s.*

Hebrew Literature Society.—Lists on application.

HEPBURN, J. C.—**A Japanese and English Dictionary.** Second Edition. Imperial 8vo, 18*s.*

A Japanese-English and English-Japanese Dictionary. Abridged by the Author. Square 16mo, 14*s.*

A Japanese-English and English-Japanese Dictionary. Third Edition. Demy 8vo, half-morocco, cloth sides. 30*s.*

HILMY, H.H. Prince Ibrahim.—**The Literature of Egypt and the Soudan.** From the Earliest Times to the Year 1885 inclusive. A Bibliography; comprising Printed Books, Periodical Writings and Papers of Learned Societies, Maps and Charts, Ancient Papyri, Manuscripts, Drawings, etc. 2 vols. Demy 4to, £3 3*s.*

Hindoo Mythology Popularly Treated. An Epitomised Description of the various Heathen Deities illustrated on the Silver Swami Tea Service presented, as a memento of his visit to India, to H.R.H. the Prince of Wales, K.G., by His Highness the Gaekwar of Baroda. Small 4to, 3*s.* 6*d.*

HODGSON, B. H.—**Essays on the Languages, Literature, and Religion of Nepal and Tibet.** Together with further Papers on the Geography, Ethnology, and Commerce of those Countries. Royal 8vo, 14*s.*

HOPKINS, F. L.—**Elementary Grammar of the Turkish Language.** With a few Easy Exercises. Crown 8vo, 3*s.* 6*d.*

HUNTER, Sir William Wilson.—The Imperial Gazetteer of India. New Edition. In 14 vols. With Maps. 1886-87. Half-morocco, £3 3*s.*

The Indian Empire: Its People, History, and Products. Second and Revised Edition, incorporating the general results of the Census of 1881. With Map. Demy 8vo, £1 1*s.*

A Brief History of the Indian People. Fourth Edition. With Map. Crown 8vo, 3*s.* 6*d.*

The Indian Musalmans. Third Edition. 8vo, 10*s.* 6*d.*

Famine Aspects of Bengal Districts. A System of Famine Warnings. Crown 8vo, 7*s.* 6*d.*

A Statistical Account of Bengal. In 20 vols. 8vo, half-morocco, £5.

A Statistical Account of Assam. 2 vols. With 2 Maps. 8vo, half-morocco, 10*s.*

Catalogue of Sanskrit Manuscripts (Buddhist). Collected in Nepal by B. H. Hodgson. 8vo, 2*s.*

India.—Publications of the Geographical Department of the India Office, London. A separate list, also list of all the Government Maps, on application.

India.—Publications of the Geological Survey of India. A separate list on application.

India Office Publications :—

Aden, Statistical Account of. 5*s.*

Baden Powell. Land Revenues, etc., in India. 12*s.*

    Do.   Jurisprudence for Forest Officers. 12*s.*

Beal's Buddhist Tripitaka. 4*s.*

Bombay Code. 21*s.*

Bombay Gazetteer. Vol. II. 14*s.* Vol. VIII. 9*s.* Vol. XIII. (2 parts) 16*s.* Vol. XV. (2 parts) 16*s.*

    Do.   do.   Vols. III. to VII., and X., XI., XII., XIV., XVI. 8*s.* each.

    Do.   do.   Vols. XXI., XXII., and XXIII. 9*s.* each.

Burgess' Archæological Survey of Western India.

                                      Vol. II. 63*s.*

    Do.   do.   do.   Vol. III. 42*s.*

    Do.   do.   Vols. IV. and V. 126*s.*

    Do.   do.   Southern India.
                                         Vol. I. 84*s.*

Burma (British) Gazetteer. 2 vols. 50*s.*

India Office Publications—*continued.*

    Corpus Inscriptionem Indicarum. Vol. I. 32*s.* Vol. III. 50*s.*

    Cunningham's Archæological Survey. Vols. I. to XXIII. 10*s.* and 12*s.* each.

        Do.   Index to Vols. I. to XXIII. 12*s.*

    Finance and Revenue Accounts of the Government of India for 1883-4. 2*s.* 6*d.*

    Gamble. Manual of Indian Timbers. 10*s.*

    Indian Education Commission, Report of the. 12*s.* Appendices. 10 vols. 10*s.*

    Jaschke's Tibetan-English Dictionary. 30*s.*

    Liotard's Silk in India. Part I. 2*s.*

    Loth. Catalogue of Arabic MSS. 10*s.* 6*d.*

    Markham's Abstract of Reports of Surveys. 1*s.* 6*d.*

    Mitra (Rajendralala), Buddha Gaya. 60*s.*

    Moir. Torrent Regions of the Alps. 1*s.*

    Mueller. Select Plants for Extra-Tropical Countries. 8*s.*

    Mysore and Coorg Gazetteer. Vols. I. and II. 10*s.* each.

    Do.   do.   Vol. III. 5*s.*

    N. W. P. Gazetteer. Vols. I. and II. 10*s.* each.

    Do.   do.   Vols. III. to XI., XIII. and XIV. 12*s.* each.

    Oudh   do.   Vols. I. to III. 10*s.* each.

    Rajputana Gazetteer. 3 vols. 15*s.*

    Saunders' Mountains and River Basins of India. 3*s.*

    Taylor. Indian Marine Surveys. 2*s.* 6*d.*

    Trigonometrical Survey, Synopsis of Great. Vols. I. to VI. 10*s.* 6*d.* each.

    Trumpp's Adi Granth. 52*s.* 6*d.*

    Waring. Pharmacopœia of India (The). 6*s.*

    Watson's Tobacco. 5*s.*

    Wilson. Madras Army. Vols. I. and II. 21*s.*

International Numismata Orientalia (The). Royal 4to, in paper wrapper. Part I. Ancient Indian Weights. By E. THOMAS, F.R.S. With a Plate and Map of the India of Manu. 9*s.* 6*d.* Part II. Coins of the Urtukí Turkumáns. By STANLEY LANE POOLE. With 6 Plates. 9*s.* Part III. The Coinage of Lydia

International Numismata Orientalia (The)—*continued.*
and Persia, from the Earliest Times to the Fall of the Dynasty of the Achæmenidæ. By BARCLAY V. HEAD. With 3 Autotype Plates. 10s. 6d. Part IV. The Coins of the Tuluni Dynasty. By EDWARD THOMAS ROGERS. 1 Plate. 5s. Part V. The Parthian Coinage. By PERCY GARDNER. 8 Autotype Plates. 18s. Part VI. The Ancient Coins and Measures of Ceylon. By T. W. RHYS DAVIDS. 1 Plate. 10s.

Vol. I. Containing the first six parts, as specified above. Royal 4to, half-bound, £3 13s. 6d.

Vol. II. **Coins of the Jews.** Being a History of the Jewish Coinage and Money in the Old and New Testaments. By F. W. MADDEN, M.R.A.S. With 279 Woodcuts and a Plate of Alphabets. Royal 4to, £2.

Vol. III. Part I. **The Coins of Arakan, of Pegu, and of Burma.** By Lieut.-General Sir ARTHUR PHAYRE, C.B. Also contains the Indian Balhara, and the Arabian Intercourse with India in the Ninth and following Centuries. By EDWARD THOMAS, F.R.S. With 5 Autotype Illustrations. Royal 4to, 8s. 6d.

Vol. III. Part II. **The Coins of Southern India.** By Sir W. ELLIOT. With Map and Plates. Royal 4to, 25s.

JÄSCHKE, H. A.—**A Tibetan-English Dictionary.** With special reference to the Prevailing Dialects. To which is added an English-Tibetan Vocabulary. Imperial 8vo, £1 10s.

Jataka (The), together with its **Commentary.** Being Tales of the Anterior Birth of Gotama Buddha. Now first published in Pali, by V. FAUSBÖLL. Text. 8vo. Vol. I. 28s. Vol. II. 28s. Vol. III. 28s. Vol. IV. 28s. Vol. V., completing the work, is in preparation.

JENNINGS, Hargrave.—**The Indian Religions ;** or, Results of the Mysterious Buddhism. Demy 8vo, 10s. 6d.

JOHNSON, Samuel.—**Oriental Religions and their Relation to Universal Religion.** Persia. Demy 8vo, 18s.

KISTNER, Otto.—**Buddha and his Doctrines.** A Bibliographical Essay. 4to, 2s. 6d.

KNOWLES, J. H.—**Folk-Tales of Kashmir.** Post 8vo, 16s.

KOLBE, F. W.—**A Language-Study based on Bantu ;** or, An Inquiry into the Laws of Root-Formation. Demy 8vo, 6s.

KRAPF, L.—**Dictionary of the Suahili Language.** 8vo, 30s.

LEGGE, James.—**The Chinese Classics.** With a Translation, Critical and Exegetical. In 7 vols. Vols. I.-V. in 8 Parts, published. Royal 8vo, £2 2s. each part.

LEGGE, James—continued.

The Chinese Classics, translated into English. With Preliminary Essays and Explanatory Notes. Popular Edition. Crown 8vo. Vol. I. Life and Teachings of Confucius. Sixth Edition. 10s. 6d. Vol. II. Works of Mencius. 12s. Vol. III. She-King; or, Book of Poetry. 12s.

LILLIE, Arthur, M.R.A.S.—The Popular Life of Buddha. Containing an Answer to the Hibbert Lectures of 1881. With Illustrations. Crown 8vo, 6s.

Buddhism in Christendom ; or, Jesus the Essene. With Illustrations. Demy 8vo, 15s.

LOBSCHEID, W.—Chinese and English Dictionary, arranged according to the Radicals. Imperial 8vo, £2 8s.

English and Chinese Dictionary, with the Punti and Mandarin Pronunciation. Folio, £8 8s.

Maha-vira-Charita ; or, The Adventures of the Great Hero Rama. An Indian Drama. Translated from the Sanskrit of BHAVA-BHÜTI. By JOHN PICKFORD. Crown 8vo, 5s.

MARIETTE-BEY, Auguste.—The Monuments of Upper Egypt. A Translation of the "Itinéraire de la Haute Egypt" of AUGUSTE MARIETTE-BEY. By ALPHONSE MARIETTE. Crown 8vo, 7s. 6d.

MARSDEN, William.—Numismata Orientalia Illustrata : The Plates of the Oriental Coins, Ancient and Modern, of the Collection of the late WILLIAM MARSDEN, F.R.S. Engraved from Drawings made under his Directions. 57 Plates. 4to, 31s. 6d.

MASON, F.—Burma : Its People and Productions ; or, Notes on the Fauna, Flora, and Minerals of Tenasserim, Pegu, and Burma. Vol. I. Geology, Mineralogy, and Zoology. Vol. II. Botany. Rewritten by W. THEOBALD. 2 vols. Royal 8vo, £3.

MAXWELL, W. E.—A Manual of the Malay Language. Second Edition. Crown 8vo, 7s. 6d.

MAYERS, Wm. Fred.—The Chinese Government. A Manual of Chinese Titles. Second Edition. Royal 8vo, 15s.

Megha-Duta (The). (Cloud Messenger.) By KĀLIDĀSA. Translated from the Sanskrit into English Verse by the late H. H. WILSON, F.R.S. The Vocabulary by FRANCIS JOHNSON. New Edition. 4to, 10s. 6d.

MOCKLER, E.—A Grammar of the Baloochee Language, as it is spoken in Makran (Ancient Gedrosia), in the Persia-Arabic and Roman characters. Fcap. 8vo, 5s.

MUIR, John.—Original Sanskrit Texts, on the Origin and History of the People of India. Translated by JOHN MUIR, LL.D.

MUIR, John—continued.

Vol. I. Mythical and Legendary Accounts of the Origin of Caste, with an Inquiry into its Existence in the Vedic Age. Third Edition. 8vo, £1 1s.

Vol. II. The Trans-Himalayan Origin of the Hindus, and their Affinity with the Western Branches of the Aryan Race. Second Edition. 8vo, £1 1s.

Vol. III. The Vedas: Opinions of their Authors, and of later Indian Writers, on their Origin, Inspiration, and Authority. Second Edition. 8vo, 16s.

Vol. IV. Comparison of the Vedic with the Later Representation of the Principal Indian Deities. Second Edition. 8vo, £1 1s.

Vol. V. Contributions to a Knowledge of the Cosmogony, Mythology, Religious Ideas, Life and Manners of the Indians in the Vedic Age. Third Edition. 8vo, £1 1s.

MÜLLER, F. Max.—Outline Dictionary, for the Use of Missionaries, Explorers, and Students of Language. 12mo, morocco, 7s. 6d.

The Sacred Hymns of the Brahmins, as preserved in the Oldest Collection of Religious Poetry, the Rig-Veda-Sanhita. Translated by F. MAX MÜLLER. Vol. I. Hymns to the Maruts, or the Storm-Gods. 8vo, 12s. 6d.

The Hymns of the Rig-Veda, in the Samhita and Pada Texts. 2 vols. Second Edition. 8vo, £1 12s.

Nágánanda; or, The Joy of the Snake World. A Buddhist Drama. Translated from the Sanskrit of Sri-Harsha-Deva, with Notes. By P. BOYD. Crown 8vo, 4s. 6d.

NEWMAN, Francis William.—A Handbook of Modern Arabic. Post 8vo, 6s.

A Dictionary of Modern Arabic. Anglo-Arabic Dictionary and Arabo-English Dictionary. 2 vols. Crown 8vo, £1 1s.

Oriental Text Society's Publications. A list may be had on application.

PALMER, the late E. H.—A Concise English-Persian Dictionary. With a Simplified Grammar of the Persian Language. Royal 16mo, 10s. 6d.

A Concise Persian-English Dictionary. Second Edition. Royal 16mo, 10s. 6d.

PRATT, George.—A Grammar and Dictionary of the Samoan Language. Second Edition. Crown 8vo, 18s.

REDHOUSE, J. W.—The Turkish Vade-Mecum of Ottoman Colloquial Language. English and Turkish, and Turkish and English. The whole in English Characters, the Pronunciation being fully indicated. Third Edition. 32mo, 6s.

REDHOUSE, J. W.—continued.

> On the History, System, and Varieties of Turkish Poetry. Illustrated by Selections in the Original and in English Paraphrase. 8vo, 2s. 6d. ; wrapper, 1s. 6d.

> A Tentative Chronological Synopsis of the History of Arabia and its Neighbours, from B.C. 500,000 (?) to A.D. 679. Demy 8vo, 1s.

Rig-Veda-Sanhita. A Collection of Ancient Hindu Hymns. Translated from the Sanskrit by the late H. H. WILSON, F.R.S. Edited by E. B. COWELL and W. F. WEBSTER. In 6 vols. 8vo, cloth. Vols. I., II., III. 21s. each. Vol. IV. 14s. Vols. V. and VI. 21s. each.

*SACHAU, Edward.—***Albêrûnî's India.** An Account of the Religion, Philosophy, Literature, Geography, Chronology, Astronomy, Customs, Laws, and Astrology of India, about A.D. 1030. Edited in the Arabic Original by Dr. EDWARD SACHAU. 4to, £3 3s.

> An English Edition. With Notes and Indices. 2 vols. Post 8vo, 36s.

*SALMONÉ, H. A.—***An Arabic-English Dictionary.** Comprising about 120,000 Arabic Words, with an English Index of about 50,000 Words. 2 vols. Post 8vo, 36s.

*SATOW, Ernest Mason.—***An English-Japanese Dictionary of the Spoken Language.** Second Edition. Imperial 32mo, 12s. 6d.

*SCHLAGINTWEIT, Emil.—***Buddhism in Tibet.** Illustrated by Literary Documents and Objects of Religious Worship. With a Folio Atlas of 20 Plates, and 20 Tables of Native Print in the Text. Royal 8vo, £2 2s.

*SCOTT, James George.—***Burma as it was, as it is, and as it will be.** Cheap Edition. Crown 8vo, 2s. 6d.

*SHERRING, M. A.—***The Sacred City of the Hindus.** An Account of Benares in Ancient and Modern Times. With Illustrations. 8vo, 21s.

*STEELE, Th.—***An Eastern Love-Story.** Kusa Játakaya. Crown 8vo, 6s.

*SUYEMATZ, K.—***Genji Monogatari.** The Most Celebrated of the Classical Japanese Romances. Translated by K. SUYEMATZ. Crown 8vo, 7s. 6d.

*TARRING, C. J.—***A Practical Elementary Turkish Grammar.** Crown 8vo, 6s.

Vazir of Lankuran. A Persian Play. A Text-Book of Modern Colloquial Persian. Edited by W. H. HAGGARD and G. LE STRANGE. Crown 8vo, 10s. 6d.

WATSON, John Forbes.—Index to the Native and Scientific Names of Indian and other Eastern Economic Plants and Products. Imperial 8vo, £1 11s. 6d.

WHEELER, J. Talboys.—The History of India from the Earliest Ages. Demy 8vo. Vol. I. Containing the Vedic Period and the Mahá Bhárata. With Map. Vol. II. The Ramayana, and the Brahmanic Period. With 2 Maps. 21s. Vol. III. Hindu, Buddhist, Brahmanical Revival. With 2 Maps. 8vo, 18s. This volume may be had as a complete work with the following title, "History of India: Hindu, Buddhist, and Brahmanical." Vol. IV. Part I. Mussulman Rule. 14s. Vol. IV. Part II. Completing the History of India down to the time of the Moghul Empire. 12s.

Early Records of British India. A History of the English Settlements in India, as told in the Government Records, and other Contemporary Documents, from the earliest period down to the rise of British Power in India. Royal 8vo, 15s.

WHITNEY, W. D.—A Sanskrit Grammar, including both the Classical Language and the older Dialects of Veda and Brahmana. Second Edition. 8vo, 12s.

WHITWORTH, George Clifford.—An Anglo-Indian Dictionary: a Glossary of Indian Terms used in English, and of such English or other Non-Indian Terms as have obtained special meanings in India. Demy 8vo, cloth, 12s.

WILLIAMS, S. Wells.—A Syllabic Dictionary of the Chinese Language; arranged according to the Wu-Fang Yuen Yin, with the Pronunciation of the Characters as heard in Pekin, Canton, Amoy, and Shanghai. 4to, £5 5s.

WILSON.—Works of the late Horace Hayman Wilson.

Vols. I. and II. Essays and Lectures chiefly on the Religion of the Hindus. Collected and Edited by Dr. REINHOLD ROST. 2 vols. Demy 8vo, 21s.

Vols. III., IV., and V. Essays Analytical, Critical, and Philological, on Subjects connected with Sanskrit Literature. Collected and Edited by Dr. REINHOLD ROST. 3 vols. Demy 8vo, 36s.

Vols. VI., VII., VIII., IX., and X. (2 parts). Vishnu Puráná, a System of Hindu Mythology and Tradition. From the original Sanskrit. Illustrated by Notes derived chiefly from other Puránás, Edited by FITZEDWARD HALL, D.C.L. Vols. I. to V. (2 parts). Demy 8vo, £3 4s. 6d.

Vols. XI. and XII. Select Specimens of the Theatre of the Hindus. From the original Sanskrit. Third Edition. 2 vols. Demy 8vo, 21s.

WRIGHT, W.—The Book of Kalilah and Dimnah. Translated from Arabic into Syriac. Demy 8vo, 21s.

TRUBNER'S ORIENTAL SERIES.

Essays on the Sacred Language, Writings, and Religion of the Parsis. By MARTIN HAUG, Ph.D. Third Edition, Edited and Enlarged by E. W. WEST. 16s.

Texts from the Buddhist Canon, commonly known as Dhammapada. Translated from the Chinese by S. BEAL. 7s. 6d.

The History of Indian Literature. By ALBRECHT WEBER. Translated from the German by J. MANN and Dr. T. ZACHARIAE. Second Edition. 10s. 6d.

A Sketch of the Modern Languages of the East Indies. With 2 Language Maps. By ROBERT CUST. 7s. 6d.

The Birth of the War-God. A Poem. By KÁLIDÁSÁ. Translated from the Sanskrit by RALPH T. H. GRIFFITHS. Second Edition. 5s.

A Classical Dictionary of Hindu Mythology and History, Geography and Literature. By JOHN DOWSON. 16s.

Metrical Translations from Sanskrit Writers. By J. MUIR. 14s.

Modern India and the Indians. Being a Series of Impressions, Notes, and Essays. By Sir MONIER MONIER-WILLIAMS. Fourth Edition. 14s.

The Life or Legend of Gaudama, the Buddha of the Burmese. By the Right Rev. P. BIGANDET. Third Edition. 2 vols. 21s.

Miscellaneous Essays, relating to Indian Subjects. By B. H. HODGSON. 2 vols. 28s.

Selections from the Koran. By EDWARD WILLIAM LANE. A New Edition. With an Introduction by STANLEY LANE POOLE. 9s.

Chinese Buddhism. A Volume of Sketches, Historical and Critical. By J. EDKINS, D.D. 18s.

The Gulistan; or, Rose Garden of Shekh Mushliu-'d-Din Sadi of Shiraz. Translated from the Atish Kadah, by E. B. EASTWICK, F.R.S. Second Edition. 10s. 6d.

A Talmudic Miscellany; or, One Thousand and One Extracts from the Talmud, the Midrashim, and the Kabbalah. Compiled and Translated by P. J. HERSHON. 14s.

The History of Esarhaddon (Son of Sennacherib), King of Assyria, B.C. 681–668. Translated from the Cuneiform Inscriptions in the British Museum. Together with Original Texts. By E. A. BUDGE. 10s. 6d.

Buddhist Birth-Stories; or, Jātaka Tales. The Oldest Collection of Folk-Lore extant: being the Jātakatthavannanā. Edited in the original Pali by V. FAUSBÖLL, and translated by T. W. RHYS DAVIDS. Translation. Vol. I. 18*s.*

The Classical Poetry of the Japanese. By BASIL CHAMBERLAIN. 7*s.* 6*d.*

Linguistic and Oriental Essays. By R. CUST, LL.D. First Series, 10*s.* 6*d.*; Second Series, with 6 Maps, 21*s.*

Indian Poetry. Containing "The Indian Song of Songs," from the Sanskrit of the Gîta Govinda of Jayadeva; Two Books from "The Iliad of India" (Mahábhárata); and other Oriental Poems. By Sir EDWIN ARNOLD, K.C.I.E. Third Edition. 7*s.* 6*d.*

The Religions of India. By A. BARTH. Translated by Rev. J. WOOD. Second Edition. 16*s.*

Hindū Philosophy. The Sānkhya Kārikā of Iswara Krishna. An Exposition of the System of Kapila. By JOHN DAVIES. 6*s.*

A Manual of Hindu Pantheism. The Vedantasara. Translated by Major G. A. JACOB. Second Edition. 6*s.*

The Mesnevī (usually known as the Mesnevīyi Sherīf, or Holy Mesnevī) of Mevlānā (Our Lord) Jelālu-'d-Din Muhammed, Er-Rūmī. Book the First. Illustrated by a Selection of Characteristic Anecdotes as collected by their Historian Mevlānā Shemsu-'d-Dīn Ahmed, El Eflākī El Arifī. Translated by J. W. REDHOUSE. £1 1*s.*

Eastern Proverbs and Emblems illustrating Old Truths. By the Rev. J. LONG. 6*s.*

The Quatrains of Omar Khayyám. A New Translation. By E. H. WHINFIELD. 5*s.*

The Quatrains of Omar Khayyám. The Persian Text, with an English Verse Translation. By E. H. WHINFIELD. 10*s.* 6*d.*

The Mind of Mencius; or, Political Economy founded upon Moral Philosophy. A Systematic Digest of the Doctrines of the Chinese Philosopher Mencius. The Original Text Classified and Translated by the Rev. E. FABER. Translated from the German, with Additional Notes, by the Rev. A. B. HUTCHINSON. 10*s.* 6*d.*

Yúsuf and Zulaika. A Poem by JAMI. Translated from the Persian into English Verse by R. T. H. GRIFFITH. 8*s.* 6*d.*

Tsuni- || Goam, the Supreme Being of the Khoi-Khoi. By THEOPHILUS HAHN. 7*s.* 6*d.*

A Comprehensive Commentary to the Quran. With SALE's Preliminary Discourse, and Additional Notes. By Rev. E. M. WHERRY. Vols. I., II., and III. 12*s.* 6*d.* each. Vol. IV. 10*s.* 6*d.*

Hindu Philosophy: The Bhagavad Gîtâ; or, The Sacred Lay. A Sanskrit Philosophical Lay. Translated by JOHN DAVIES. 8s. 6d.

The Sarva-Darsana-Samgraha; or, Review of the Different Systems of Hindu Philosophy. By MADHAVA ACHARYA. Translated by E. B. COWELL and A. E. GOUGH. 10s. 6d.

Tibetan Tales. Derived from Indian Sources. Translated from the Tibetan of the Kay-Gyur by F. ANTON VON SCHIEFNER. Done into English from the German by W. R. S. RALSTON. 14s.

Linguistic Essays. By CARL ABEL. 9s.

The Indian Empire: Its History, People, and Products. By Sir WILLIAM WILSON HUNTER, K.C.S.I. 21s.

History of the Egyptian Religion. By Dr. C. P. TIELE, Leiden. Translated by J. BALLINGAL. 7s. 6d.

The Philosophy of the Upanishads. By A. E. GOUGH. 9s.

Udanavarga. A Collection of Verses from the Buddhist Canon. Compiled by DHARMATRÂTA. Translated from the Tibetan by W. WOODVILLE ROCKHILL. 9s.

A History of Burma, including Burma Proper, Pegu, Taungu, Tenasserim, and Arakan. From the Earliest Time to the End of the First War with British India. By Lieut.-General Sir ARTHUR P. PHAYRE, C.B. 14s.

A Sketch of the Modern Languages of Africa. Accompanied by a Language Map. By R. N. CUST. 2 vols. With 31 Autotype Portraits. 18s.

Religion in China. Containing a Brief Account of the Three Religions of the Chinese. By JOSEPH EDKINS, D.D. Third Edition. 7s. 6d.

Outlines of the History of Religion to the Spread of the Universal Religions. By Prof. C. P. TIELE. Translated from the Dutch by J. ESTLIN CARPENTER. Fourth Edition. 7s. 6d.

Si-Yu-Ki. Buddhist Records of the Western World. Translated from the Chinese of HIUEN TSIANG (A.D. 629). By SAMUEL BEAL. 2 vols. With Map. 24s.

The Life of the Buddha, and the Early History of his Order. Derived from Tibetan Works in the Bkah-Hgyur and the Bstan-Hgyur. By W. W. ROCKHILL. 10s. 6d.

The Sankhya Aphorisms of Kapila. With Illustrative Extracts from the Commentaries. Translated by J. R. BALLANTYNE, LL.D. Third Edition. 16s.

The Ordinances of Manu. Translated from the Sanskrit. With an Introduction by the late A. C. BURNELL, C.I.E. Edited by EDWARD W. HOPKINS. 12s.

The Life and Works of Alexander Csoma De Körös between 1819 and 1842. With a Short Notice of all his Works and Essays, from Original Documents. By T. DUKA, M.D. 9*s.*

Ancient Proverbs and Maxims from Burmese Sources; or, The Niti Literature of Burma. By JAMES GRAY. 6*s.*

Manava-Dharma-Castra. The Code of Manu. Original Sanskrit Text, with Critical Notes. By Prof. J. JOLLY, Ph.D. 10*s.* 6*d.*

Masnavi I Ma'navi. The Spiritual Couplets of Maulána Jalálu-'d-Dín Muhammad I Rúmí. Translated and Abridged. By E. H. WHINFIELD. 7*s.* 6*d.*

Leaves from my Chinese Scrap-Book. By F. H. BALFOUR. 7*s.* 6*d.*

Miscellaneous Papers relating to Indo-China. Reprinted from "Dalrymple's Oriental Repertory," "Asiatick Researches," and the "Journal of the Asiatic Society of Bengal." 2 vols. 21*s.*

Miscellaneous Essays on Subjects connected with the Malay Peninsula and the Indian Archipelago. From the "Journals" of the Royal Asiatic, Bengal Asiatic, and Royal Geographical Societies; the "Transactions" and "Journal" of the Asiatic Society of Batavia, and the "Malayan Miscellanies." Edited by R. ROST. Second Series. 2 vols. With 5 Plates and a Map. £1 5*s.*

The Satakas of Bhartrihari. Translated from the Sanskrit by the Rev. B. HALE WORTHAM. 5*s.*

Albêrûnî's India. An Account of the Religion of India: its Philosophy, Literature, Geography, Chronology, Astronomy, Customs, Law, and Astrology, about A.D. 1030. By EDWARD SACHAU. 2 vols. 36*s.*

The Folk-Tales of Kashmir. By the Rev. J. HINTON KNOWLES. 16*s.*

Mediæval Researches from Eastern Asiatic Sources. Fragments towards the Knowledge of the Geography and History of Central and Western Asia from the Thirteenth to the Seventeenth Century. By E. BRETSCHNEIDER, M.D. 2 vols. With 2 Maps. 21*s.*

The Life of Hiuen-Tsiang. By the Shamans HWUI LI and YEN-TSUNG. With an Account of the Works of I-Tsing. By Prof. SAMUEL BEAL. 10*s.*

English Intercourse with Siam in the Seventeenth Century. By J. ANDERSON, M.D., LL.D., F.R.S. 15*s.*

Bihar Proverbs. By JOHN CHRISTIAN. [*In preparation.*

Original Sanskrit Texts on the Origin and History of the
People of India : Their Religion and Institutions. Collected,
Translated, and Illustrated. By J. MUIR, LL.D. Vol. I.
Mythical and Legendary Accounts of the Origin of Caste, with
an inquiry into its existence in the Vedic Age. Third Edition.
21*s.*

MILITARY WORKS.

BRACKENBURY, Col. C. B., R.A. — Military Handbooks for
Regimental Officers.

> I. Military Sketching and Reconnaissance. By Col.
> F. J. Hutchison and Major H. G. MacGregor. Fifth
> Edition. With 16 Plates. Small crown 8vo, 4*s.*

> II. The Elements of Modern Tactics Practically
> applied to English Formations. By Lieut.-Col.
> Wilkinson Shaw. Seventh Edition. With 25 Plates and
> Maps. Small crown 8vo, 9*s.*

> III. Field Artillery. Its Equipment, Organization and Tactics.
> By Lieut.-Col. Sisson C. Pratt, R.A. Fourth Edition.
> Small crown 8vo, 6*s.*

> IV. The Elements of Military Administration. First
> Part : Permanent System of Administration. By Major
> J. W. Buxton. Small crown 8vo, 7*s.* 6*d.*

> V. Military Law : Its Procedure and Practice. By
> Lieut.-Col. Sisson C. Pratt, R.A. Fifth Edition. Revised.
> Small crown 8vo, 4*s.* 6*d.*

> VI. Cavalry in Modern War. By Major-General F. Chenevix
> Trench, C.M.G. Small crown 8vo, 6*s.*

> VII. Field Works. Their Technical Construction and Tactical
> Application. By the Editor, Col. C. B. Brackenbury, R.A.
> Small crown 8vo, in 2 parts, 12*s.*

BROOKE, Major, C. K. — A System of Field Training. Small
crown 8vo, cloth limp, 2*s.*

Campaign of Fredericksburg, November—December, 1862.
A Study for Officers of Volunteers. By a Line Officer. With
5 Maps and Plans. Second Edition. Crown 8vo, 5*s.*

CLERY, C. Francis, Col. — Minor Tactics. With 26 Maps and Plans.
Eighth Edition, Revised. Crown 8vo, 9*s.*

COLVILE, Lieut.-Col. C. F. — Military Tribunals. Sewed, 2*s.* 6*d.*

CRAUFURD, Capt. H. J.—Suggestions for the Military Training of a Company of Infantry. Crown 8vo, 1s. 6d.

HAMILTON, Capt. Ian, A.D.C.—The Fighting of the Future. 1s.

HARRISON, Col. R.—The Officer's Memorandum Book for Peace and War. Fourth Edition, Revised throughout. Oblong 32mo, red basil, with pencil, 3s. 6d.

Notes on Cavalry Tactics, Organisation, etc. By a Cavalry Officer. With Diagrams. Demy 8vo, 12s.

PARR, Col. H. Hallam, C.M.G.—The Dress, Horses, and Equipment of Infantry and Staff Officers. Crown 8vo, 1s.

Further Training and Equipment of Mounted Infantry. Crown 8vo, 1s.

PATERSON, Lieut.-Colonel William.—Notes on Military Surveying and Reconnaissance. Sixth Edition. With 16 Plates. Demy 8vo, 7s. 6d.

SCHAW, Col. H.—The Defence and Attack of Positions and Localities. Fourth Edition. Crown 8vo, 3s. 6d.

STONE, Capt. F. Gleadowe, R.A.—Tactical Studies from the Franco-German War of 1870-71. With 22 Lithographic Sketches and Maps. Demy 8vo, 10s. 6d.

WILKINSON, H. Spenser, Capt. 20th Lancashire R.V.—Citizen Soldiers. Essays towards the Improvement of the Volunteer Force. Crown 8vo, 2s. 6d.

EDUCATIONAL.

ABEL, Carl, Ph.D.—Linguistic Essays. Post 8vo, 9s.

Slavic and Latin. Ilchester Lectures on Comparative Lexicography. Post 8vo, 5s.

ABRAHAMS, L. B.—A Manual of Scripture History for Use in Jewish Schools and Families. With Map and Appendices. Crown 8vo, 1s. 6d.

AHN, F.—A Concise Grammar of the Dutch Language, with Selections from the best Authors in Prose and Poetry. After Dr. F. Ahn's Method. 12mo, 3s. 6d.

Practical Grammar of the German Language. Crown 8vo, 3s. 6d.

AHN, F.—continued.

New, Practical, and Easy Method of Learning the German Language. First and Second Courses in 1 vol. 12mo, 3s.

Key to Ditto. 12mo, 8d.

Manual of German and English Conversations, or Vade Mecum for English Travellers. 12mo, 1s. 6d.

New, Practical, and Easy Method of Learning the French Language. First Course and Second Course. 12mo, each 1s. 6d. The Two Courses in 1 vol. 12mo, 3s.

New, Practical, and Easy Method of Learning the French Language. Third Course, containing a French Reader, with Notes and Vocabulary. 12mo, 1s. 6d.

New, Practical, and Easy Method of Learning the Italian Language. First and Second Courses. 12mo, 3s. 6d.

Ahn's Course. Latin Grammar for Beginners. By W. IHNE, Ph.D. 12mo, 3s.

*BARANOWSKI, J. J.—*Anglo-Polish Lexicon. Fcap. 8vo, 12s.

Slownik Polsko-Angielski. (Polish-English Lexicon.) Fcap. 8vo, 12s.

*BELLOWS, John.—*French and English Dictionary for the Pocket. Containing the French-English and English-French divisions on the same page; conjugating all the verbs; distinguishing the genders by different types; giving numerous aids to pronunciation; indicating the *liaison* or *non-liaison* of terminal consonants; and translating units of weight, measure, and value by a series of tables. Second Edition. 32mo, roan, 10s. 6d.; morocco tuck, 12s. 6d.

Tous les Verbes. Conjugations of all the Verbs in the French and English Languages. 32mo, 6d.

*BOJESEN, Maria.—*A Guide to the Danish Language. Designed for English Students. 12mo, 5s.

*BOLIA, C.—*The German Caligraphist. Copies for German Handwriting. Oblong 4to, 1s.

*BOWEN, H. C., M.A.—*Studies in English. For the use of Modern Schools. Tenth Thousand. Small crown 8vo, 1s. 6d.

English Grammar for Beginners. Fcap. 8vo, 1s.

Simple English Poems. English Literature for Junior Classes. In four parts. Parts I., II., and III., 6d. each. Part IV., 1s. Complete, 3s.

BRETTE, P.H., and THOMAS, F.—French Examination Papers set at the University of London. Arranged and Edited by the Rev. P. H. ERNEST BRETTE, B.D., and FERDINAND THOMAS, B.A. Part I. Matriculation, and the General Examination for Women. Crown 8vo, 3*s.* 6*d.*

French Examination Papers set at the University of London. Key to Part I. Edited by the Rev. P. H. E. BRETTE and F. THOMAS. Crown 8vo, 5*s.*

French Examination Papers set at the University of London. Edited by the Rev. P. H. ERNEST BRETTE and FERDINAND THOMAS. Part II. Crown 8vo, 7*s.*

BUTLER, F.—The Spanish Teacher and Colloquial Phrase Book. 18mo, half-roan, 2*s.* 6*d.*

BYRNE, James.—General Principles of the Structure of Language. 2 vols. Demy 8vo, 36*s.*

The Origin of Greek, Latin, and Gothic Roots. Demy 8vo, 18*s.*

CAMERINI, E.—L'Eco Italiano. A Practical Guide to Italian Conversation. With a Vocabulary. 12mo, 4*s.* 6*d.*

CONTOPOULOS, N.—A Lexicon of Modern Greek-English and English-Modern Greek. 2 vols. 8vo, 27*s.*

CONWAY, R. Seymour.—Verner's Law in Italy. An Essay in the History of the Indo-European Sibilants. Demy 8vo, 5*s.*

The Italic Dialects. I. The Text of the Inscriptions. II. An Italic Lexicon. Edited and arranged by R. SEYMOUR CONWAY. 8vo. *[In preparation.*

DELBRÜCK, B.—Introduction to the Study of Language. The History and Methods of Comparative Philology of the Indo-European Languages. 8vo, 5*s.*

D'ORSEY, A. J. D.—A Practical Grammar of Portuguese and English. Adapted to Ollendorff's System. Fourth Edition. 12mo, 7*s.*

Colloquial Portuguese ; or, The Words and Phrases of Every-day Life. Fourth Edition. Crown 8vo, 3*s.* 6*d.*

DUSAR, P. Friedrich.—A Grammar of the German Language. With Exercises. Second Edition. Crown 8vo, 4*s.* 6*d.*

A Grammatical Course of the German Language. Third Edition. Crown 8vo, 3*s.* 6*d.*

Education Library. Edited by Sir PHILIP MAGNUS :—

An Introduction to the History of Educational Theories. By OSCAR BROWNING, M.A. Second Edition. 3*s.* 6*d.*

Education Library—*continued.*

Industrial Education. By Sir PHILIP MAGNUS. 6*s.*

Old Greek Education. By the Rev. Prof. MAHAFFY, M.A. Second Edition. 3*s.* 6*d.*

School Management. Including a general view of the work of Education, Organization, and Discipline. By JOSEPH LANDON. Seventh Edition. 6*s.*

EGER, Gustav.—Technological Dictionary in the English and German Languages. Edited by GUSTAV EGER. 2 vols. Royal 8vo, £1 7*s.*

ELLIS, Robert.—Sources of the Etruscan and Basque Languages. Demy 8vo, 7*s.* 6*d.*

FRIEDRICH, P.—Progressive German Reader. With Copious Notes to the First Part. Crown 8vo, 4*s.* 6*d.*

FRŒMBLING, Friedrich Otto.—Graduated German Reader. A Selection from the most Popular Writers ; with a Vocabulary for the First Part. Tenth Edition. 12mo, 3*s.* 6*d.*

Graduated Exercises for Translation into German. Consisting of Extracts from the best English Authors; with Idiomatic Notes. Crown 8vo, 4*s.* 6*d.* Without Notes, 4*s.*

GARLANDA, Federico.—The Fortunes of Words. Letters to a Lady. Crown 8vo, 5*s.*

The Philosophy of Words. A Popular Introduction to the Science of Language. Crown 8vo, 5*s.*

GELDART, E. M.—A Guide to Modern Greek. Post 8vo, 7*s.* 6*d.* Key, 2*s.* 6*d.*

GOWAN, Major Walter E.—A. Ivanoff's Russian Grammar. (16th Edition.) Translated, enlarged, and arranged for use of Students of the Russian Language. Demy 8vo, 6*s.*

HODGSON, W. B.—The Education of Girls; and the Employment of Women of the Upper Classes Educationally considered. Second Edition. Crown 8vo, 3*s.* 6*d.*

KARCHER, Theodore.—Questionnaire Francais. Questions on French Grammar, Idiomatic Difficulties, and Military Expressions. Fourth Edition. Crown 8vo, 4*s.* 6*d.* ; interleaved with writing-paper, 5*s.* 6*d.*

LANDON, Joseph.—School Management ; Including a General View of the Work of Education, Organization, and Discipline. Seventh Edition. Crown 8vo, 6*s.*

LANGE, F. K. W.—Germania. A German Reading-Book Arranged Progressively. Part I. Anthology of German Prose and Poetry, with Vocabulary and Biographical Notes. 8vo, 3*s.* 6*d.* Part II. Essays on German History and Institutions, with Notes. 8vo, 3*s.* 6*d.* Parts I. and II. together, 5*s.* 6*d.*

LANGE, F. K. W.—continued.
    German Grammar Practice. Crown 8vo, 1*s.* 6*d.*
    Colloquial German Grammar. Crown 8vo, 4*s.* 6*d.*

LE-BRUN, L.—Materials for Translating from English into French. Seventh Edition. Post 8vo, 4*s.* 6*d.*

Little French Reader (The). Extracted from "The Modern French Reader." Third Edition. Crown 8vo, 2*s.*

MAGNUS, Sir Philip.—Industrial Education. Crown 8vo, 6*s.*

MASON, Charlotte M.—Home Education : a Course of Lectures to Ladies. Crown 8vo, 3*s.* 6*d.*

MILLHOUSE, John.—Pronouncing and Explanatory English and Italian Dictionary. 2 vols. 8vo, 12*s.*

    Manual of Italian Conversation. 18mo, 2*s.*

Modern French Reader (The). A Glossary of Idioms, Gallicisms, and other Difficulties contained in the Senior Course of the Modern French Reader. By CHARLES CASSAL. Crown 8vo, 2*s.* 6*d.*

Modern French Reader (The). Prose. Junior Course. Tenth Edition. Edited by CH. CASSAL and THÉODORE KARCHER. Crown 8vo, 2*s.* 6*d.*

    Senior Course. Third Edition. Crown 8vo, 4*s.*

Modern French Reader. Senior Course and Glossary combined. 6*s.*

NUGENT.—Improved French and English and English and French Pocket Dictionary. 24mo, 3*s.*

OLLENDORFF.—Metodo para aprender a Leer, escribir y hablar el Inglés segun el sistema de Ollendorff. Por RAMON PALENZUELA y JUAN DE LA CARREÑO. 8vo, 4*s.* 6*d.* Key to ditto. Crown 8vo, 3*s.*

    Metodo para aprender a Leer, escribir y hablar el Frances, segun el verdadero sistema de Ollendorff. Por TEODORO SIMONNÉ. Crown 8vo, 6*s.* Key to ditto. Crown 8vo, 3*s.* 6*d.*

OTTÉ, E. C.—Dano-Norwegian Grammar. A Manual for Students of Danish based on the Ollendorffian System. Third Edition. Crown 8vo, 7*s.* 6*d.* Key to above. Crown 8vo, 3*s.*

PONSARD, F.—Charlotte Corday. A Tragedy. Edited, with English Notes and Notice on Ponsard, by Professor C. CASSAL, LL.D. Third Edition. 12mo, 2*s.* 6*d.*

    L'Honneur et l'Argent. A Comedy. Edited, with English Notes and Memoir of Ponsard, by Professor C. CASSAL, LL.D. Second Edition. 12mo, 3*s.* 6*d.*

RASK, Erasmus.—Grammar of the Anglo-Saxon Tongue. from the Danish of ERASMUS RASK. By BENJAMIN THORPE. Third Edition. Post 8vo, 5*s.* 6*d.*

RIOLA, Henry.—How to Learn Russian. A Manual for Students, based upon the Ollendorffian System. With Preface by W. R. S. RALSTON. Fourth Edition. Crown 8vo, 12*s*.

　　Key to the above. Crown 8vo, 5*s*.

A Graduated Russian Reader. With a Vocabulary. Crown 8vo, 10*s*. 6*d*.

ROCHE, A.—A French Grammar. Adopted for the Public Schools by the Imperial Council of Public Instruction. Crown 8vo, 3*s*.

Prose and Poetry. Select Pieces from the best English Authors, for Reading, Composition, and Translation. Second Edition. Fcap. 8vo, 2*s*. 6*d*.

ROSING, S.—English-Danish Dictionary. Crown 8vo, 8*s*. 6*d*.

SAYCE, A. H.—An Assyrian Grammar for Comparative Purposes. Crown 8vo, 7*s*. 6*d*.

The Principles of Comparative Philology. Third Edition. Crown 8vo, 10*s*. 6*d*.

SINCLAIR, F.—A German Vocabulary. Crown 8vo, 2*s*.

SMITH, M., and HORNEMAN, H.—Norwegian Grammar. With a Glossary for Tourists. Post 8vo, 2*s*.

THOMPSON, A. R.—Dialogues, Russian and English. Crown 8vo, 5*s*.

TOSCANI, Giovanni.—Italian Conversational Course. Fourth Edition. 12mo, 5*s*.

Italian Reading Course. Fcap. 8vo, 4*s*. 6*d*.

Trübner's Catalogue of Dictionaries and Grammars of the Principal Languages and Dialects of the World. Second Edition. 8vo, 5*s*.

Trübner's Collection of Simplified Grammars of the Principal Asiatic and European Languages. Edited by REINHOLD ROST, LL.D. Crown 8vo.

　　I.　Hindustani, Persian, and Arabic. By E. H. PALMER. Second Edition. 5*s*.

　　II.　Hungarian. By I. SINGER. 4*s*. 6*d*.

　　III.　Basque. By W. VAN EYS. 3*s*. 6*d*.

　　IV.　Malagasy. By G. W. PARKER. 5*s*.

　　V.　Modern Greek. By E. M. GELDART. 2*s*. 6*d*.

　　VI.　Roumanian. By R. TORCEANU. 5*s*.

　　VII.　Tibetan Grammar. By H. A. JÄSCHKE. 5*s*.

　　VIII.　Danish. By E. C. OTTÉ. 2*s*. 6*d*.

　　IX.　Turkish. By J. W. REDHOUSE. 10*s*. 6*d*.

Trübner's Collection of Simplified Grammars of the Principal Asiatic and European Languages—*continued.*

X. Swedish. By E. C. OTTÉ. 2*s.* 6*d.*

XI. Polish. By W. R. MORFILL. 3*s.* 6*d.*

XII. Pali. By E. MÜLLER. 7*s.* 6*d.*

XIII. Sanskrit. By H. EDGREN. 10*s.* 6*d.*

XIV. Grammaire Albanaise. Par P. W. 7*s.* 6*d.*

XV. Japanese. By B. H. CHAMBERLAIN. 5*s.*

XVI. Serbian. By W. R. MORFILL. 4*s.* 6*d.*

XVII. Cuneiform Inscriptions. By GEORGE BERTIN, 5*s.*

XVIII. Panjābī Language. By the Rev. W. ST. CLAIR TISDALL. 7*s.* 6*d.*

XIX. Spanish. By W. F. HARVEY. 3*s.* 6*d.*

VAN LAUN.—Grammar of the French Language. Crown 8vo. Parts I. and II. Accidence and Syntax. 4*s.* Part III. Exercises. 3*s.* 6*d.*

VELASQUEZ, M., de la Cadena.—A Dictionary of the Spanish and English Languages. For the Use of Young Learners and Travellers. In 2 parts. I. Spanish-English. II. English-Spanish. Crown 8vo, 6*s.*

A Pronouncing Dictionary of the Spanish and English Languages. 2 parts in one volume. Royal 8vo, £1 4*s.*

New Spanish Reader. Passages from the most approved Authors, in Prose and Verse. With Vocabulary. Post 8vo, 6*s.*

An Easy Introduction to Spanish Conversation. 12mo, 2*s.* 6*d.*

VELASQUEZ and SIMONNÉ.—New Method to Read, Write, and Speak the Spanish Language. Adapted to Ollendorff's System. Post 8vo, 6*s.* Key. Post 8vo, 4*s.*

VIEYRA.—A New Pocket Dictionary of the Portuguese and English Languages. In 2 parts. Portuguese-English and English-Portuguese. 2 vols. Post 8vo, 10*s.*

WELLER, E.—An Improved Dictionary. English and French, and French and English. Royal 8vo, 7*s.* 6*d.*

WHITNEY, W. D.—Language and the Study of Language. Twelve Lectures on the Principles of Linguistic Science. Fourth Edition. Crown 8vo, 10*s.* 6*d.*

Language and its Study, with especial reference to the Indo-European Family of Languages. Lectures. Edited by the Rev. R. MORRIS, LL.D. Second Edition. Crown 8vo, 5*s.*

WHITNEY, *Prof. William Dwight.*—Essentials of English Grammar, for the Use of Schools. Second Edition. Crown 8vo, 3s. 6d.

YOUMANS, *Eliza A.*—First Book of Botany. Designed to cultivate the Observing Powers of Children. With 300 Engravings. New and Cheaper Edition. Crown 8vo, 2s. 6d.

POETRY.

ADAMS, *Estelle Davenport.*—Sea Song and River Rhyme, from Chaucer to Tennyson. With 12 Etchings. Large crown 8vo, 10s. 6d.

ALEXANDER, *William, D.D., Bishop of Derry.*—St. Augustine's Holiday, and other Poems. Crown 8vo, 6s.

ARNOLD, *Sir Edwin, C.S.I.*—In my Lady's Praise. Being Poems Old and New, written to the Honour of Fanny, Lady Arnold. Imperial 16mo, parchment, 3s. 6d.

Poems: National and Non-Oriental. With some New Pieces. Selected from the Works of Sir EDWIN ARNOLD, C.S.I. Crown 8vo, 7s. 6d.

**** See also under ORIENTAL.

BADDELEY, *St. Clair.*—Lotus Leaves. Fcap. folio, boards, 8s. 6d.

BARNES, *William.*—Poems of Rural Life, in the Dorset Dialect. New Edition, complete in one vol. Crown 8vo, 6s.

BLUNT, *Wilfrid Scawen.* — The Wind and the Whirlwind. Demy 8vo, 1s. 6d.

The Love Sonnets of Proteus. Fifth Edition. Elzevir 8vo, 5s.

In Vinculis. With Portrait. Elzevir 8vo, 5s.

A New Pilgrimage, and other Poems. Elzevir 8vo, 5s.

BRYANT, *W. C.*—Poems. Cheap Edition, with Frontispiece. Small crown 8vo, 3s. 6d.

CODD, *John.*—A Legend of the Middle Ages, and other Songs of the Past and Present. Crown 8vo, 4s.

DASH, *Blancor.*—Tales of a Tennis Party. Small crown 8vo, 5s.

DAWE, *William.*—Sketches in Verse. Small crown 8vo, 3s. 6d.

DAWSON, *C. A.*—Sappho. Small crown 8vo, 5s.

DE VERE, Aubrey.—Poetical Works.

    I. THE SEARCH AFTER PROSERPINE, etc. 3s. 6d.
    II. THE LEGENDS OF ST. PATRICK, etc. 3s. 6d.
    III. ALEXANDER THE GREAT, etc. 3s. 6d.

The Foray of Queen Meave, and other Legends of Ireland's Heroic Age. Small crown 8vo, 3s. 6d.

Legends of the Saxon Saints. Small crown 8vo, 3s. 6d.

Legends and Records of the Church and the Empire. Small crown 8vo, 3s. 6d.

DOBSON, Austin.—Old World Idylls, and other Verses. Elzevir 8vo, gilt top, 6s.

At the Sign of the Lyre. Elzevir 8vo, gilt top, 6s.

DOYLE, J.—Cause. Small crown 8vo, 6s.

DURANT, Héloïse.—Dante. A Dramatic Poem. Small crown 8vo, 5s.

DUTT, Toru.—A Sheaf Gleaned in French Fields. Demy 8vo, 10s. 6d.

Ancient Ballads and Legends of Hindustan. With an Introductory Memoir by EDMUND GOSSE. 18mo. Cloth extra, gilt top, 5s.

Elegies and Memorials. By A. and L. Fcap. 8vo, 2s. 6d.

ELLIOTT, Ebenezer, The Corn Law Rhymer.—Poems. Edited by his son, the Rev. EDWIN ELLIOTT, of St. John's, Antigua. 2 vols. Crown 8vo, 18s.

English Verse. Edited by W. J. LINTON and R. H. STODDARD. 5 vols. Crown 8vo, cloth, 5s. each.

    I. CHAUCER TO BURNS.
    II. TRANSLATIONS.
    III. LYRICS OF THE NINETEENTH CENTURY.
    IV. DRAMATIC SCENES AND CHARACTERS.
    V. BALLADS AND ROMANCES.

FIFE-COOKSON, Lieut.-Col.—The Empire of Man. Small crown 8vo, 2s. 6d.

GARRICK, H. B. W.—India. A Descriptive Poem. Crown 8vo, 7s. 6d.

GOSSE, Edmund.—New Poems. Crown 8vo, 7s. 6d.

Firdausi in Exile, and other Poems. Second Edition. Elzevir 8vo, gilt top, 6s.

On Viol and Flute: Lyrical Poems. With Frontispiece by L. ALMA TADEMA, R.A., and Tailpiece by HAMO THORNYCROFT, R.A. Elzevir 8vo, 6s.

G

GRAY, Maxwell.—Westminster Chimes, and other Poems. Small crown 8vo, 5*s.*

GURNEY, Rev. Alfred.—The Vision of the Eucharist, and other Poems. Crown 8vo, 5*s.*

A Christmas Faggot. Small crown 8vo, 5*s.*

Voices from the Holy Sepulchre. Crown 8vo, 5*s.*

HARRISON, Clifford.—In Hours of Leisure. Second Edition. Crown 8vo, 5*s.*

HEINE, Heinrich.—The Love-Songs of. Englished by H. B. BRIGGS. Post 8vo, parchment, 3*s.* 6*d.*

HUES, Ivan.—Heart to Heart. Small crown 8vo, 5*s.*

INGLEBY, Holcombe.—Echoes from Naples, and Other Poems. With Illustrations by his Wife. Crown 8vo, 3*s.* 6*d.*

KEATS, John.—Poetical Works. Edited by W. T. ARNOLD. Large crown 8vo, choicely printed on hand-made paper, with Portrait in *eau-forte.* Parchment or cloth, 12*s.* ; vellum, 15*s.* New Edition. Crown 8vo, cloth, 3*s.* 6*d.*

KING, Mrs. Hamilton.—The Disciples. Tenth Edition. Small crown 8vo, 5*s.* Elzevir Edition. Cloth extra, 6*s.*

A Book of Dreams. Third Edition. Crown 8vo, 3*s.* 6*d.*

The Sermon in the Hospital (from "The Disciples"). Fcap. 8vo, 1*s.* Cheap Edition for distribution 3*d.*, or 20*s.* per 100.

Ballads of the North, and other Poems. Crown 8vo, 5*s.*

LANG, A.—XXXII. Ballades in Blue China. Elzevir 8vo, 5*s.*

Rhymes à la Mode. With Frontispiece by E. A. ABBEY. Second Edition. Elzevir 8vo, cloth extra, gilt top, 5*s.*

Living English Poets MDCCCLXXXII. With Frontispiece by WALTER CRANE. Second Edition. Large crown 8vo. Printed on hand-made paper. Parchment or cloth, 12*s.* ; vellum, 15*s.*

LOCKER, F.—London Lyrics. Tenth Edition. With Portrait, Elzevir 8vo, cloth extra, gilt top, 5*s.*

LULWORTH, Eric.—Sunshine and Shower, and other Poems. Small crown 8vo, 5*s.*

LYALL, Sir Alfred.—Verses written in India. Elzevir 8vo, gilt top, 5*s.*

MASSEY, Gerald.—My Lyrical Life. Poems Old and New. Two Series. Fcap. 8vo, 5*s.* each.

MEREDITH, Owen [The Earl of Lytton].—Lucile. New Edition. With 32 Illustrations. 16mo, 3*s.* 6*d.* Cloth extra, gilt edges, 4*s.* 6*d.*

MORRIS, *Lewis.*—**Poetical Works of.** New and Cheaper Editions. In 5 vols., 5*s.* each.

Vol. I. contains "Songs of Two Worlds." Thirteenth Edition.
Vol. II. contains "The Epic of Hades." Twenty-third Edition.
Vol. III. contains "Gwen" and "The Ode of Life." Seventh Edition.
Vol. IV. contains "Songs Unsung" and "Gycia." Fifth Edition.
Vol. V. contains "Songs of Britain." Third Edition. Fcap. 8vo, 5*s.*

Poetical Works. Complete in 1 vol. Crown 8vo, 6*s.*

The Epic of Hades. With 16 Autotype Illustrations, after the Drawings of the late George R. Chapman. 4to, cloth extra, gilt leaves, 21*s.*

The Epic of Hades. Presentation Edition. 4to, cloth extra, gilt leaves, 10*s.* 6*d.*

The Lewis Morris Birthday Book. Edited by S. S. COPE-MAN, with Frontispiece after a Design by the late George R. Chapman. 32mo, cloth extra, gilt edges, 2*s.* ; cloth limp, 1*s.* 6*d.*

OWEN, *John.*—**Verse Musings on Nature.** Faith and Freedom. Crown 8vo, 7*s.* 6*d.*

PFEIFFER, *Emily.*—**Flowers of the Night.** Crown 8vo, 6*s.*

PIERCE, *J.*—**In Cloud and Sunshine.** A Volume of Poems. Fcap. 8vo, 5*s.*

POE, *Edgar Allan.*—**The Raven.** With Commentary by JOHN H. INGRAM. Crown 8vo, parchment, 6*s.*

Rare Poems of the 16th and 17th Centuries. Edited by W. J. LINTON. Crown 8vo, 5*s.*

ROWBOTHAM, *J. F.*—**The Human Epic.** Canto i. Crown 8vo, 1*s.* 6*d.*

RUNEBERG, *Johan Ludvig.*—**Nadeschda.** A Romantic Poem in Nine Cantos. Translated from the Swedish by Miss MARIE A. BROWN (Mrs. JOHN B. SHIPLEY). With Illustrations. 8vo.
[In preparation.

SCOTT, *G. F. E.*—**Sursum Corda** ; or, Songs and Service. Small crown 8vo, 5*s.*

SEARELLE, *Luscombe.*—**The Dawn of Death.** Crown 8vo, 4*s.* 6*d.*

SYMONDS, *John Addington.*—**Vagabunduli Libellus.** Crown 8vo, 6*s.*

TAYLOR, *Sir H.*—**Works.** Complete in Five Volumes. Crown 8vo, 30*s.*

Philip Van Artevelde. Fcap. 8vo, 3*s.* 6*d.*

The Virgin Widow, etc. Fcap. 8vo, 3*s.* 6*d.*

TRENCH, Archbishop.—**Poems.** Collected and Arranged anew. Tenth Edition. Fcap, 8vo, 7s. 6d.

Poems. Library Edition. 2 vols. Small crown 8vo, 10s.

Sacred Latin Poetry. Chiefly Lyrical, Selected and Arranged for Use. Third Edition, Corrected and Improved. Fcap. 8vo, 7s.

Twilight and Candleshades. By Exul. With 15 Vignettes. Small crown 8vo, 5s.

TYNAN, Katherine.—**Louise de la Valliere,** and other Poems. Small crown 8vo, 3s. 6d.

Shamrocks. Small crown 8vo, 5s.

WADDIE, John.—**Divine Philosophy.** Small crown 8vo, 5s.

WILSON, Crawford.—**Pastorals and Poems.** Crown 8vo, 7s. 6d.

Wordsworth Birthday Book (The). Edited by Adelaide and Violet Wordsworth. 32mo, limp cloth, 1s. 6d. ; cloth extra, 2s.

Wordsworth, Selections from. By Wm. Knight and other members of the Wordsworth Society. Large crown 8vo. Printed on hand-made paper. With Portrait. Parchment, 12s. ; vellum, 15s.

YEATS, W. B.—**The Wanderings of Oisin,** and other Poems. Small crown 8vo, 5s.

NOVELS AND TALES.

BANKS, Mrs. G. L.—**God's Providence House.** Crown 8vo, 6s.

BILLER, Emma.—**Ulli.** The Story of a Neglected Girl. Translated from the German by A. B. Daisy Rost. Crown 8vo, 6s.

CABLE, G. W.—**Strange True Stories of Louisiana.** 8vo, 7s. 6d.

CAIRD, Mona.—**The Wing of Azrael.** Crown 8vo, 6s.

COLERIDGE, Hon. Stephen.—**The Sanctity of Confession.** A Romance. Crown 8vo, 5s.

CRAWFURD, Oswald.—**Sylvia Arden.** With Frontispiece. Crown 8vo, 1s.

DERING, Ross George.—**Giraldi ;** or, The Curse of Love. A Tale of the Sects. 2 vols. Crown 8vo, 12s.

EBERS, Georg.—**Margery.** A Tale of Old Nuremberg. Translated from the German by Clara Bell. 2 vols. 8s. ; paper, 5s.

ECKSTEIN, Ernst.—**Nero.** A Romance. Translated from the German by CLARA BELL and MARY J. SAFFORD. 2 vols. Paper, 5*s.*

FLETCHER, J. S.—**Andrewlina.** Crown 8vo, cloth, 1*s.* 6*d.* ; paper covers, 1*s.*

The Winding Way. Crown 8vo.

FRANCIS, Frances.—**Mosquito.** A Tale of the Mexican Frontier. Crown 8vo, 3*s.* 6*d.*

GALDOS, B. Perez.—**Leon Roche.** A Romance. From the Spanish by CLARA BELL. 2 vols. 16mo, cloth, 8*s.* ; paper, 5*s.*

GARDINER, Linda.—**His Heritage.** With Frontispiece. Crown 8vo, 6*s.*

GRAY, Maxwell.—**The Reproach of Annesley.** With Frontispiece. Crown 8vo, 6*s.*

Silence of Dean Maitland. With Frontispiece. Crown 8vo, 6*s.*

GREY, Rowland.—**In Sunny Switzerland.** A Tale of Six Weeks. Second Edition. Small crown 8vo, 5*s.*

Lindenblumen and other Stories. Small crown 8vo, 5*s.*

By Virtue of his Office. Crown 8vo, 6*s.*

Jacob's Letter, and other Stories. Crown 8vo, 6*s.*

HARRIS, Emily Marion.—**Lady Dobbs.** A Novel. In 2 vols. 21*s.*

HUNTER, Hay, and WHYTE, Walter.—**My Ducats and My Daughter.** With Frontispiece. Crown 8vo, 6*s.*

INGELOW, Jean.—**Off the Skelligs.** A Novel. With Frontispiece. Crown 8vo, 6*s.*

LANG, Andrew.—**In the Wrong Paradise, and other Stories.** Crown 8vo, 6*s.*

MACDONALD, G.—**Donal Grant.** A Novel. With Frontispiece. Crown 8vo, 6*s.*

Home Again. With Frontispiece. Crown 8vo, 6*s.*

Castle Warlock. A Novel. With Frontispiece. Crown 8vo, 6*s.*

Malcolm. With Portrait of the Author engraved on Steel. Crown 8vo, 6*s.*

The Marquis of Lossie. With Frontispiece. Crown 8vo, 6*s.*

St. George and St. Michael. With Frontispiece. Crown 8vo, 6*s.*

What's Mine's Mine. With Frontispiece. Crown 8vo, 6*s.*

Annals of a Quiet Neighbourhood. With Frontispiece. Crown 8vo, 6*s.*

The Seaboard Parish : a Sequel to "Annals of a Quiet Neighbourhood." With Frontispiece. Crown 8vo, 6*s.*

MACDONALD, G.—continued.

Wilfred Cumbermede. An Autobiographical Story. With Frontispiece. Crown 8vo, 6s.

Thomas Wingfold, Curate. With Frontispiece. Crown 8vo, 6s.

Paul Faber, Surgeon. With Frontispiece. Crown 8vo, 6s.

The Elect Lady. With Frontispiece. Crown 8vo, 6s.

MALET, Lucas.—**Colonel Enderby's Wife.** A Novel. With Frontispiece. Crown 8vo, 6s.

A Counsel of Perfection. With Frontispiece. Crown 8vo, 6s.

MULHOLLAND, Rosa.—**Marcella Grace.** An Irish Novel. Crown 8vo, 6s.

A Fair Emigrant. With Frontispiece. Crown 8vo, 6s.

OGLE, Anna C.—**A Lost Love.** Small crown 8vo, 2s. 6d.

PONTOPIDDAN, Henrik. — **The Apothecary's Daughters.** Translated from the Danish by GORDIUS NIELSEN. Crown 8vo, 3s. 6d.

ROBINSON, Sir J. C.—**The Dead Sailor,** and other Stories. Crown 8vo, 5s.

SAVILE, Ames.—**A Match Pair.** 2 vols. 21s.

SEVERNE, Florence.—**The Pillar House.** With Frontispiece. Crown 8vo, 6s.

SHAW, Flora L.—**Castle Blair:** a Story of Youthful Days. Crown 8vo, 3s. 6d.

STRETTON, Hesba.—**Through a Needle's Eye.** A Story. With Frontispiece. Crown 8vo, 6s.

TASMA.—**A Sydney Sovereign,** and other Tales. Crown 8vo, cloth, 6s.

Uncle Piper of Piper's Hill. An Australian Novel. Third Edition. Crown 8vo, 6s.

In her Earliest Youth. 3 vols. Crown 8vo, 31s. 6d.

TAYLOR, Col. Meadows, C.S.I., M.R.I.A.—**Seeta.** A Novel. With Frontispiece. Crown 8vo, 6s.

Tippoo Sultaun: a Tale of the Mysore War. With Frontispiece. Crown 8vo, 6s.

Ralph Darnell. With Frontispiece. Crown 8vo, 6s.

A Noble Queen. With Frontispiece. Crown 8vo, 6s.

The Confessions of a Thug. With Frontispiece. Crown 8vo, 6s.

Tara: a Mahratta Tale. With Frontispiece. Crown 8vo, 6s.

TOORGEYNIEFF, Ivan.—The Unfortunate One. A Novel. Translated from the Russian by A. R. THOMPSON. Crown 8vo, 3s. 6d.

TREHERNE, Mrs.—A Summer in a Dutch Country House. Crown 8vo, 6s.

Within Sound of the Sea. With Frontispiece. Crown 8vo, 6s.

BOOKS FOR THE YOUNG.

Brave Men's Footsteps. A Book of Example and Anecdote for Young People. By the Editor of "Men who have Risen." With 4 Illustrations by C. DOYLE. Ninth Edition. Crown 8vo, 2s. 6d.

COXHEAD, Ethel.—Birds and Babies. With 33 Illustrations. Second Edition. Imp. 16mo, cloth, 1s.

DAVIES, G. Christopher.—Rambles and Adventures of our School Field Club. With 4 Illustrations. New and Cheaper Edition. Crown 8vo, 3s. 6d.

EDMONDS, Herbert.—Well-Spent Lives: a Series of Modern Biographies. New and Cheaper Edition. Crown 8vo, 3s. 6d.

MAC KENNA, S. J.—Plucky Fellows. A Book for Boys. With 6 Illustrations. Fifth Edition. Crown 8vo, 3s. 6d.

MALET, Lucas.—Little Peter. A Christmas Morality for Children of any Age. With numerous Illustrations. Fourth Thousand. 5s.

REANEY, Mrs. G. S.—Waking and Working; or, From Girlhood to Womanhood. New and Cheaper Edition. With a Frontispiece. Crown 8vo, 3s. 6d.

    Blessing and Blessed: a Sketch of Girl Life. New and Cheaper Edition. Crown 8vo, 3s. 6d.

    Rose Gurney's Discovery. A Story for Girls. Dedicated to their Mothers. Crown 8vo, 3s. 6d.

    English Girls: their Place and Power. With Preface by the Rev. R. W. Dale. Fifth Edition. Fcap. 8vo, 2s. 6d.

    Just Anyone, and other Stories. Three Illustrations. Royal 16mo, 1s. 6d.

    Sunbeam Willie, and other Stories. Three Illustrations. Royal 16mo, 1s. 6d.

    Sunshine Jenny, and other Stories. Three Illustrations. Royal 16mo, 1s. 6d.

STORR, Francis, and TURNER, Hawes.—Canterbury Chimes; or, Chaucer Tales re-told to Children. With 6 Illustrations from the Ellesmere Manuscript. Third Edition. Fcap. 8vo, 3s. 6d.

 A List of

STRETTON, *Hesba.*—David Lloyd's Last Will. With 4 Illustrations. New Edition. Royal 16mo, 2*s.* 6*d.*

WHITAKER, *Florence.*—Christy's Inheritance. A London Story. Illustrated. Royal 16mo, 1*s.* 6*d.*

PERIODICALS.

Amateur Mechanical Society's Journal.—Irregular.

Anthropological Institute of Great Britain and Ireland (Journal of).—Quarterly, 5*s.*

Architect (American) and Building News.—Contains General Architectural News, Articles on Interior Decoration, Sanitary Engineering, Construction, Building Materials, etc. 4 full-page Illustrations accompany each Number. Weekly. Annual Subscription, 38*s.* Post free.

Bibliotheca Sacra.—Quarterly, 3*s.* 6*d.* Annual Subscription, 14*s.* Post free.

British Archæological Association (Journal of).--Quarterly, 8*s.*

British Chess Magazine.—Monthly, 8*d.*

British Homœopathic Society (Annals of).—Half-yearly, 2*s.* 6*d.*

Browning Society's Papers.—Irregular.

Calcutta Review.—Quarterly, 6*s.* Annual Subscription, 24*s.* Post free.

Cambridge Philological Society (Proceedings of).—Irregular.

Englishwoman's Review. — Social and Industrial Questions. Monthly, 6*d.*

Geological Magazine, or Monthly Journal of Geology, 1*s.* 6*d.* Annual Subscription, 18*s.* Post free.

Index Medicus.—A Monthly Classified Record of the Current Medical Literature of the World. Annual Subscription, 50*s.* Post free.

Indian Antiquary.—A Journal of Oriental Research in Archæology, History, Literature, Languages, Philosophy, Religion, Folk-Lore, etc. Annual Subscription, £2. Post free.

Indian Evangelical Review.—Annual Subscription, 10*s.*

Indian Magazine. Monthly, 6*d.*

Library Journal.—Official Organ of the Library Associations of America and of the United Kingdom. Monthly, 2*s.* 6*d.* Annual Subscription, 20*s.*, or with Co-operative Index, 25*s.* Post free.

Mathematics (American Journal of).—Quarterly, 7s. 6d. Annual Subscription, 24s. Post free.

Meister (The).—Journal of the Wagner Society. 4to, 1s.

Nineteenth Century.—Monthly, 2s. 6d.

Orientalist (The).—Monthly. Annual Subscription, 12s.

Orthodox Catholic Review.—Irregular.

Philological Society (Transactions and Proceedings of).—Irregular.

Psychical Research (Society of), Proceedings of.

Publishers' Weekly: The American Book-Trade Journal.—Annual Subscription, 18s. Post free.

Punjab Notes and Queries.—Monthly. Annual Subscription, 10s.

Revue Internationale.—Issued on the 10th and 25th of each Month. Annual Subscription, including postage, 36s.

Scientific American.—Weekly. Annual Subscription, 18s. Post free.

Supplement to ditto.—Weekly. Annual Subscription, 25s. Post free.

Science and Arts (American Journal of).—Monthly, 2s. 6d. Annual Subscription, 30s.

Speculative Philosophy (Journal of).—Quarterly, 4s. Annual Subscription, 16s. Post free, 17s.

Sun Artists.—Quarterly, 5s.

Sunday Review.—Organ of the Sunday Society for Opening Museums and Art Galleries on Sunday. Quarterly, 1s. Annual Subscription, 4s. 6d. Post free.

Theosophist (The).—Magazine of Oriental Philosophy, Art, Literature, and Occultism. Monthly, 2s.

Trübner's Record.—A Journal devoted to the Literature of the East, with Notes and Lists of Current American, European, and Colonial Publications. Small 4to, 2s. per number. Annual Subscription, 10s. Post free.

MESSRS.

KEGAN PAUL, TRENCH, TRÜBNER & CO.'S

(LIMITED)

EDITIONS OF

SHAKSPERE'S WORKS.

THE PARCHMENT LIBRARY EDITION.

THE AVON EDITION.

The Text of these Editions is mainly that of Delius.   Wherever a variant reading is adopted, some good and recognized Shaksperian Critic has been followed.   In no case is a new rendering of the text proposed; nor has it been thought necessary to distract the reader's attention by notes or comments

[P. T. O.

SHAKSPERE'S WORKS.

THE AVON EDITION.

Printed on thin opaque paper, and forming 12 handy volumes, cloth, 18*s.*, or bound in 6 volumes, 15*s.*

The set of 12 volumes may also be had in a cloth box, price 21*s.*, or bound in Roan, Persian, Crushed Persian Levant, Calf, or Morocco, and enclosed in an attractive leather box at prices from 31*s.* 6*d.* upwards.

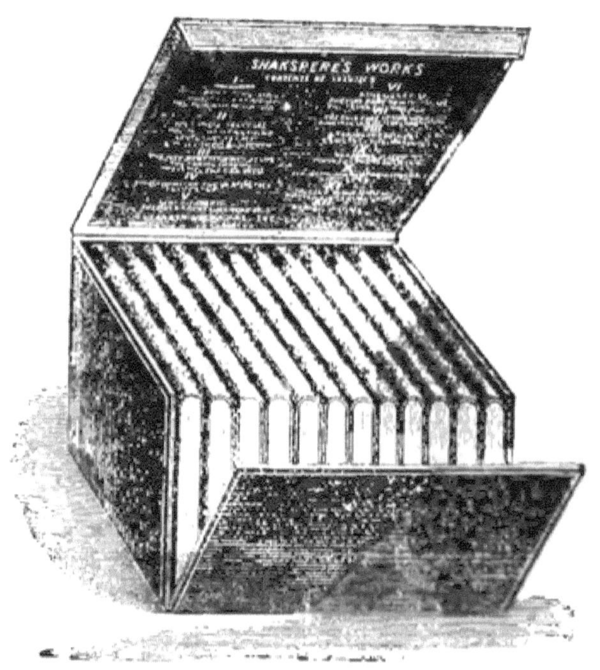

SOME PRESS NOTICES.

"This edition will be useful to those who want a good text, well and clearly printed, in convenient little volumes that will slip easily into an overcoat pocket or a travelling-bag."—*St. James's Gazette.*

"We know no prettier edition of Shakspere for the price."—*Academy.*

"It is refreshing to meet with an edition of Shakspere of convenient size and low price, without either notes or introductions of any sort to distract the attention of the reader."—*Saturday Review.*

"It is exquisite. Each volume is handy, is beautifully printed, and in every way lends itself to the taste of the cultivated student of Shakspere."—*Scotsman.*

LONDON : KEGAN PAUL, TRENCH, TRÜBNER & CO., LTD.

SHAKSPERE'S WORKS.

THE PARCHMENT LIBRARY EDITION.

In 12 volumes Elzevir 8vo., choicely printed on hand-made paper, and bound in parchment or cloth, price £3 12s., or in vellum, price £4 10s.

The set of 12 volumes may also be had in a strong cloth box, price £3 17s., or with an oak hanging shelf, £3 18s.

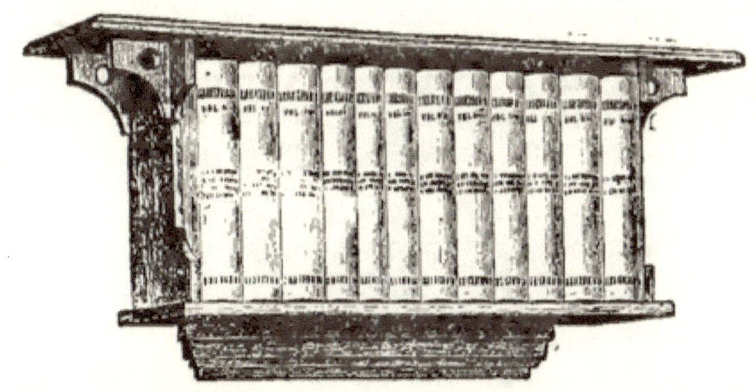

SOME PRESS NOTICES.

". . . There is, perhaps, no edition in which the works of Shakspere can be read in such luxury of type and quiet distinction of form as this, and we warmly recommend it."—*Pall Mall Gazette.*

"For elegance of form and beauty of typography, no edition of Shakspere hitherto published has excelled the 'Parchment Library Edition.' . . . They are in the strictest sense pocket volumes, yet the type is bold, and, being on fine white hand-made paper, can hardly tax the weakest of sight. The print is judiciously confined to the text, notes being more appropriate to library editions. The whole will be comprised in the cream-coloured parchment which gives the name to the series."—*Daily News.*

"The Parchment Library Edition of Shakspere needs no further praise."—*Saturday Review.*

Just published. Price 5s.

AN INDEX TO THE WORKS OF SHAKSPERE.

Applicable to all editions of Shakspere, and giving reference, by topics, to notable passages and significant expressions; brief histories of the plays; geographical names and historic incidents; mention of all characters and sketches of important ones; together with explanations of allusions and obscure and obsolete words and phrases.

By EVANGELINE M. O'CONNOR.

LONDON: KEGAN PAUL, TRENCH, TRÜBNER & CO., LT^D.

SHAKSPERE'S WORKS.

SPECIMEN OF TYPE.

  Salar.   My wind, cooling my broth,
Would blow me to an ague, when I thought
What harm a wind too great might do at sea.
I should not see the sandy hour-glass run
But I should think of shallows and of flats,
And see my wealthy Andrew, dock'd in sand,
Vailing her high-top lower than her ribs
To kiss her burial.   Should I go to church
And see the holy edifice of stone,
And not bethink me straight of dangerous rocks,
Which touching but my gentle vessel's side,
Would scatter all her spices on the stream,
Enrobe the roaring waters with my silks,
And, in a word, but even now worth this,
And now worth nothing ?   Shall I have the thought
To think on this, and shall I lack the thought
That such a thing bechanc'd would make me sad ?
But tell not me : I know Antonio
Is sad to think upon his merchandise.
  Ant. Believe me, no : I thank my fortune for it,
My ventures are not in one bottom trusted,
Nor to one place ; nor is my whole estate
Upon the fortune of this present year :
Therefore my merchandise makes me not sad.
  Salar. Why, then you are in love.
  Ant.   Fie, fie !
  Salar. Not in love neither ?   Then let us say you
      are sad,
Because you are not merry ; and 'twere as easy
For you to laugh, and leap, and say you are merry,
Because you are not sad.   Now, by two-headed
      Janus,
Nature hath fram'd strange fellows in her time :
Some that will evermore peep through their eyes
And laugh like parrots at a bag-piper ;
And other of such vinegar aspect

LONDON : KEGAN PAUL, TRENCH, TRÜBNER & CO., LT^{D.}

PRINTED BY WILLIAM CLOWES AND SONS, LIMITED,
LONDON AND BECCLES.

PRINTED BY WILLIAM CLOWES AND SONS, LIMITED,
LONDON AND BECCLES.